MADISON HORTON

KINGDOM
OF THE
SEA

First edition: June 2023

Cover design by MiblArt
Map by FantasyMapShop

ISBN 979-8-9871968-0-9 (hardback)
ISBN 979-8-9871968-1-6 (paperback)
ISBN 979-8-9871968-2-3 (ebook)

www.madisonhortonauthor.com

For Grandma

*You've read so many books, it's about time you had one
dedicated to you!*

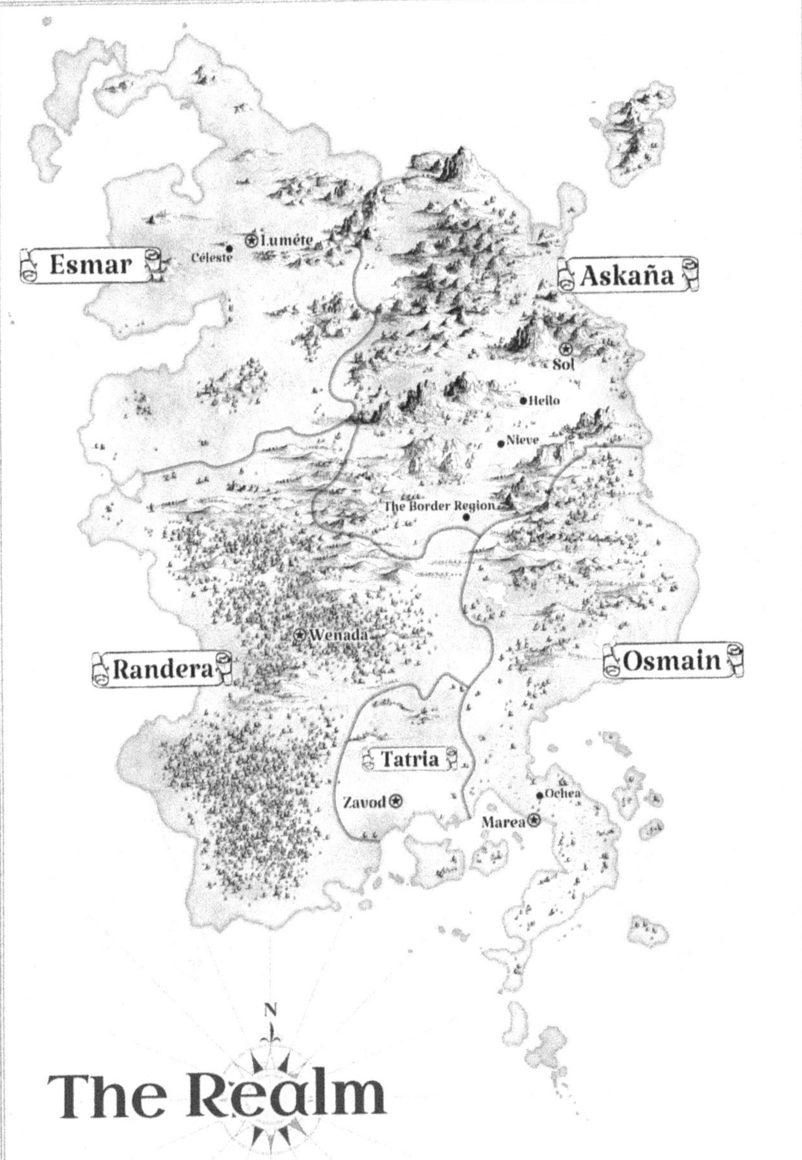

Esmar
Askaña
Céleste
Luméte
Sol
Hello
Nieve
The Border Region
Wenada
Randera
Osmain
Tatria
Zavod
Ochea
Marea
N
The Realm

1

Year 738

Day 14 of Summer

*L*uciana knew without a doubt that she was born to rule. Even at twelve years old, there had been no question in her mind—she was a natural leader.

She had been a natural when learning to ride, with dancing, reading and writing, and every other subject in which a young lady should be proficient. She'd excelled with music, too, mastering both violin and flute in just one year.

Luciana prided herself on being the best. With her nature inclining her toward being the picture of Askanese perfection, it was a shame she was only second in line to inherit the throne.

But as Luciana took a deep breath, she reminded herself perhaps she could change that if she simply excelled beyond what anyone expected from her. If she was already the best at everything she tried, maybe she could be the best at ruling, too.

Her lady's maid, Alora, gently tied Luciana's dress in place. The rich crimson of the velvet made Luciana look like the perfect future Reina of Askaña. Luciana never appeared in public with anything out of place, and today would be no exception.

"Alora?" Luciana asked.

"Yes, Your Highness?" Alora replied cheerfully. Alora was the best maid Luciana could ever ask for. She'd served Luciana since Luciana had outgrown her governess, Alora's mother, several years ago. The two had practically grown up together.

"What is on my agenda for today?"

"Not as much as you'd prefer, I'm sure," Alora laughed. Luciana sighed impatiently and waited. "The royals from Osmain are coming to visit today. That is all."

"That is hardly nothing!" A new list was already forming in Luciana's head. It was likely all taken care of already, but she'd still have to make sure the servants had arranged everything appropriately. Luciana didn't take diplomacy lightly, and she didn't want anything to go wrong.

"Don't worry, Your Highness," Alora said, moving to work on Luciana's dark, curly hair. "Your uncle has already taken care of everything. All you need to do is play the part of hostess."

Luciana sighed. Of course Nicolas had already seen to everything. He managed his household perfectly, as one would expect from the Rey of a country as large as Askaña. Still, it pained Luciana to be shoved to the back-burner. Askaña was her home, and she wanted to help as much as possible.

"Do you know Camila's schedule, then?" Camila was Luciana's older sister by two years and, since Uncle Nicolas had never married, next in line for the throne.

"Her Highness should be in her study. She intends to tend to her daily duties until the Osmainians arrive." Alora finished pinning the last few strands of hair into place, then set Luciana's small golden tiara on her head.

"The Osmainians," Luciana mused aloud. "They haven't visited Askaña in several years."

"I can't remember the last time they came to visit," Alora agreed.

Luciana considered that. "Have you heard anything about the reason for their trip?"

"Not this time," Alora said as she expertly applied a faint blush to Luciana's cheeks.

"Come on, Alora! In the busy servants' quarters, you haven't even heard a whisper?"

Alora's face went blank as she tried to remember conversations heard in passing. Luciana didn't try to call her on a bluff like she would if any other servant had claimed ignorance. But Alora didn't listen in on others. She only noticed things that were meant for her ears. While that was a quality Luciana usually valued, it didn't help in situations like this one.

"Nothing?" Luciana finally asked.

Alora shook her head sadly. "I'm sorry. I can try to listen and report back to you later if you'd like?"

"There's no time," Luciana said, shaking her head. "I'll just find Condesa Esmeralda. I'm sure she'll know."

Condesa Esmeralda had set up residence at the castillo two years ago at Camila's request. She seemed to have ears everywhere and know everyone's secrets. Luciana didn't know how Esmeralda did it, one of the many reasons that Luciana kept her ambitions close to her chest.

Alora shrugged. "You'll find out what the Osmainians want soon enough, anyway."

"Yes, but I want to be prepared."

"Well, you'll at least look presentable. My work here is done. Is there anything else I can do for you?" Alora asked.

"That will be all, Alora. Thank you," Luciana answered. Alora curtsied and dismissed herself. Luciana took a deep breath, then swept out of her chamber. She needed to find Esmeralda.

THE CARRIAGE WHEEL caught on a stone in the road, nearly tossing Daniel into his father's arms. Given the circumstances of the ride, hugging his father was the last thing the young man wanted to do. He adjusted his position to keep himself as far away from his father as possible. It was insulting that he'd been dragged all the way to Askaña like an animal, with no choice in the matter.

It wasn't as if Daniel hadn't been away from his home in Osmain before. Only a year ago he'd been serving a respectable term in the military, surrounded by men his own age who cared so much for their country. Of course, being next in line for the throne of Osmain, he'd never engaged in actual combat, but it had been humbling, nevertheless. Daniel only hoped he could serve his fellows well one day.

Unfortunately, as soon as Daniel's stint in service had ended, his father had started pestering him to get married.

"You're twenty-five now, son," he had said. "It's high time you produced an heir."

Daniel wasn't averse to marriage. Most of the memories he had of his parent's marriage were positive ones.

He just didn't want to marry someone he didn't know. Yet here he was, on his way to the Askanese Castillo to meet his future bride, less than a season before their wedding was to take place.

"You look as if you're about ready to throw a punch at any moment," Antonio said.

"Don't tempt me" was all Daniel said in response. He did not want his father to think he'd accepted his fate. Imperatore Antonio was a good man and, usually, a good father, but no one would guess it from his looks. While Daniel shared his father's olive skin and dark, curly hair, that was just about all he'd inherited. An easily intimidated man might run away screaming if Antonio glared at him. Daniel wasn't an easily intimidated man, despite his friendlier face and more approachable nature.

Antonio sighed. "I know this isn't exactly the marriage you were hoping for—"

"A love-match, you mean? Like you and Mother had? No, how dare I want a happy union?"

Bringing up his mother was the only way to strike a chord with Antonio. Daniel had been poking at his father's weak spot for the late Imperatrice since the betrothal was conceived, hoping the objections might eventually work and get him out of the arrangement.

"Need I remind you," Antonio continued, unswayed,

"that your mother and I were arranged to marry as well? We just gave each other a chance."

"Like you could have changed it if you wanted," Daniel retorted.

"No, that is true. But I am not like my father, Daniel. I will not force you to wed if you do not think you could be happy with the Princesa."

Daniel's heart skipped a beat, and he almost did a double take. Could this really be happening? Had all of his incessant nagging and complaining finally paid off? Daniel fought the urge to smile in victory. Antonio wasn't entirely unreasonable, after all.

"Then turn the damn carriage around and let's go home!"

"Not so fast," Antonio said firmly. "You still need to meet her. Give it until the engagement ball. That's all I ask. If after that time you still don't think you'll suit one another, you can come home. No questions asked."

"But—"

"This is my compromise, son. Do not make me change my mind."

Daniel considered his options, but there was really no alternative. He would just have to hate the Princesa. He nodded. "Deal."

"Good," said Antonio, "because it looks like we're arriving at the castillo now."

As Luciana expected, Camila's study was empty. Luciana fought the urge to smile as she quietly stepped up to her elder sister's desk. Camila was hardly ever in her study. In fact, Luciana was there more than anyone else in the castillo.

Politics weren't exactly a part of Luciana's set curriculum, but they were certainly a part of Camila's, and Luciana was going to exploit her sister's absence while she could. Every day, Luciana would sneak in to read the briefing letters that were delivered to Camila to inform her of the news and pressing issues. Most people would have found them boring, but Luciana enjoyed learning about things like the annual crop yields and tax income. Her sister never read any of it, but Luciana knew everything that the documents contained.

Luciana picked up the day's news. The headline read, "Strike Turns Deadly in the Border Regions." Luciana had been keeping up with the recent unrest in the outlying cities, but most of the rumblings had been peaceful until now. The rebels were citing that Rey Nicolas had been taxing them out of their homes and having the royal guard publicly slaughter those who couldn't pay. Luciana doubted these accusations, the executions at the very least. She'd yet to hear an account that could prove them. Minor rebellions like this popped up every few years and nothing ever came of them. They either fizzled out on their own or were crushed by the militia. As disturbing as a rebellion could be, this one was not yet a cause for concern.

The next article wasn't much better. A drought had swept through the northeast territories, hurting crop yields, and causing a chain reaction of supply shortages and an economic downturn. It pained Luciana to read about the sad state of her homeland, but there was truly nothing that she could do about it. Her uncle would never listen to Luciana on matters of politics. As heir to the throne, Camila was the only one invited to participate in discussions on affairs of state, and often those invitations were wasted. Camila had never offered an opinion on any political issues.

Camila's resistance to prepare herself to become Reina was perhaps the biggest reason Luciana wanted to change the line of succession. It wouldn't be easy. Lines could only be changed from the top down. Her uncle, Rey Nicolas, could remove someone from the line if he saw them unfit to rule. Otherwise, changes could only be made if someone in line took themselves out of the running by treason, abdicating, or death. But Luciana had decided long ago that she would never kill Camila.

No, she would have to outshine her sister so much that her uncle could not ignore Luciana's abilities and remove Camila from the line entirely. Camila could keep living her life in the castillo without responsibilities, and Luciana could finally be respected in the political sphere. There was still danger in this plan, of course. If she was exposed as a threat to her sister, she could be tried for treason or expelled from the royal family. So, Luciana kept her ambitions quiet. For now, she had to make her political interest look innocent.

Careful to replace the papers exactly where she had found them, Luciana slipped back out of the study. She used her key to lock the door, making the study look untouched.

Now to find Esmeralda. Luciana had barely left the corridor before the guardhouse bells sounded, signaling the arrival of the Osmainians. Already? She'd thought she'd have at least another hour or two, but at least she was ready to receive guests. It would make both Askaña and herself look bad if she were not presentable for the sovereign ruler of the neighboring kingdom upon his arrival. Luciana just hoped Camila was ready as well. As much as Luciana wanted to outshine her sister, the last thing Askaña needed was to insult the Osmainians.

Luciana walked to the great hall at a speed that would get her there quickly, but just slowly and gracefully enough that not a single hair would fall out of place. By the time she arrived, only her uncle Nicolas and her mother were there. Camila was nowhere to be seen. Luciana took a deep breath and put on her most pleasant face.

"Good afternoon, Uncle, Mother." Luciana curtsied.

They turned to face her. Nicolas and Natalia looked so similar, with their dark hair and fair skin, that it never surprised anyone to learn that they were siblings. Now that Luciana's father was gone, the darker skin she had inherited from him made her stick out like a sore thumb.

"Oh, good. You're here," grumbled Nicolas. Luciana ignored him. He was always in a foul mood.

Luciana's mother, however, gave her a smile. "That color looks lovely on you, dear," she said.

"Thank you, Mother," said Luciana. The compliment from Natalia left Luciana momentarily off-balance. They rarely spoke, only really making conversation at family dinners. Luciana could only barely remember a time when they'd been close.

Before the death of Luciana's father, their family had been full of love and laughter. But as soon as her husband had died, Natalia shut herself off from her daughters. At first, Luciana had thought it was just grief. But as Natalia's mourning period ended, nothing improved with her daughters. The only explanation Luciana could think of was that their looks were too close to that of their father. It must have hurt her mother to look at two girls who were nearly identical to her deceased husband. Luciana didn't have much sympathy. She'd essentially lost both parents at once to her mother's selfishness. But maybe there was still something to be salvaged here. Perhaps this was a change in the right direction.

"Where is Camila?" Nicolas huffed, looking to his sister and Luciana for answers.

"Tending to her duties, I'm sure," Natalia said calmly.

"This *is* her duty," Nicolas said, crossing his arms angrily.

Luciana cleared her throat. "Perhaps if you were to make me one of your advisors and distribute some of her duties to me, she would be more available during the day for meetings like this one?"

Nicolas turned to Luciana and stepped toward her, sneering. "Askaña won't need two Reinas, now will it? Why don't you do what Princesas do best and keep your mouth shut?"

Luciana formed fists at her side to keep from shaking. She should have been used to his dismissals by now, but it felt like a slap in the face every time he degraded her like this.

At that moment, a small page peeked out from behind the tall double doors that led to the long hallway outside. Nicolas motioned for Natalia and Luciana to sit, and the two women followed his lead, sitting on their thrones. He cleared his throat. "Your Majesty, may

I present to you His Majesty, Imperatore Antonio Riccardo Lorenzo DiAngelo of Osmain, and His Royal Highness, Principe Daniel Leonardo Gabriel DiAngelo of Osmain!"

Luciana fought back a smile at the length of the recitation. She'd heard that Osmainian names were sometimes ridiculously long, but these were better than she could have ever imagined. The Askanese hardly used any names other than their given one and any official title. She was a bit impressed that the page could even remember the absurdly long Osmainian names.

The double doors opened with a flourish. The first man who entered was clearly the Imperatore. He stood a good head taller than even the tallest of the Askanese, and his muscular form was draped in the finest purple robe Luciana had ever seen. He had a stern face, but the laugh lines around his eyes betrayed him to be a man Luciana shouldn't fear.

At his left walked a young man, appearing to be just a few years older than Luciana. That must have been the Principe. He was almost as tall as his father, and while he was not as bulky, he clearly had a muscular build under his own purple robes. His hair fell around his face in warm chocolate ringlets, and even from a distance Luciana could tell that he had striking eyes the color of fresh honey.

It dawned on Luciana that she still had no idea as to

the reason for their visit. Anxiety churned in Luciana's stomach. It could be something routine, like the renewal of a treaty, but it could also be something more serious. They could be planning to overtake the entire realm, for all Luciana knew, and she didn't like being left out of their plans. Nicolas nodded to the Osmainians, his grumbly mood hidden so well that anyone besides his family would have never assumed his attitude had switched entirely. "Your Majesty, Your Highness, welcome to Askaña," he said. "It has been a while since I have seen you."

The Imperatore bowed in response. "We are honored to be here, Your Majesty. And Your Highness Natalia, it is wonderful to see you." The Imperatore spoke with a thick Osmainian accent, but overall, his Askanese was better than Luciana had expected. She had prepared herself to have to communicate with them in their native tongue, as she'd had to do with the Randerans during their last visit. It had taken Luciana years to learn all five languages of the realm, but it had already paid dividends. She'd been able to form a friendship with Prince Wes of Randera, a political ally that would be helpful were she to become Reina.

Mother smiled. "It has been far too long! Not since your dashing son was born, I believe."

"Indeed." The Imperatore turned to Luciana before any further introductions could be made, saying, "Your

Highness, it is a pleasure to make your acquaintance. I have heard many good things about you, and I must say, you will make a fine Reina one day."

The color drained from Luciana's face, and she was without words. He thought she was Camila. She supposed that made sense. Camila wasn't there, after all, and even if she had been, no one could deny that Luciana's presence was more regal than her sister's. Not wanting to correct the Imperatore, Luciana stayed silent.

Nicolas opened his mouth, she assumed to clarify, but before he could, the Imperatore continued. "Where is the youngest Princesa? I am sure she will be eager to meet my son, in light of their engagement."

Luciana fought to keep her jaw from dropping, as a weighted feeling spread throughout her body. Engagement? Luciana could not even consider the prospect of marriage right now. Not while she was working her hardest to prove that she was capable of being the Reina. If Luciana married the Principe, he would whisk her away to Osmain, and while she would be their Imperatrice eventually, the thought of leaving Askaña in Camila's disinterested hands was frightening, to say the least. She couldn't leave Askaña to her sister unless there was already nothing left of it.

Nicolas finally found his voice. "The Princesa Camila is not here. She is tending to matters of state." Luciana fought the urge to scoff at his blatant lie, but she held her tongue. "Imperatore, may I present Princesa Luciana."

The Imperatore bowed to Luciana. "My apologies, Your Highness."

Luciana sucked in a deep breath. Despite the bile rising in her throat, she managed to say, "That is quite alright."

Antonio motioned to his son. "May I introduce to you my son, Principe Daniel of Osmain."

Luciana felt like all the air had been sucked out of her lungs. How could she possibly greet the man who had shown up at her doorstep to ruin her life? Luciana found that all she could do was nod. She hoped it was respectful enough.

Nicolas cleared his throat. "Your Highness, I would like to present to you Princesa Luciana of Askaña."

"It is a pleasure to meet you, Your Highness," the Principe said, bowing. Luciana stayed silent. She feared if she opened her mouth she might vomit.

Nicolas and the Imperatore began to prattle on about wedding preparations, and despite her best efforts to listen to the two men bartering away her future, Luciana had to tune them out. It was dehumanizing to hear about the land and money Askaña would gain from sending her away as if she were no more than cattle. She wouldn't marry the Principe. She wouldn't. Luciana stared straight ahead, her posture perfect, breathing perfectly timed to keep her heart from beating out of control.

Then Luciana made the mistake of glancing at the Principe, and their eyes met briefly. He did not appear surprised at the announcement. In fact, his gaze seemed calm and respectful, almost as though he were looking upon her as an equal. As if he wasn't going to fight anyone to end the abomination of an engagement. And more than anything so far, that was what made Luciana's blood boil.

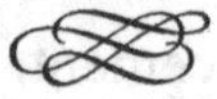

2

Day 14 of Summer

"You should have seen the way she looked at me, Father," Daniel said. "She hid it well, but there was no love in her eyes. Not even mild interest. There was nothing there but cold hard malice."

Daniel didn't want to admit it, but he had been disappointed by Princesa Luciana's icy gaze. He didn't want to marry a stranger, that much was true. But he hadn't considered that his intended bride-to-be would be just as opposed to the marriage as he was. Maybe even more so.

When he'd first seen the Princesa, she'd been so proper, so perfect, sitting upon her throne that Daniel couldn't help but stare. He'd heard stories, of course, about the beauty of the Princesas of Askaña, but he'd thought it was all an exaggeration. The sisters were the only Princesas eligible for marriage across the five kingdoms, and that would skew anyone's perspective.

But Princesa Luciana… she was even more beautiful than he could have imagined. She reminded him of Esmar. He'd visited that kingdom years ago during the winter, and they'd had their first snowfall during his visit. It was the only time he'd ever seen snow—beautiful but colder than he'd imagined. Intimidating. But he'd wanted to go out in the blizzard anyway, just to experience everything the snow had to offer.

His father could never know any of this, Daniel decided. He couldn't show any indication that his first impression of the Princesa had been so remarkable or favorable. Daniel had promised Antonio that he would have a chance to get to know her, but based on the shivers she had sent down his spine, he had a feeling he wasn't likely to find a wife in Luciana.

Antonio turned to his son. "Remember our deal? Last until the ball. It's only ten days."

"Do you really have to go so soon?" Daniel asked. "If you stay until the ball, then we can leave together."

"You know I cannot. I wanted to see you safely to Askaña so that I might go over terms of the marriage contract before the official betrothal. But now that the contract has been negotiated, I must return to our people as soon as possible," Antonio answered.

"But—"

"I leave in the morning. That is final."

The two men sat in silence for a moment. Daniel pulled out his leatherbound journal, flipping through the pages until he found an empty page.

Antonio leaned over Daniel's shoulder and said, "You really ought to talk to her, you know."

"Can't you give me one blasted hour of peace?"

"You must try in earnest to to make a fair decision or I will end our deal. Your engagement will become public knowledge immediately, and she will be your wife by the end of the season."

Daniel sighed. "I will, trust me. Let me just rest from the journey for a moment, please."

"You're angry with me," Antonio said. "I remember when I first met your mother. I wasn't excited about the arrangement myself."

Daniel sighed. He'd heard his parents' love story on more than one occasion. He'd once found it charming… or at least he had before his mother had died and left Antonio and Daniel alone with their grief. It hadn't been easy for Daniel to lose his mother, but he'd fared better than Antonio, who had been utterly destroyed by her death. That kind of sadness was enough to taint any love story.

"I know this has been a point of contention for us this past season," Antonio continued. "I must always balance what's good for our people with what is best for you. I expect a great deal from you because our people will, too. But you should know that I do wish for your happiness."

Antonio left without another word. Daniel sighed. His father was right. It was his duty to marry, and he had to consider his kingdom's needs above his own. That didn't mean Daniel had to be happy about it.

Daniel decided he would hide in his room until dinner, taking his time to get settled in. The deal with his father would have to be proven later. Despite this, he didn't rest. He couldn't. Pulling out his journal, Daniel flipped to an open page, but his quill hovered just inches above the page, never touching the paper. What could he possibly write about when he could not stop thinking of the Princesa's glare? She had been so cold. What could he have possibly done in those brief seconds to invoke her hatred so quickly?

She was likely surprised by the news, but perhaps there was more to it. Maybe she was in love with another or perhaps she had an affinity for women instead. The thoughts swirled around in his head as he stared at the empty page. He was thinking too much about the Princesa. There had been so many things to see on the carriage ride to Askaña. He should write about them instead. Much like Osmain, Askaña was full of green rolling hills, but it was much cooler in Askaña. He had been grateful for his cape by the time he reached the castillo.

Daniel scratched out a few words.

> *Askaña is cold in more ways than one. Even in the summer, I shivered upon entering their castillo. As if I wasn't chilly enough already, the Princesa here seems to hate me.*

Back to the Princesa already? He scratched out the line. His journal was his pride and joy, writing a habit he'd picked up during his time in the military. It was something he intended to share with his future family to describe his travels, and he didn't need a perfectly good journal ruined with descriptions of the Princesa of Askaña.

Daniel threw his quill down. This Princesa was already distracting him, and he had never even spoken to her.

~

As soon as the Osmainians left the throne room, Luciana turned to face her mother and her uncle. "What was that?"

"It was a marriage contract negotiation, Luciana. I thought you were smart enough to figure that out," Nicolas said, dropping all pleasantries.

"I can't marry the Principe!" Luciana protested.

"Of course, you can, dear," her mother said calmly. "He is a perfect match for you."

"You just met him today, Mother. You said so yourself. How can you say we are well-suited?"

"He is from a wealthy country that Askaña could use a stronger alliance with. You will be well cared for in Osmain. That's all I need to know," Natalia said, shrugging.

Luciana's heart sank. So much for strengthening the relationship with her mother. She didn't seem to care about Luciana's wishes at all, only what was easiest. Luciana had to admit the match was advantageous for Askaña, but she couldn't just give up on becoming Reina.

"I don't belong in Osmain, Mother. I belong here... in Askaña. This is my home," Luciana said, hoping against all odds that they would see reason.

"You will always have a home here, darling. But you must learn to live in Osmain," her mother persisted.

"I won't go through with this engagement," Luciana said, standing. "You can't make me."

Nicolas rose from his throne, towering over Luciana. "You will marry him."

Luciana opened her mouth to retort, but as her uncle scowled at her, she found herself speechless. He continued, "You are a Princesa. The property of Askaña. Your duty to your country is to secure an alliance with Osmain. If you refuse the Principe, you refuse your title. I will have no choice but to banish you from Askaña."

"No!" Luciana shouted, shocked. This was unfair. She was being bartered away like cattle, her chances of becoming Reina slipping away more and more by the minute.

"I don't want to hear any more complaints about the arrangement," Nicolas said sternly. "Now, get out of my sight."

Luciana was disappointed with herself when she followed his command and left the throne room. She had to find Camila. Her sister was the only person in the castillo who might understand her heartache.

She finally found Camila and Esmeralda in the gardens. As soon as she entered the flower-lined pathways, she heard the faint sounds of her sister's laughter. Luciana turned the corner to see Camila sitting on the edge of a fountain. Like Luciana, Camila had the same pale brown skin and curly hair. They even had the same blue eyes, which were unusual for Askanese. The combination of their dark skin and bright eyes made them both stand out in any crowd.

Camila smiled when she spotted Luciana and said, "Come join us, dear sister!" Condesa Esmeralda stood next to the fountain, holding a blooming red rose. She gave Luciana a friendly nod and smile.

Luciana did not return either of their smiles. In fact, Luciana had been fighting the urge to cry for over an hour now. "Where have you been, Camila?" Luciana demanded.

Camila frowned. "What happened?"

"What happened? They have thrown me into a marriage that I don't want, and you have been missing all day!"

Camila looked at Esmeralda, wide-eyed panic in her expression.

Esmeralda said gently, "That is my fault. Her absence, anyway. Why don't you tell us what happened?"

Luciana told them almost everything. She told them about the Imperatore and the Principe and the impending marriage, decidedly leaving her real reason for her being upset. She didn't tell them anything that might even lead them to think that. The last thing she needed was Esmeralda figuring out her secret desires and telling everyone in the castillo. By the end of her tale, Camila and Esmeralda looked just as sick as Luciana had felt in the throne room.

Camila held out her arms and Luciana fell into them. Luciana refused to cry, but she trembled against her own will. It had been one thing to keep hoping in vain that Nicolas would see her as a more suitable heir and remove Camila from the line of succession and another entirely to have that hope torn to shreds. What would she do now?

Her sister's embrace was warm and calming, and Luciana remembered why she loved Camila. It was easy to criticize Camila for her leadership skills, but Luciana couldn't deny that she was a more empathetic soul and Luciana was grateful for it. Without saying a word, she could lift the spirits of anyone around.

Camila's voice wavered, but she tried to comfort Luciana. "I'm sure it will turn out alright."

"Why don't you try to get to know him?" Esmeralda chimed in.

"I hardly see the point in that. Looks like I'll have an entire lifetime to do so, whether I want to or not," Luciana grumbled.

"Then take the rest of the day for yourself. Get your mind off of it. Why don't you go riding? That usually clears your head. Or you could go down to the little creek? It's warm enough to swim today."

As much as Luciana hated to admit it, Esmeralda was

right. Seeing Camila had helped her mood considerably, but it might be good to get away for a while.

"Camila and I will cover for you if you'd like to skip dinner?"

Luciana never missed dinner, especially when guests were at the castillo, and despite her situation, Luciana would not start tonight. "That's alright. I don't want to offend the Osmainians. I'll pull myself together before then," Luciana said. Camila pursed her lips and Esmeralda opened her mouth to object, but Luciana excused herself from the garden and made her way to the music room.

The music room was a special place in the castillo for Luciana. It was only accessible through hidden passageways, yet its window overlooked a beautiful courtyard. She didn't know why there was a hidden room in the castillo. She could only imagine it was used for a treasure room or bunker of some kind. It was perfect for Luciana, though. When the cold seasons came, it was the perfect place to watch the snow fall. It was also the only place that no one else in the family seemed to know about. It had taken Luciana and Alora hours to smuggle the pieces of a piano through the passageways, but now that she sat on the bench and prepared her fingers to play, she was glad they had made the effort.

She had performed on her violin for the Randerans when they'd visited three years ago, making no secret of her musical talents, but she didn't play the piano in front of others. It was her favorite instrument, and her fingers could fly over the keys like birds in the spring. But she didn't want anyone to know. Despite the benefits that might come from showing off her skills, it was nice to have something that was just hers.

Luciana collapsed onto her bench and selected a piece with a dark melody. She began to play it softly, but as her thoughts swirled around in her head, she pounded the keys harder and harder, the music growing louder. There had to be some way to get out of the marriage, surpass Camila in line for the throne, and become Reina of Askaña. Minutes turned into hours, and as the tips of her fingers finally grew sore from all the playing, she looked out the window to see the golden rays of the setting sun. It was time for dinner.

Luciana gathered her skirts, closing the lid of the piano and slipping into the passageway. She wasn't looking forward to dinner. Her only plan for the occasion was to sit in silence and avoid conversations with the Osmainians. While there would inevitably be some interaction between herself and the Principe, that didn't mean she had to seek his company.

～

DANIEL GLANCED around the quiet dinner table. He sat next to his father, who occasionally complimented the food. Rey Nicolas and his sister made muted small talk. And Luciana—well, she was still a mystery. He'd tried multiple times to meet Luciana's gaze, but she seemed to look anywhere else other than at him. Despite his frustration, Daniel glanced her way every once in a while, hoping against all odds that she'd return the look. A small part of him hoped he'd see something behind her eyes other than contempt.

Also at the table was the older Princesa, Camila. The future Reina of Askaña. She and her sister looked remarkably similar, but there was more kindness in her eyes. The last face at the table was also new, a young woman who had briefly been introduced as Condesa Esmeralda. She and Camila seemed to be close, so Daniel could only assume that she was a close friend of the Royal family. Esmeralda was clearly as close to the family as one could get without being born royal, but that still left her the lowest ranked of anyone in the room, and so she said nothing.

And Princesa Luciana didn't utter a word to anyone. The girl could not have been more obvious about her opposition towards the marriage arrangement, but nothing she did was inherently impolite. She sat up straight, put a pleasant smile on her face, and pretended to be present in the moment.

Finally, Nicolas cleared his throat and addressed the table. "It is an honor to be in the company of such distinguished men tonight."

Antonio nodded politely. "My son and I could not be happier to be in your beautiful kingdom. We don't have nearly as many mountains back home in Osmain. They are majestic."

Princesa Camila finally joined the conversation. "Oh, but they get tiring after a while. I'm sure the beaches of your kingdom are much more interesting."

"I have no doubt," Daniel piped up. "I've heard tales of your winters."

And he had. All of Osmain had. It was widely known that traversing Askaña in the cold season was a death wish. Between the heavy snow, avalanches, and steep slopes, many Osmainians had perished during their visits. It was easy to believe that Askaña could be that deadly. But as beautiful as it was outside now, he understood why people might choose to visit.

Condesa Esmeralda finally spoke. "The winters in our kingdom are harsh, but they constantly remind us that the sun will rise again. They remind us to be grateful for what we have."

Daniel understood why the Askanese kept Condesa Esmeralda around. She had an infectious way of speaking that urged him to listen.

She continued, "I have also heard tales of your great

nation. I have a cousin who lives there, and he reports your shorelines are the finest in all the realm."

"We would like to think so," laughed Antonio. "Is your cousin a man of status? Perhaps I might know him from court."

"He is the current Visconte of Ochea."

Daniel's breath caught in his throat. "You don't mean Capitano Quirino, do you?"

Esmeralda's face lit up. "You know him?"

"Know him? I was in the military with him!"

They had been as close as brothers while Daniel served. Ochea was a region of Osmain further north than where Daniel had taken up residence, a few hours' away by carriage. Quirino's time in the military had ended with the sudden death of his father, forcing him to return home to inherit and manage the estate. Daniel had left the service himself shortly after Quirino's departure. As heirs to powerful men, neither Daniel nor Quirino had been allowed to anything life-threatening during their service, and with his friend gone, the military had lost some of its appeal.

"How is your cousin? I have not heard from him in some time," Daniel said.

"Doing well, last I heard." Esmeralda shrugged.

"It truly is the smallest of realms," Natalia said from across the table, taking a sip of her wine.

"Still not married?" Daniel asked.

"Certainly not," Esmeralda laughed. "Can you imagine...?"

Esmeralda didn't finish her sentence, but Daniel knew what she meant. Quirino liked to play the field, and he'd yet to find anyone he took seriously enough to marry. Daniel had spent some of his wildest nights in taverns with Quirino, drunkenly flirting with potential partners. If Quirino knew where Daniel was right now, he'd probably laugh. Unlike Quirino, Daniel had never felt indifferent towards love. On the contrary, he believed in it more than anything. He imagined Quirino would find it hilarious that Daniel was being forced to court a girl who hated him. How was he to fulfill his part of the deal with his father if his bride-to-be wouldn't even look at him? She was clearly against the marriage, too. If he could only find a chance to speak with her...

He would just have to follow her after dinner. Find her alone, explain the deal, and then they would be out of the whole mess in a matter of days.

Daniel wasn't surprised when Luciana was the first to excuse herself from dinner. She hadn't said a word the entire night. Daniel considered waiting a few minutes before leaving himself, so as not to seem suspicious, but then decided that following Luciana might be useful to his claims when it came time to call off the betrothal. If he showed that he was trying, then his father would believe him when he said he'd done his best to get to know the Princesa. On top of that, the corridors of the castillo were long and winding. Daniel had been in the castillo for less than a day, and if he waited, he would probably get lost and never find her.

So Daniel excused himself as well, slipping out right behind her. She walked quickly, faster than most girls of her station would normally walk. Even with skirts as full and billowing as hers, she was remarkably nimble. Unless he broke into a run, Daniel would never catch up. Luciana rounded the corner and Daniel ran after her, but by the time he turned the corner, she was gone.

3

Day 15 of Summer

When Luciana awoke the next morning, she decided that today would be different. She had a plan. Last night's near run-in with the Principe had been too close for her liking. She'd only just been able to close the door to the hidden passageway before he could catch up to her. She was just grateful he hadn't called out to her. Luciana could be blunt, but she prided herself on following social protocol exactly. She had been careful to follow every rule of etiquette at dinner, so that no one could accuse her of being rude to their guests. She had vowed not to speak unless spoken to, and no one had spoken to her. But if Daniel had called out to her in the hall, she would have been forced to respond.

Today, Luciana had requested the darkest shade of red dress she owned. She did not want to wear black and appear too obviously in mourning, but she was going to get as close to it as she could. And, as if knowing her exact thoughts, Alora delivered the best possible option. The gown was the deep color of wine and remarkably plain compared to Luciana's usual decadence. Other than the fact that it was made from a fine silk, there was not an ounce of decadence to the dress. It was perfectly acceptable, perfectly regal, and perfectly angry.

As usual, Camila was not in her study when Luciana entered. Camila had certainly been in the room that morning, though, as the pillows on her small couch were ruffled and out of order. Careful not to disturb the mess, Luciana stepped over to the desk, tucking her copy of the key to Camila's study away. The day's briefing papers were about the rebels again. Apparently, they were moving north and they had slaughtered several noble households on the way. She scanned the list of names and her stomach turned. She recognized several of them and some of the names she knew were those of young children.

She'd known these people. And those poor children. Innocent—but still dead.

It was strange that Nicolas hadn't spoken about it at all. If she hadn't snuck in to read the briefings, she never would have known. It bothered Luciana to no end that Nicolas was so proud that he didn't allow her into his team of advisors. She was sure she could bring ideas to the table that would help fix her home.

Luciana had to remind herself that, as angry as she was at being left out, the military would soon put an end to the rebellion. They would bring the criminals to justice, and Askaña would be peaceful again. Still disturbed by the news, Luciana decided she'd had enough for the day, stealthily left Camila's study, and made her way to the library. She often visited the royal library when no one else was there, and during some of those trips she would brush up on her knowledge of Askanese law. Knowing the ins and outs of her country would surely be useful one day, so she never let her knowledge of it grow stale. Today, however, she was looking for something very specific—something that could help her get out of the marriage.

She had a good idea of where to look and retrieved the enormous volume of laws regarding marriages, heirs, and the order of precedence in Askaña. Luciana dropped the book on a table with a loud thud and flipped through the pages, looking for anything that might be relevant to a Princesa refusing a suitor. She knew the basics of Askanese royal marriage and inheritance law. The firstborn child would always inherit the throne unless they abdicated it or were removed from the line by the current ruler. At least one child was expected to marry and carry on the line, but if there was more than one child of the monarchs, the firstborn would be allowed to rule alone if they chose.

That was what her uncle had done. Nicolas had never married nor had children, choosing instead to be an Ambassador of the Sun. Ambassadors of the Sun were the closest thing the Askanese had to gods, and the opportunity to become one was only ever offered to the Rey or Reina. There could be entire generations that passed with no Ambassador, as choosing to pass the line to a sibling's children and dedicating your life to the people of Askaña at the expense of your own happiness was a tremendous sacrifice, one that the people respected. Ambassadors had temples built in their honor, statues erected. Luciana was fairly certain her uncle had at least one temple in one of the bigger cities.

There were caveats to this, of course. Say an Ambassador was sworn in and then their younger siblings died before producing an heir. It would immediately void the vow of chastity. That ruler would still be respected for their decision to become an Ambassador but would lose the title and be expected to marry and have children. Or if a monarch died before producing heirs and their younger sibling was no longer pure, that sibling wouldn't be able to have the option to become an Ambassador at all.

Someday, if Luciana became Reina, she would have to make the same choice to either have a family of her own or be an Ambassador. She knew what she would choose. Unless someone swept her off her feet before she could say her vow of chastity, she'd choose to be an Ambassador. Knowing the type of men who would covet Luciana's hand, she'd be forced to share her power. The men that chased after her would be men like the Principe —after her title and nothing more or looking for a match designed for political advantage. And there was no one she trusted to govern Askaña more than herself.

Luciana was just happy she wasn't attracted to women. That would have been the biggest torture. There was no happy ending for an heir that was attracted to the same sex. Not that those relationships were forbidden among the Askanese. Most people didn't really care. But since a union with a woman would still break Luciana's vow of chastity and a woman could never give Luciana an heir, it would be a sad existence indeed.

On the other hand, if Luciana failed to become Reina instead of Camila, Luciana had always imagined that her sister would choose to marry. Men loved Camila's gentle nature and sweet smile, and while she'd never returned an interest in any of them, Camila loved children. She'd undoubtedly want some, and it seemed as if Nicolas shared Luciana's assumption. Otherwise, he wouldn't marry Luciana off to a foreign prince and muddle their line. If Luciana married Daniel, their children would be Osmainian, not eligible to rule Askaña. For all intents and purposes, Camila would be an only child under the eyes of the law. Becoming an Ambassador wouldn't be an option for her.

Luciana quickly scanned the pages of the leather-bound tome, flipping quickly from one to the next. How many pages had she read now? Five? Ten? Fifty? Luciana glanced at the page numbers.

413.

414.

415.

418.

418? She must have read this book a hundred times, and she'd never noticed the jump in numbers. She ran her fingertips along the side of page 415, and it seemed thicker than the rest. Almost as if it were two pages stuck together. Luciana furrowed her brow. What could be between them? Her heart leapt into her throat as she imagined what she might find written on those hidden sheets. Perhaps the loophole she needed in order to become Reina!

Her nail didn't work to pry them apart, but Luciana

was too excited by the potential to worry about preserving the book now. Her hands shook with anticipation. Wincing, Luciana tore the page clean out of the binding. Once out, the pages separated easily, and she quickly scanned the missing information. It was a list of the rules surrounding heirs, nothing new—firstborns either had to marry someone who could produce an heir or become an Ambassador. Luciana shrugged it off. She already knew that.

But there was something far more interesting tucked away between the glued-together pages. A small letter pressed so flat that it hadn't been detectable from simply reading the book.

This letter must have been intentionally concealed and concealed well. Luciana knew she was the only one who poked around in these Askanese law books. Anyone who needed to know the law either had their own copies or learned the law from a tutor. This letter could have been there for years without being discovered. Luciana carefully picked it up and read it to herself. It was written in Askanese, but some of the prose was poor—a couple of misspelled words. This was the writing of someone lower-class, with a poor education—or someone whose first language wasn't Askanese.

Day 16 of Winter, Year 730

Father,

The rumors are all true. I do indeed exist. I had hoped you'd have known by now considering my mother's repeated attempts to inform you, but it saddened me to hear that you'd written them off as slander.

While I do lament that it will ruin your reputation once I reveal myself to the public, I must say that it is all your own doing. I do not understand your unwillingness to marry my mother, but rest assured, you will pay for it. I am fully prepared to tell the entire realm the truth, and when I do, you will be denounced and I will be the rightful Reina of Askaña.

If you try to have me killed, I will reveal the news twice as fast. I have a circle of people willing to reveal the truth should anything happen to me. Perhaps we can come to an agreement to buy my silence. You know where to find me.

Your loving daughter

AT THE END of the letter was a signature so illegible that Luciana could not make out even a single letter.

Luciana dropped the letter in shock. Written eight years ago, concealed at some point after that. The only person this letter could have been addressed to was Nicolas. He was the only man in the Royal line who would be ruined by having a bastard daughter—and a daughter who had a claim to the throne. The hot-tempered, rule-enforcing man who ran Askaña had broken his sacred vow of chastity, and now there was someone else vying for the crown.

Or at least there had been.

Who was this mysterious woman? And where was she now? Why had her letter been hidden here instead of being destroyed? If Nicolas had received the letter, then it seemed Nicolas was the only one who knew of the writer's existence. Anything Camila knew, so did Luciana, so she was obviously still oblivious. As for Natalia... it was possible she knew, but she had mentioned nothing.

Had Nicolas killed his own daughter to silence her? Was she rotting somewhere in the royal prison? Or had he given her what she wanted in return for silence? Luciana shook from the weight of what she'd found. It was difficult enough trying to prove that she should be Reina with only one person in her way. The thought of two people being ahead of her in line for the throne made her stomach churn.

Luciana's mind swirled with all of the new information. Perhaps she should talk with Esmeralda, as she seemed to know everyone's secrets. Luciana's eyes grew wide. Esmeralda. She had been a close acquaintance of Camila's for years, but they hadn't become inseparable until around the time the letter from Nicolas's daughter was written. Could it be a coincidence that Esmeralda had started coming around the castillo more or could there be more to it?

It was certainly unusual to have a guest stay for more than a season, and Esmeralda had been at the castillo for two years now. Was it possible that Esmeralda was only spending time with Camila to get closer to the crown? Luciana shuddered. She knew she couldn't avoid Esmeralda without also avoiding Camila, but Luciana would have to be extra careful not to reveal any of her ambitions to Esmeralda until she had more solid proof of her identity.

A loud knock at the door startled Luciana, and she

quickly pocketed the letter before turning around to see the Principe standing in the doorway. There were no passages that she could get to without him noticing, and the last thing she wanted was for him to figure out her secrets. She would have to speak to him. There was no getting out of this one. Luciana casually closed the book, tucking the ripped pages inside, and placed it back on the shelf where she'd found it. She hoped he hadn't noticed what she had been reading.

"I was sorry to miss you last night," he said, still lingering in the doorway.

"I haven't any idea what you mean," she said, putting on a pleasant face.

"I think you do. After dinner. You disappeared."

"The castillo is large. Were you following me?"

"I…" His voice broke off. Of course, she knew he'd been following her, but it was satisfying to make him admit it. "I simply wished to introduce myself," he finally said.

"That's very kind, but hardly necessary. Your page did that job for you."

"I know, but I just thought—"

"We will have plenty of time to get to know each other, don't you think?"

The Principe finally left the doorframe and came closer to Luciana. Now was her time to run, but she would have to approach her escape carefully. She had made her opinion perfectly clear, but she did not wish to offend him. Luciana did not want to trigger any political conflicts with Osmain because of her actions.

"I can tell you don't like this arrangement," the Principe said.

Luciana spoke very slowly, trying to calculate her words carefully. "What gave you that impression?"

"Everything you've done since I arrived. Either you're particularly cold to everyone or you don't care to marry me. I'd like to think it's the latter."

"I hope you don't think poorly of me."

"Not at all."

The Principe smiled at her, and as his eyes found hers, she couldn't look away. He had the kindest eyes. Even though she'd been avoiding him, he still had no hint of hatred in his gaze. He also had a lovely smile, the kind that was obviously genuine. Luciana was sure that he must be the pride and joy of Osmain and probably had women lining up for his hand back home. With looks like his, how could he not? And somehow, she couldn't be sure, but it almost seemed like he understood her. The fleeting urge to stay came over Luciana but she fought it back.

Luciana gave him her most polite smile. She'd played her part. Now she needed to make her escape. "I'm glad we had this talk. See you at dinner, then?" With that, Luciana bolted from the room. The Principe was apparently too shocked by her sudden departure to call out after her, and with a smirk, Luciana rounded the corner and was out of his sight.

But with every step Luciana took, she felt like she'd made a mistake. He didn't hate her for not wanting to marry him. This should have been a relief, but instead it left Luciana conflicted. How could she hate a man who seemed to respect her feelings? She would have to step up her game. If she was to end this engagement promptly, his passive understanding wouldn't be enough. She didn't want to risk offending the Osmainians, especially since Daniel had been kind to her so far, but she only had one choice left. She would have to make Daniel hate her.

DANIEL SAT in the drawing room with his journal struggling to read what he wrote. It was late, and no one else was awake that he could tell. The Askanese rose and fell with the sun, and there were significantly fewer candles around the castillo than he was used to as a result. He didn't mind, though, as today he'd found his words. Daniel preferred to write poetry about what he experienced and felt rather than a simple recounting of his days. Tonight, he was optimistic, his language flowery and descriptive. As much as Luciana seemed to hate him and even though he hadn't been able to find her alone since the encounter in the library, he couldn't help but be hopeful. He hadn't been trying to seek her out that time. He'd merely been looking for a quiet place to write. But seeing her had been a lucky coincidence. He'd meant to tell her about his deal with his father, but she'd slipped out before he could. Then at dinner, she'd been silent, as if nothing had happened. And perhaps to her, nothing had.

But for Daniel, Luciana was a challenge, a puzzle to be solved. Daniel still intended to tell her about the deal as soon as possible, but one awkward conversation was enough for one day. Their connection was still fragile, and Daniel didn't want to push her further. But he was going to figure her out, and he was determined that by the end of their engagement, they would part as allies— if not friends. He knew little about Luciana. Even the general gossip about the Askanese princesas was scarce. All anyone seemed to know was that they were beautiful. But as he observed her, he picked up on some things. She was ladylike to a fault. She was fashionable. He had seen her smile at her sister during dinner. It was a small gesture, just a faint upturn of the lips, like she and Camila were the only ones in on a secret. Luciana actually seemed to be fairly close to her sister, and so far Camila was the only one he had seen Luciana speak to a social function.

Perhaps Princesa Camila was the answer. Camila and Condesa Esmeralda also seemed very close, and he already had the Condesa's favor thanks to his friendship with her cousin. Tomorrow, instead of searching for Luciana, he would look for Camila and Esmeralda. He was certain they were the key to figuring out Luciana.

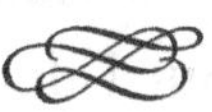

Day 16 of Summer

The next morning, Alora was silent. Luciana tried to make small talk with her maid as she got ready for the day, but Alora didn't manage more than a few words at a time. She had bags under her eyes, which were red from crying, and her uniform was more wrinkly than usual. Luciana hadn't wanted to pry. She wouldn't want Alora asking her questions if she looked upset and she wanted to extend the same courtesy to her maid, but Luciana still felt a stab of pain seeing Alora so upset.

As soon as the finishing touches were done on Luciana's outfit, she whirled around to face her maid. "Alora, what happened?"

"Nothing, Your Highness," Alora replied, her voice wavering slightly.

"Don't lie to me. I know you well enough to see you're hurting. What has happened?"

Alora took a shaky breath. "Something bad has happened back home. But I don't want to trouble you, so I should be going."

Luciana took Alora's hand and said soothingly, "If I can confide in you, you can do the same with me. Please tell me."

Alora looked like she wanted to run from the room, but after a moment her gaze softened and she slouched. "It's the rebels."

Luciana thought back to the briefings she'd read the past few days. There had been mentions of the rebels. They seemed to be a growing threat.

"What happened?" Luciana asked softly.

"My family's home… it…" Alora's voice cracked.

"Did they raid your village?" Alora's family was from Nieve, a small farming town just outside of the border regions. The food grown there supplied much of what the royal family and other nobility ate. It was no surprise that the rebels would choose to attack a village known for its loyalty to the crown.

Alora nodded as tears welled in her eyes. "They marched through. They burnt down homes. They slaughtered everyone in their path. My brother… he…

he didn't make it." She buried her head in her hands, sobbing. Luciana couldn't even imagine what Alora must be feeling. She didn't know what she would do if she lost Camila.

Luciana wrapped her maid in a hug and held her tightly. "Alora, I'm so sorry. I will speak with my uncle. Perhaps he can do something to avenge your brother's death and guarantee shelter for the rest of your family."

Alora wiped the tears from her eyes. "I'm not sure that's such a good idea, Your Highness. I don't want your request traced back to me."

"I'll keep it anonymous," Luciana said. "But I can't blindly sit by watching you suffer if I can help."

Alora nodded. "Okay."

Luciana left her maid in peace, then went to find Nicolas. He wasn't in the throne room and when she knocked on the door to his study, there was no response. She found him in his meeting room, sitting at the head of the large wooden table that took up most of the space. A few of his advisors were packing up their meeting materials around the table.

"Uncle, I require an audience with you!" Luciana said, sitting beside him at the table. The advisors that remained looked at each other with annoyance on their faces, then quickly left the room, leaving Luciana alone with her uncle.

"What is it, Luciana?" Nicolas grumbled, his cold eyes staring into Luciana's soul.

"It's the rebels. They have to be stopped. They're killing innocent civilians," Luciana said.

"Don't you think I know that?" Nicolas sneered.

"Of course, but—"

"Is it your job to worry about silly little skirmishes in the border regions?"

"Well, no. But—"

"Then shut your mouth," Nicolas said, standing.

"But your people—" Luciana said weakly.

"My people will be just fine. I will continue to lead them the same way I always have."

Luciana formed a fist at her side, trying to keep her anger in check. "If you could send your condolences to the people of Nieve, send food, and provide shelter to the survivors—"

"Now you're telling me what to do?" Nicolas leaned in close to Luciana, sending shivers down her spine. "Get out of my meeting room."

Nicolas pointed to the door, and Luciana slowly stood, sheepishly making her way to the exit. As she neared the threshold, Nicolas said from behind her, "You have no power in Askaña and you never will. The sooner you learn your place, the better off you'll be."

Luciana fought the urge to rage back at him, instead pretending that she never heard him at all. She sighed as she entered the corridor. So much for helping her people.

IT TOOK Daniel all morning to find Camila and Esmeralda. Not knowing much about either the castillo's layout or the people he was looking for, he found himself wandering down one corridor only to end up in the same place five minutes later. After nearly an hour of walking around in circles, Daniel stumbled upon the two women near the stables. It appeared as if they were just getting ready to go riding. Perfect. Daniel was an excellent rider. It would be a challenge navigating the steeper terrain of Askaña, compared to the tight streets surrounding his home in Osmain, but Daniel was certain he could manage.

"Good afternoon, Princesa Camila, Condesa Esmeralda," Daniel called out.

Camila and Esmeralda turned, looking surprised by his presence. Esmeralda smiled at him. "Good afternoon, Your Highness!" Camila gave a polite smile and nod but said nothing. These sisters were more alike than he'd thought.

"Would you mind if I join you? I just came to do a bit of riding myself."

It was an obvious lie, as he was not wearing riding

clothes. Camila and Esmeralda exchanged a look, but Esmeralda turned back to him and said politely, "Of course."

Daniel, whose horse had been sent back to Osmain with Antonio, was forced to borrow Natalia's horse, while the Askanese women mounted their own. The three of them left the stable and followed a well-worn path through the castillo grounds. It was wide enough that three of them could ride side by side, and Daniel weaseled his way in the middle.

He cleared his throat. "Thank you again for letting me ride with you."

"You never thanked us the first time," Camila remarked scornfully, looking straight ahead at the trail.

"Well... thank you now."

"What brought you out for a ride?" asked Esmeralda. Her tone was inquisitive, but Daniel could tell she was just being courteous.

"I thought I might get my mind off things."

"What kind of things?"

"I think that should be fairly obvious." And it was. Neither lady asked for any kind of clarification.

The silence loomed over them for a moment, then Camila asked, "What exactly are your intentions with my sister?"

Daniel sighed. Some voice inside told him to be honest, but he brushed it aside. "Please do not take offense, as I find your sister quite... lovely. But I was just as surprised by this engagement as she was."

"You're lying," Esmeralda said plainly. "You knew."

"What?" Daniel stammered. Perhaps he hadn't been entirely honest in the way he had phrased it, but he had been surprised when his father had told him on the way here, hadn't he?

"Let me guess. You don't want to marry her. But you've known about the plan since at least the spring," Esmeralda said, crossing her arms smugly.

"Well... um..." Shocked by her intuition, Daniel couldn't get out a single word.

"There's no shame in it." Esmeralda shrugged.

"Esme, get back to the issue at hand," Camila nudged.

"Oh, yes. Sorry. Sometimes I just get carried away," Esmeralda laughed.

"Well, anyway," Daniel cleared his throat, trying to regain his footing in the conversation. "I certainly have no intentions of hurting Princesa Luciana."

Camila smiled slowly, a devious grin. "Good. I'd hate to see what would happen to you if you broke her heart."

Daniel blinked slowly. He could hardly believe this new side of Camila. "Was that a threat?"

Camila burst out laughing. "Oh, not from me. From Luciana. She'll rip you apart if you don't watch yourself."

"I'll keep that in mind," Daniel said, searching for any

hint of sarcasm in her tone and not finding one. Message received.

"Good," Camila said. "So, why were you at the stables looking for us?"

"Because I…" Daniel snapped his mouth shut. He'd never said anything about looking for them, but she'd figured it out anyway. Camila was quicker than he'd given her credit for, and with Esmeralda there, the two could keep anyone on their toes. He wasn't fooling anyone at this point. He might as well tell the truth.

"Because I thought I might ask for advice. Your sister seems to be avoiding me. Given our situation, I only wish to get to know her. I want to know the person who I'm supposed to rule beside. I'm sure you understand."

Camila paused. She looked at Daniel and Esmeralda riding side by side. "I do. More than you know."

There was a sadness in her voice, something just under the surface of what she was saying, but Daniel didn't know what. He would worry about that later. One sister was hard enough as it was. He couldn't handle trying to decode them both.

"My sister is hardheaded," Camila continued. "If she's decided she doesn't like you, there isn't much you can do to change her mind."

"I don't need her to love me," Daniel said. Then he added, "Not yet anyway." It was best for Camila to think he had every intention of wooing Luciana. He wanted witnesses to vouch that he tried his hardest to make things work just in case his father asked.

"At least your expectations aren't too high," Esmeralda laughed. "Luciana has never been the type to fall head over heels for anyone. She doesn't even flirt."

"Never?"

"No."

"Do you think she might prefer to be alone?" Daniel asked.

Camila shrugged. "The answer to that depends on whose opinion you ask."

"She's never been interested in anyone—male, female, or otherwise," Esmeralda added. "I don't think she ever will."

"You don't know her as well as I do," Camila pointed out. "I've seen her in the ballroom. She looks at the happy couples swirling on the floor and gets this look in her eyes, as though she wants to join in but can't quite bring herself to do it. I'm not sure if she's shy or if she just hasn't found the right partner. But she certainly doesn't want to be alone. Perhaps an engagement is what she needs. It will give her a chance to participate for once."

"May I ask for your help, then?" Daniel asked.

"I'm not sure how you think we can help," Camila replied. "Luciana doesn't listen to anyone but herself."

"I only wish to spend time with her. Can you arrange

just one conversation between us?" Daniel asked.

"Our path will cross with my sister in just a moment. We were going to meet her during her ride," Camila said. She seemed to be genuinely opening up to him, like she wanted him to succeed. "The Condesa and I will do our best to give you time to get to know one another. Perhaps I can even urge her in your direction."

"Thank you. I am in your debt," Daniel said.

"Don't think a thing of it." Camila smiled warmly. It was such a different smile than the one he'd seen Luciana make when she spoke with Camila at dinner. Camila was friendly and kind, but Luciana's seemed like something rarer. Luciana wasn't inviting, but Daniel knew that her smiles would always mean more than Camila's. Camila gave hers away freely, while Luciana's were earned. Daniel was surprised at how he'd noticed that—and better yet, how he wanted to see Luciana smile for him. He shook his head. He shouldn't be thinking like this.

They had reached the base of the small hill on top which the castillo sat, mountains rising around them on all sides. The landscape seemed like an endless maze. The tops of some of the taller mountains were capped with snow, even in the heat of summer. Daniel understood why no one dared invade Askaña. In a country with this many hiding places for soldiers, not knowing the lay of the land was an excellent way to lose a war.

Not that anyone had problems with Askaña. They were usually too wrapped up in domestic affairs to bother the other kingdoms in the realm.

Daniel snapped himself back to reality as the three of them entered a small clearing. Luciana looked up as they approached, and Daniel noticed how she tried her best not to act shocked when she saw him riding alongside Camila and Esmeralda. This made him grin with satisfaction. But his grin immediately faded as he saw her in her riding clothes. He'd expected her to be in another plain velvet dress, but instead she wore riding pants and boots. Instead of riding sidesaddle like Camila and Esmeralda, she straddled the horse like a man would.

"Sister!" Camila called.

Luciana could not hide her scowl as she trotted toward the group.

"We've brought a guest," Camila continued. "We didn't think you'd mind."

Luciana's eyes flicked over to Daniel's. He'd clearly invaded her private time with her sister and friend, and Daniel almost felt bad for interfering. Almost. If Luciana had been even just a bit more agreeable, then maybe.

"Well, aren't you going to greet him? It's rude to stare," Esmeralda whispered to Luciana.

Luciana cleared her throat and said, "Well, yes. Hello, Your Highness. Let's get on with it."

Esmeralda led the way, clearly very familiar with

these trails. Camila followed, catching up to her. Luciana quickly filled the third space next to them, but the trail was too narrow for Daniel to fit in with the group. A spark of anger rose within him. He had been nothing but kind to Luciana, but she had deliberately left him behind.

He rode in silence for several minutes, listening to the women laughing up ahead. It sounded like they were gossiping about some poor nobleman, but he couldn't make out much of their conversation. Every once in a while, Esmeralda would look back at him pityingly. Finally, she gently slapped Camila on the arm and gestured to Daniel, who gave a small wave.

Camila turned to Luciana. Daniel couldn't hear what was being said between them, but a moment later Luciana slowed down to keep pace with Daniel. He fought to contain a smile from spreading across his face. Camila winked at him before she turned around, leaving him to speak to the Princesa.

Luciana stared straight ahead, her brow furrowed. Her breaths rose and fell evenly, as if she were purpose-fully regulating herself. Daniel thought about what he should say, trying to choose his words carefully. Now was not the time to tell Luciana about the deal with his father, not with Camila and Esmeralda so near. He wanted the conversation to be private, just between the two of them.

Finally, he said, "I didn't know you'd be out for a ride as well."

Luciana scoffed. "You didn't? I thought we'd already established you have a habit of following me."

"I assure you, this was a pure coincidence."

"So, you just happened to be riding with Camila and Esmeralda and on my mother's horse?" Luciana raised one of her perfectly arched eyebrows at him.

Where was this attitude coming from? It was clear that Luciana wasn't going to believe his story, no matter what he said, so he decided to change the subject. "Are you alright? After we spoke yesterday, I had assumed—"

"What? That I would suddenly be happy to marry you? You would be mistaken. All I learned from our conversation is that I should not fear being frank with you."

Daniel's heart sank. Of course, he hadn't expected Luciana to change her mind overnight, but he had at least hoped that she would become more of a partner in crime. He was more than willing to escape a marriage with this woman, but her attitude about it tempted him to push for it simply to spite her.

"I have done my best to get to know you," Daniel said quietly, his heart sinking. "What more can I do to win your favor?"

"Leave me alone," Luciana spat.

For a moment, Daniel was silent. He ignored the

shaking of his hands. He couldn't afford to give her any more power over him by appearing upset. He was perfectly prepared to give up an extremely advantageous match so that they both could find love, and here she was treating him like garbage. He was a Principe! Who gave her the right to treat him so cruelly?

Heat bubbled in his chest as Luciana looked away from him, like she didn't realize how badly she'd hurt him. Or maybe she just didn't care. He might not want her love, but he surely didn't deserve her hatred. Daniel tried to keep his breathing steady to calm himself, but he failed. Before he could decide on a tactful response, Daniel blurted out, "Oh, don't worry. As soon as I am able, I plan to run as far away from you as I can."

"What's stopping you?" Luciana spat. "Go back to Osmain."

"I am only trying to help you!"

"I don't want your help!"

"You've made that very clear. Very classy, by the way."

"You want to talk about class?" Luciana seethed, keeping her tone even as to not attract the attention of Camila and Esmeralda. "It seems pretty low to buy a bride, doesn't it? What, no one wants to sleep with you back home, so you had to come here and ruin my life?"

"You honestly think I want to marry you?" Daniel almost laughed at the absurdity of it all.

This got Luciana attention. She raised her head and opened her mouth to respond, but Daniel trampled over her words before she could make a sound. Anger had overtaken him, and he was blabbing without thought of consequence. "You're a fool, Your Highness. You think so highly of yourself that you can't fathom that I don't want you. From what I've heard about your love life, no one wants you. And as long as you're the angry, spiteful bitch that you've been to me since we met, no one ever will."

Daniel was shocked at the tone of his own voice. He looked forward to seeing if Camila or Esmeralda had heard, but thankfully they had already moved farther down the path and were out of earshot. He was glad they hadn't heard him lose his composure.

If Luciana was shaken, she didn't show it. She just gave him the same steely look she always did and said, "Good."

Then she tore off the path.

LUCIANA RODE as fast as she could through the brambles and trees, biting her lip to keep herself from shedding any tears. She supposed she had asked for that when she'd decided to make him hate her. If she could be brutal with him, she had no right to be upset when he threw it back in her face. Still, she could not bear to be in his presence one moment longer after he'd called out her actions. He was right. She had been acting cruelly. Daniel had done nothing to her but be kind and she had been remarkably mean.

The only thing worse than being embarrassed was being wrong. Luciana fought to regain her composure. She didn't like the person she was becoming. She'd always known that she couldn't become Reina without being a little ruthless, but her actions were beyond ambition. This could have ramifications for all of Askaña. If Daniel wanted to, he could use this tiff to prod his father into starting a war or imposing tariffs on their goods. How Luciana had ever thought this to be a good idea was beyond her.

Luciana tried her best to swallow her embarrassment. She couldn't tell anyone about the encounter. That evening, of course, Luciana would probably have to sit down with Camila and explain her sudden disappearance from the ride. She'd have to come up with a story less awful than the truth. Hopefully, her sister wouldn't worry that something had happened.

Luciana took her horse back to the stable and immediately left for her music room, not even bothering to change out of her riding clothes. She knew that she would be tracking mud through the tunnels and likely into her music room, but she didn't care. Her mind was still swirling, the mixture of everything and nothing filling her mind all at once convoluting any coherent thoughts.

She sat at the piano in a huff. Luciana could play hundreds of songs, but she could not even think of one she would like to play. Sighing, she banged angrily on the keys.

Then she sat in silence. It was all just too much. The marriage, her drive to become Reina, her mysterious letter-writing cousin. There were so many problems now falling on her shoulders that she did not know how she was to organize them.

Worse than anything was that she should have known better. Had she not prepared for this? All her years of training to be the perfect Princesa—the perfect Reina—had taught her the power of a clear and just mind. Now this Principe had come into her home and ruined everything. She couldn't even play her piano without thinking of him, thinking of Camila, thinking of Nicolas's daughter. With all the problems she was suddenly facing, how could she ever become Reina?

A rustling noise outside her window tore Luciana from her thoughts. The music room was close to the foundation of the castillo, the window overlooking a flower-filled courtyard. She rose from her seat and peered out to see Daniel outside. He was bent over, plucking a rose from its bush. He did not see her at first, but slowly he turned and they made eye contact. His shoulders slouched, not his usual confident posture. His brows furrowed as he took her in, and Luciana wished she could disappear underneath her piano. She could tell from the way his eyes no longer sparkled that he was hurt. She had done that, and her stomach churned like she might be sick.

Luciana sighed and left the window. This had gone too far. Her plan to make him hate her had worked, but at what cost? She'd lost herself in the process. From now on, she would have to be kinder to him. She supposed she could still oppose the marriage without making him into an enemy.

Luciana sat again. Daniel was still outside. He looked in through the window, but he wasn't staring at her exactly. It was more like he was lost in his own world and not registering what he saw. Luciana's fingers hovered over the keys, and she wracked her brain for the right piece. Slowly, she lowered her hands and began to play a sad melody.

For the most part, the room didn't carry sound well. In fact, the privacy of the space was one of her favorite parts of the music room. But as she played, Daniel looked up at her. He cocked his head to the side as if he could hear the melody, and she tried to express through the highs and lows of the music an apology that she hoped he would understand.

5

Day 17 of Summer

*D*aniel gave Luciana the rest of the day to herself. He didn't want to explode at her again, and he also didn't want to make her any more uncomfortable than she already seemed to be, so he left her alone. He'd been in Askaña for four days now and still had not managed to get Luciana alone long enough to tell her about the deal with his father. The next day, he decided, would be that day.

He didn't approach her for most of it, but after dinner, Daniel made sure he was the first to excuse himself. He needed to beat Luciana to her secret hideout.

After Luciana had ridden off into the woods the day before, Daniel had quickly alerted Camila and Esmeralda that Luciana had left the trail. Excusing himself, he then backtracked their route, riding recklessly, hoping to get back to the stables before Luciana. It worked. Then Daniel had simply waited. At first when she appeared, he'd intended to call out to her and apologize, but he didn't want to make a bigger fool of himself, so he held back. She seemed too preoccupied to notice that Daniel's horse was back in his stall, and she had stalked off toward the castillo. She had twigs in her hair and mud on her boots, but Daniel was glad he'd been able to see her like that. Luciana was such a force of nature that it was almost necessary to have that reminder that she was human.

Daniel had stood in silence as she marched off, not exactly sure what to do with himself. Then he'd moved after her and before he knew it, was following her into the castillo.

His espionage skills were sorely lacking these days, and given previous experience with Luciana, she probably knew he was behind her and just didn't care. He had been careful to take light steps, however, and to follow at such a distance that he could hide if she were to look behind her.

Luciana made a few turns down the gilded corridors. Then, in a place that had nothing interesting about it, she stopped cold. Luciana turned to look around, and Daniel ducked behind the corner to avoid being seen.

A moment later he peeked back around the corner to see Luciana carefully opening up a portion of the wall. A secret passageway! She slipped inside, shut the door soundlessly behind her, and she was gone. Where had she disappeared to? What could she possibly be hiding?

After he was sure she'd had time to move on, Daniel pushed open the same panel and closed it behind him just as carefully. The door was small, and based on her finesse climbing into the tunnel, Daniel figured Luciana must use the passage often.

He found himself in a drab hallway made entirely of black stone. There were no cobwebs, and the only dirt was from tracks that must have come from her riding boots. The only source of light was a small candle on the wall, which he carefully lifted and carried with him as he trod along the secret path. After the exceptionally small door to get in, the hallway had expanded to a comfortable height inside.

Daniel walked as slowly and quietly as he could down the endless hallway until he finally reached a dead end. He had passed plenty of forks in the path along his way, but not wanting to get lost in the labyrinthine tunnels, he had turned to go back the way he came.

That was when he had heard it. A loud banging noise, almost like the sound of piano keys.

Daniel had turned toward the source of the sound, a

doorway along the hall and to his left. Daniel cautiously opened the small door, grateful when it did not squeak.

It had opened into a well-lit room with similar décor to the rest of the castillo. The light from the midday sun illuminated the red walls and the gold furniture inside the room, giving it a heavenly glow. He strained to see through the window. He was curious what it looked out to, but he was too far back to see.

Luciana sat at a piano in the center of the room, her back turned to the door. She sat on her bench like a wilted flower, beautifully tragic and vulnerable, and still covered in grime from her ride through the woods. Daniel certainly had not meant to follow her this far, and it was strange to see her like this, with her guard down. She certainly would never want to be seen that way. He closed the door and exited the passageway the same way he'd come in.

His next step had been to find that window. Just because he didn't want to interrupt Luciana's moment didn't mean he wasn't curious about her secret. He was on the lowest level of the castillo, which meant he just needed to circle the grounds to find the music room and its arched window. He started his trek around the castillo, peering in windows to see if any of them contained Luciana and her piano. He tried to keep his face hidden just in case he was to be seen wandering around the estate by a member of the nobility. It wouldn't be fun to explain his midday adventures to everyone at dinner.

There were few windows on the ground floor and those that were had shades drawn over them. Back home in Osmain, those rooms would have been the rooms of the nobility. The closer to sea level the chambers were, the higher-ranking the official. But here in Askaña, his room had been several flights up, and it seemed like the Rey was even higher than he was. Based on this, he figured the rooms he passed must have been servants quarters or kitchens. He'd been shocked to discover that he had been given a room here on one of the upper levels of the castillo. In Osmain his bedroom had always been at sea level.

With no help coming from the windows, it had taken Daniel the better part of thirty minutes to stumble upon a tall window facing a rose garden. He picked a lush red rose from a well-manicured bush outside and looked over to see Luciana staring at him through the glass.

He instinctively turned away. Had she seen him following her? He stood still for a moment, half expecting her to yell at him through the window. Instead, after a moment, he heard a soft melody. The sound was muffled by the walls, but he could hear enough to know she was very talented. When he'd looked back through the window, he'd seen Luciana, still covered in mud and twigs still in her hair, playing the loveliest song he'd ever heard. She was absolutely exquisite and her icy blue eyes shone like diamonds as the sunlight wafted in through the window.

He'd been too busy trying to get out of the marriage to notice that she was the kind of girl who would have turned his head back home. If he'd met Luciana under different circumstances, he probably wouldn't have needed any prodding to be interested in getting to know her. As if his situation couldn't get more complicated, he was actually attracted to Luciana. Just his luck.

EVEN THE NEXT DAY, as Daniel now prepared to find Luciana alone, he just couldn't shake the memory of what he'd seen. Luciana had a hobby that she seemed to keep for herself, and judging by the fact that there was only one visible door, a whole hidden room. His mind was abuzz all throughout dinner, and he could hardly concentrate on the conversion.

He'd spoken to Camila and Esmeralda, and they assured him that they would keep Luciana busy all day so she would want to spend time away from everyone else after dinner. Daniel was still patting himself on the back for getting the Crown Princesa on his side. He was only hoping that Luciana would choose to spend her free time in her hidden space. He was buzzing with anticipation to see her alone, and as soon as he'd finished his food, Daniel excused himself from the dinner table. Not that it mattered much but Daniel wanted to be the first one to arrive in the music room.

He made his way as quickly as he could back to where he'd entered the tunnels the day before, creeping down the same passageways as he had before.

When Daniel reached the door to the piano room, he pushed it ajar. The room seemed to be empty. He'd arrived before Luciana. He opened the door completely and stepped into the small space. The sunset cast a golden glow through the room, and Daniel sat in a large, cushy chair overlooking the garden. It was surprisingly comfortable and he found himself settling in as he glanced out of the window. In the heat of the summer, everything was in full bloom. He could only imagine that this view would be much bleaker during Askaña's notoriously brutal winters. Besides a few evergreen trees, everything would most likely be dead and covered in snow.

Looking around the room, he saw several more instruments on shelves or in corners. A violin, a flute, even a guitar. Luciana was apparently a woman of many talents. A cello rested next to the chair, and he imagined that was the only reason Luciana had even bothered bringing one in. He couldn't imagine she received very many visitors down here, and by the looks of things, there was only one door—the secret passageway itself.

It was not Daniel's place to question the layout of Askaña's castillo, but it made him wonder about the Osmainian palazzo. Did they also have secret passages just out of reach, whole rooms in his home that he had never seen?

Daniel heard a creaking noise, and he perked up as the secret door opened.

LUCIANA DUCKED as she passed through the entryway, looked up to see Daniel sitting in her chair, then fell flat on her face.

Daniel jumped up to help her. "Are you alright?"

Luciana fought to keep herself from blushing. How embarrassing to trip on her own gown! But then again, she wouldn't have been startled if Daniel hadn't been sitting in her private space.

"What are you doing here?" Luciana shrieked, scrambling to regain her composure. How dare he enter her secret room? How had he even found it? Had he been following her? Luciana furrowed her brow as her thoughts swarmed around in her mind. Surprise turned to anger, which turned to curiosity.

Daniel had a remarkably calm exterior as he said, "I came to speak with you."

"You couldn't have done that anywhere else?" Luciana crossed her arms.

"Given your habit of running away from me, no."

Luciana couldn't keep the heat from rising to her cheeks this time, and she averted her gaze in embarrassment. "I apologize for running from you yesterday."

"And I apologize for losing my temper with you."

Daniel helped Luciana to her feet, then he took a seat in her chair, crossing his legs and looking far too comfortable. "Please have a seat," Daniel said.

Without thinking, Luciana sat at her piano bench. Then she scowled as she realized she'd actually listened to his command. "How did you get in here?" Luciana asked. She'd been so shocked at his presence that she still hadn't been able to ask all of her questions.

"Same way as you," Daniel explained calmly. "The passageways."

"Well, obviously, but how did you—"

"I saw you use one. Then yesterday when I saw you playing in here, I was able to figure it out." Daniel shrugged. Luciana thought back to the mud that had caked her riding boots the day before. She must have led him right to her.

Luciana squirmed in her seat. How had she been so

careless? She wasn't usually hiding anything. She just liked her space. Only now she had the letter from her supposed cousin rolled up tight and shoved inside her flute for safe keeping. When her eyes darted over to where the flute was stored, it didn't seem to be disturbed.

Luciana cleared her throat. "So, what did you wish to talk about?"

Daniel laughed. "Oh, now you'd like to know. I kept trying to pull you aside to tell you sooner."

"Tell me what?" Luciana asked impatiently.

"I made a deal with my father on our way here," he said.

Luciana sighed. "What does that have to do with me?"

"Everything." Daniel smiled.

Luciana motioned for him to continue.

"I don't wish to marry you any more than you wish to marry me. I've been trying my best to get to know you this week, but it's only because my father gave me an exit opportunity. Should I dislike you, we can cancel the engagement."

Luciana's eyes widened. "What do you mean?"

"I mean, I have until the night of our engagement ball to decide as long as I pursue you in earnest. If we don't have a connection by then, I will be allowed to return to Osmain alone, and we will both be free to go about our lives. I only hope Rey Nicolas won't be offended when the contract is left unsigned."

"Given my behavior toward you, why haven't you simply given up already?"

"Because that was his stipulation. I had to try. I can't just give up before the ball. I could lie, but my father would see through that in an instant. With my servants here and your family watching our every move, I've tried to make our interactions very public until now. I'm sorry, but this was the only way to get your attention. If we don't agree to his terms, you and I will be married by the end of the season."

Luciana practically choked. "That soon?"

"That is the plan. Didn't you listen to your uncle discussing it with my father upon our arrival?"

"My mind was somewhere else."

"Clearly."

Luciana was growing impatient. What was he trying to say? "Get to the point. You made a deal, then what?"

"Well, I figured I would give you a chance. I obviously didn't know what you'd be like and I certainly didn't expect what I got."

"I'll take that as a compliment."

"I wouldn't," Daniel laughed.

Luciana couldn't think of a retort fast enough, so she sputtered, "What happened next?"

"I'm getting there!" Daniel leaned forward, and

Luciana's heart skipped a beat. "Maybe if you stopped interrupting me…"

Luciana wanted to say more just to spite him, but as long as their eyes were locked together, she couldn't come up with words. She was speechless as they sat there, Daniel daring her to say anything else. She simply crossed her arms and that seemed to satisfy him.

Daniel cleared his throat dramatically before he continued.

"Anyway, I've always had a fantasy of marrying for love. My parents loved each other, and I want the same for myself and my future bride. But I suppose I waited too long to find her, and the next thing I knew, my father was dragging me here."

Luciana knew how he felt. She had never really thought much about marriage, always found herself much too busy to fool around with the idiots in the Askanese court. Still, if she married, she would want it to be because she loved her husband.

Luciana smiled a bit as she said, "My mother loved my father, too. They made it look so easy." Then she paused, remembering how it had been when her father had passed away, how deeply her mother had grieved. "I miss him." She looked up as Daniel's chair scraped against the wooden floors, inching it closer to her. There was a certain look in his eyes. It wasn't pity, as she had expected, but understanding. She should have been disgusted that he was coming closer to her or terrified that she didn't want him to move away. But try as she might, she couldn't look away from him.

Then once again, he seemed to look right through her. "I lost my mother, too," he whispered.

Luciana, for the first time, gave Daniel a smile. A real one. It wasn't exactly ideal to bond over the deaths of their parents, but somehow it was comforting to know that someone else besides Camila had experienced the same pain as her.

Luciana's father had always been so lively, and when he'd gotten sick, her family might as well have, too. Nothing had been the same since he'd died. Natalia was distant from her daughters, serving as a mother only when eyes were trained in her direction. Luciana had to remind herself every once in a while that her father would never truly disappear. He lived on through Camila and Luciana—especially Luciana. She was the spitting image of her father, and the only bit of Natalia that Luciana had inherited were her uncommon blue eyes.

The prick of tears formed in said eyes, and she quickly changed the subject. "Anyway, I get what you mean. About wanting to marry for love."

Daniel looked as if he'd just been snapped out of a trance, his look of concern replaced with business-like swagger. Their time for grief was over and it was back to the matter at hand— their marriage. "Yes. So, as I was saying, I was willing to take the chance and get to know you. But your total disinterest has decided for me. I'll call off our wedding at the engagement ball."

Luciana didn't react at all for a moment. Was he joking? But no, he sat there, entirely serious, and a tremendous weight lifted off her shoulders. This would make her appeal to become Reina much easier. Reina. Perhaps Daniel could help her there, too. He seemed to understand her so well already, perhaps if she simply told him…

"Are you alright?" Daniel asked.

"Yes, quite," said Luciana unconvincingly.

"What is it? Isn't this what you want?"

Luciana just nodded and made up her mind. She couldn't tell him about her desire to be Reina. As much as he seemed sympathetic to her right now, they weren't friends. A secret that big could only be told to someone who could be trusted.

"It's settled then," Daniel said. "I'll call it all off and you and I can part as friends."

"Is there a catch?" Luciana asked. It seemed almost too good to be true.

Daniel smiled, a grin that caused nervous butterflies in Luciana's stomach. "Of course," he said. "Spend time with me."

Luciana bit her lip, weighing her options. She didn't

want anyone to see her with the Principe. They would have to hide away in the music room. But it was still better than marrying him.

"Deal," Luciana said, extending her hand for a shake. "You get thirty minutes."

6

Day 18 of Summer

The bells from the watchtower tolled, signaling a guest entering the castillo grounds. Luciana looked up from her daily paper in shock. She hadn't expected a visitor today. Alora hadn't said anything about it either, although she was still grieving the loss of her brother. Things were bound to slip through the cracks.

Luciana walked as quickly as she could to the throne room, prepared to greet whoever might be entering the castillo. When she arrived, she found herself to be the only one present. Camila's absence was to be expected at this point, so that didn't surprise Luciana in the slightest. Her mother must have heard about the visit and decided not to attend the meeting, meaning it probably wasn't someone of great importance. As for her uncle…

He would undoubtedly be there to greet his guests, right? Luciana sat on her throne, anxious. As the minutes ticked by and no one came inside, she found herself squirming in her seat. Who could these visitors be?

The door opened slowly and a page stepped forward. As he saw only Luciana sitting on her throne, his eyes widened in surprise. He cleared his throat.

"Your Highness," he said, "I present to you, the Barón of Heilo!"

A small elderly man hobbled into the throne room. He was so feeble he could barely bow before Luciana. He eyed her up and down, and she stared right back at him. She'd met the Barón once, but it had been several years ago, and without Nicolas there to greet him, Luciana felt awkward.

"It's wonderful to see you, señor," Luciana said as diplomatically as possible. "What brings you to the castillo today?"

"I must speak with Rey Nicolas immediately," the Barón said.

"I understand," Luciana said. "I'm sure he will be here any moment now. In the meantime, can I help you?"

"With all due respect, Your Highness, I must speak with someone who has the power to help me."

Luciana narrowed her eyes. "Perhaps I can relay a message."

"You'll tell him my request?" The Barón asked.

"Of course," Luciana said. "I'd do anything to help my people. What exactly do you need?"

The Barón shook his head. In disappointment or disbelief, Luciana wasn't sure. But in the end he said, "Alright."

Luciana sat up straight, ready to listen. She'd prepared her whole life for this. Now here she was speaking with a nobleman about his concerns. It was exhilarating.

"It's the rebels," he said.

Luciana's heart dropped as he said it. She seemed to be hearing more and more about the rebels each day.

"What's happened?" Luciana said, trying to keep her voice calm.

"Nothing yet, Your Highness. But they seem to be slowly marching across Askaña. They've been burning villages and our already sparse crops."

"So I've heard. I was very saddened to hear about what happened in Nieve," Luciana said.

"A horrible tragedy, indeed. I've come here today to avoid that fate for Heilo. We are positioned between Nieve and the castillo, and as such we are likely to be in the direct path of the rebels' attack. I cannot defend my land and my tenants without assistance from your uncle and his militia," the Barón explained.

"I understand completely," Luciana said, nodding in sympathy. "I don't wish for any more innocent blood to be spilt or for any more food to be destroyed. I will speak to him as soon as possible to work on a solution to your problem."

"Thank you, Your Highness," the Barón said, "but that's only part of the issue."

Before Luciana could decipher what that meant, her uncle entered the throne room.

"The Barón of Heilo," Nicolas said, sweeping through the room and onto his throne. "Greetings, Señor! I apologize for my tardiness. I've had much to attend to this morning. What's the occasion for your surprise visit?"

The Barón said, "I've just explained some of it to Princesa Luciana, but I was just getting to my largest concern."

"Which is?"

"My people are turning on me," he said solemnly.

"Turning on you?" Nicolas asked, a slight hint of annoyance in his tone.

"Yes, my tenants are dividing amongst themselves. Most are still loyal to the crown, but there are some who have decided to join the rebellion. And their numbers are growing. I am worried about the fate of Heilo. Either the rebels will burn my land down from the outside, or they will destroy it from within. I've already heard stories of nobility in the border regions slain by their own subjects who turned to the rebellion. I need your help to ensure that doesn't happen to me, too," the Barón said.

Luciana shook her head. This went deeper than she'd thought. First the border regions, then Nieve, and now Heilo. The rebellion was like a plague spreading throughout Askaña.

"That does seem concerning," Nicolas said, considering the Barón's request. "But it also seems like your problem. I can provide some men as personal defense to keep you and your estate safe, but as for your rowdy tenants, I can't help you with that, can I?"

Luciana wanted to argue that he *could*, in fact, help. He could figure out why people were joining the rebellion, meet their demands, and let them fizzle out on their own. Luciana knew she was on shaky ground with Nicolas already. She knew he was growing tired of her constant nagging to help him around the castillo. So, despite every fiber of her being telling her to speak out against her uncle, she stayed silent.

"Please," the Barón said. "I need help to keep things under control. Personal protection can only go so far. I need to keep people from joining the rebellion or the situation will only get worse."

"It is not my job to make sure you do your duty," Nicolas said coldly. "Now I believe we're done here."

Without saying another word, he stood and left the throne room. Luciana looked at the Barón, sadness in her eyes. As he turned to leave, he said, "Thank you for trying, Your Highness."

As Luciana continued about her day, she couldn't help but feel a sense of dread. The rebellion was becoming a big problem and Nicolas refused to fix it.

"I CAN'T EVEN IMAGINE what Esmeralda is going to be saying about us," Luciana said that evening as she sank onto her piano bench.

Daniel shrugged from the chair he'd begun to claim as his in the corner. "Who cares?"

"I do. It matters to me that any talk surrounding me is true," Luciana said.

Doing his best impression of Esmeralda, he said, "Did you hear? The Principe and the Princesa sit in silence at dinner and glare at each other! How romantic!"

Luciana rolled her eyes, but she couldn't prevent a small laugh from escaping. When he put it that way she did sound a bit ridiculous, but this was Esmeralda they were talking about. She could make a compelling story out of anything.

"She's probably going to start telling people that we sneak off together after dinner," Luciana said.

"That's technically true," Daniel replied.

"But they won't know that talking is all we're doing. We could be… well…" Luciana trailed off, the heat of a blush rising in her cheeks. She'd managed to avoid thinking of Daniel in any kind of romantic way up until this point and she didn't plan to start now. But she would have to make sure no rumors had spread that she'd lost her innocence. If she wanted any chance at all of being an Ambassador of the Sun, she'd have to make sure her image stayed completely clean.

"We could be," Daniel agreed. "But instead, we're in here, doing absolutely nothing."

"We can't very well go outside together," she objected. "Someone could see, and I don't want anyone getting the wrong idea about us. They can't have any hope that it will work out."

"We will have to be more cordial at meals. I think if you write him a letter confirming that we spent time together he will believe it, but I want to have a few accounts from other people that we were friendly just in case he asks."

"That's fine." Luciana shrugged. It could be worse.

"It's not exactly what I had in mind, but we will do something in here," Daniel said.

Luciana looked around. "There's nothing in here but instruments. Besides, you get thirty minutes. That's all. What exactly could we do in thirty minutes?"

Daniel didn't respond, but he grinned awkwardly, his eyes wide. As soon as she'd said it, Luciana realized exactly what two people could do in thirty minutes. Especially if marriage was in their future. She bit her lip. This might complicate things. She had to spend time with him to get out of the marriage—that wasn't an option. But if they were caught, this would practically guarantee that she would have to marry if she ever became Reina, whether she'd done anything or not.

Daniel cleared his throat. "We don't have to talk if you don't want to."

"So, we'll sit here in silence?"

"Just do what you'd do if I weren't here," Daniel said. She knew he was just trying to make her feel more comfortable, but it put pressure on her instead. What exactly would she be doing if she were alone?

Her eyes drifted to the piano in front of her. She'd almost certainly be practicing. But she couldn't just play the piano for Daniel. He'd already heard her play once, and that should have been enough.

"I don't know what I'd be doing," she lied.

"None at all?" Daniel said, leaning forward almost as

though he were making a challenge. "All these instruments in here and you wouldn't be playing even one?" His gaze swept the room. "How many do you even have? I can see five just from here."

"There are seven," Luciana corrected.

"Seven?" Daniel said, raising his eyebrows. "How are you not known for your music talents throughout the realm?" He looked impressed, which made the corners of Luciana's mouth curl into a small grin.

"I just like having this to myself. As far as the rest of the realm knows, I only play the violin."

"And you're an expert at them all?" Daniel asked, amazed. Luciana couldn't help it as a swell of pride made her smile.

"I'm better at some more than others," Luciana admitted. "But I can play a few pieces on each."

Daniel smiled. "Show me what you can do."

"I can't," Luciana said.

"Why not?"

"I just told you. It's very personal for me."

"I've already heard you play," Daniel reminded her, smiling devilishly. He had dimples when he smiled. Luciana had never noticed them before. She'd spent so much time pushing him away that she'd forgotten to look at the little things. It unsettled her that she'd been so blind.

"That was different," Luciana said, crossing her arms.

"Why?"

A great question. Luciana couldn't just admit that she'd meant the last time as an apology. It seemed silly. She shook her head and tried to deflect, saying, "How would you feel if you had something deeply personal. Something you kept for yourself, that you'd never shared with anyone, and suddenly it was on display for everyone to see?"

Daniel shrugged. "I'd be nervous, but I'd do it anyway. What's the point of having a talent if you never share it?"

"Spoken like a man with no hobbies," Luciana huffed.

Daniel held a hand to his chest in a dramatic gesture. "Rude!"

"Am I wrong?"

"I'll have you know, I write—"

"Books?" Now he'd piqued Luciana's interest.

"I've been keeping a journal for the past two years."

Luciana giggled. "Really?"

Daniel nodded.

"And you've never shared this with anyone?"

"Nope. I mean, people know I keep the journal. It would be crazy if they didn't. But no one has ever read my writings."

"I have to see it!" Luciana laughed, delighted.

"No way," Daniel said lightheartedly.

"What's the matter?" Luciana teased. "Afraid to share?"

"No, I just... it's silly, but I'd like to share it later. When it's finished. I'm writing down everything notable in my life so I can tell the stories to my children, you know?" Daniel said, suddenly serious.

Luciana imagined an older version of Daniel, sitting by a fireplace, reading his journal aloud with a smile on his face. The thought was unexpectedly charming. "I can respect that," she said. "But if you want me to play for you, I'll need to hear some of your writing in exchange."

"I don't have my journal with me right now," Daniel protested.

"But you brought it with you to Askaña?"

"It's in my chamber."

Luciana cocked her head and said, "If I play something tonight, will you bring your journal here tomorrow?"

Daniel considered this for a moment, then said, "It's a deal."

Luciana smiled. This was the perfect test to determine his trustworthiness. If he brought his journal tomorrow and shared his most intimate writings with her, she might consider asking for his help to claim her throne.

"What instrument do you want me to play?" she asked, taking stock of her options.

"Piano is fine," he said. "I'd like an encore."

Luciana didn't know why, but his request made her blush. She nodded. "Piano it is." She looked through her sheet music. "What do you want to hear?" she asked. "Something dramatic? Something sad? Something upbeat?"

Daniel leaned forward, looking into her eyes. Luciana's breath caught in her throat as his eyes darted to her lips. He was close enough to touch as he said, "Play something beautiful."

7

Day 19 of Summer

After taking her time at the breakfast table, Luciana stood and made her way to Camila's study. She'd purposely lingered this morning so she could give her sister time to attend to any duties she might wish to. Camila would likely spend the rest of her morning in the garden after that, giving Luciana time to read the morning post uninterrupted. Ideally she would have woken up early and gone before breakfast, but she was tired from the night before. She'd only promised Daniel thirty minutes a day until the ball, now five days away, but they'd stayed in the music room much later than she'd intended.

Daniel was an excellent audience. Every time she glanced over at him, she'd seen him listening intently.

He seemed to enjoy listening to her play, and to her surprise, she enjoyed showing off her skills. There was something satisfying about seeing all of her practice pay off. Losing track of time had come at a cost, but his smile as her fingers floated along the keys made it all worth it. Luciana stifled a yawn as she shuffled towards Camila's study. She hoped something interesting had happened in the realm, otherwise she wasn't sure that she could stay awake.

Reaching Camila's door, Luciana slowly turned the key and opened the door slightly, peeking in as she always did to ensure the room was empty. Luciana did not see Camila, but she did see a bodice thrown haphazardly to the ground. Luciana furrowed her brows. This was unusual. Luciana soundlessly stepped inside, and as she stepped closer, recognized it as the same garment her sister had been wearing just that morning. She picked it up. It seemed to have been unlaced in a hurry and tossed aside. Luciana heard a rustling noise from behind the couch and stopped in her tracks. Something was wrong.

What was Camila doing down there? Was she alright? Luciana silently edged her way toward the couch.

"Camila?" She called softly.

The faint scent of perfume and sweat filled Luciana's nose. She edged around the couch and caught sight of her sister. Luciana's hand flew to her mouth and she instinctively stepped back, a cornered animal, frozen in place. Camila and Esmeralda sat up. They had both lost their gowns, their hair tousled as if they'd been...

No.

She had to be imagining things. There had to be a different explanation. Except there were the faintest beginnings of a love bite forming on the exposed flesh of Camila's neck.

No, this was real. Camila and Esmeralda had been having sex. And Luciana had walked in on it. Luciana's face burned red-hot. She was vaguely aware of her mouth falling open somewhere in the process, but she didn't care. She couldn't look away from the scene.

"Luciana?" said Camila, sitting up slowly.

"Don't mind me. I was just going," Luciana said, edging toward the door.

But Esmeralda, who was quicker than Luciana in her shocked state, dashed to the door and slammed it, blocking Luciana's exit.

Luciana and Esmeralda stared at each other for a second that stretched into an eternity. Luciana could think of nothing to say, and apparently neither could anyone else. She found herself hoping that the castillo would swallow her whole so she could escape from the humiliation. She supposed this did eliminate Esmeralda as a suspect for Nicolas's daughter, but that was hardly a consolation given the circumstances.

Finally, Esmeralda said, "Kindly give Camila her bodice back, please."

Luciana slowly obliged, crossing the room, and handing Camila her bodice. She had forgotten that poor Camila was still topless, but then again, Esmeralda wasn't exactly fully clothed either. Her shoes and petticoat were missing, and her top was gone, leaving her in a thin shift. Camila snatched her garment from Luciana's hands and put it back on the best she could manage by herself.

"What were you doing in here?" Esmeralda demanded.

Luciana should have been rattled by so direct a question, but all she could manage was a gesture at Camila, who was trying desperately to appear as if she and Esmeralda hadn't just been on the floor together. "I could ask you the same question."

"I don't know what you think you saw but—"

Luciana cut Esmeralda off. "I know very well what I saw, thank you." That seemed to shut her up.

"Please, Luciana, you mustn't tell," Camila begged.

"Is this a common occurrence? Or was this just a temporary lapse of judgment?" Luciana asked.

"Luciana—"

"Need I remind you, you cannot marry a woman!

She cannot give you a blood heir, and after what I've seen today, you could never be an Ambassador of the Sun."

"I love her!" Camila cried.

When Luciana looked at Esmeralda, her cheeks were bright red, but her lips curled into a soft smile. So, it was true. Luciana had known they loved each other. She just assumed the affection was sisterly. Luciana's heart melted at her sister's desperation. Camila was a traitor to her title, but she'd found something genuine in Esmeralda. She had no right to judge Camila for what her heart wanted.

Luciana sat on the floor with her sister and wrapped her in a tight hug. "Camila, I am so happy for you. I wish I could find a love of my own as deep as yours and Esmeralda's."

Camila's tears fell onto Luciana's gown. She was undoubtedly afraid and rightfully so. If her secret was to be made public, she could be cast from the family for betraying her title. Or maybe this could be the ticket to Luciana taking the throne in her sister's place. Her heart fluttered at the thought.

"Camila, look at me," Luciana said. "I would never do anything to hurt you. You needn't worry about me."

Camila nodded in response. Her eyes were red and puffy from crying, her corset askew, her hair in tangles. She looked like a mess. Esmeralda no longer blocked the door but stood over Luciana, almost daring her to try anything.

Luciana looked back and forth between the two of them. "How did this happen?" she demanded.

"It was two years ago," Esmeralda said. "I had already begun living here at the castillo."

Luciana remembered the time well. Esmeralda's parents had been caught in a nasty winter storm on their trip home from Osmain and perished on the treacherous mountain slopes. Following their deaths and thanks to Camila's long friendship with their daughter, Nicolas had offered Esmeralda a room in his home. The two of them had been inseparable since childhood, and now Esmeralda performed her duties as Condesa from the comfort of the castillo.

"We went for a walk in the garden and something just clicked. It was as if I could suddenly see the world the way it was meant to be seen. Beautiful and full of life, and it was all because of Camila. She brought me out of my despair."

"I didn't care what might happen. All I knew was I wanted her. The rest is history," Camila cut in.

Luciana saw the way they looked at each other, as if she wasn't in the room at all. She wondered how she'd been so blind to this in the past.

"Who else knows?" Luciana asked.

"Not a soul," said Esmeralda, "and we had intended

to keep it that way."

"But now that you know, we won't have to hide in front of you any longer! I am truly happy you know. I just wish things were different for us, so we didn't have to hide at all," Camila said, taking Luciana's hands and giving her the most genuine smile she'd ever seen.

"Perhaps…" Luciana said softly. "Perhaps you could just tell everyone. Then you could be together without hiding."

"I'm going to be Reina one day," Camila said. "I don't want to abandon my title."

Luciana fought to keep her composure at Camila's blatant dismissal of the obvious solution, but nevertheless, her gaze became steely. "So, then what do you intend to do? Keep this a secret forever?" Luciana asked, dropping Camila's hands and crossing her arms.

"Essentially," Esmeralda said. "Camila and I will choose husbands eventually, and hopefully we will take residence close enough that we will be able to still see each other."

That was a horribly bleak outcome to imagine, the two of them sneaking around behind the backs of their husbands and children forever. Luciana made a mental note to search the law books for anything that might help them. "Surely you're not going to settle for that," Luciana said.

"That is our only option," Camila said sadly.

But it wasn't. Luciana wanted to grab Camila by the shoulders and shake her until she came to her senses. It made so much more sense to simply allow Luciana to take her place as Reina. Being unable to take the throne due to a scandal and giving it up willingly with a strong reputation were two entirely different things. Abdicating the throne and granting the title to the next person in line was considered just fine under Askanese law. As long as Camila waited a few more years to announce her relationship with Esmeralda, Luciana could be Reina and Camila could be with the woman she loved. Luciana pursed her lips.

Camila looked at her with pleading eyes. "I'm begging you, Luciana. Don't tell anyone."

Luciana had no words left to say. She had barely had time to process anything that had happened. It seemed that Camila and Esmeralda were done, too. Luciana picked up a petticoat from the ground and tossed it to Esmeralda, who quickly put it on.

"I should go," Luciana said. "Your secret is safe with me."

Before they could say anything else, Luciana bolted from the room.

In the shock of everything, Luciana had forgotten to check the post.

~

LUCIANA WAS ALREADY WAITING for Daniel when he ducked under the door. They'd been friendly at dinner, but that hadn't been enough for Daniel. It would satisfy his father, but Daniel wanted to speak to her freely. He was tired of calling her "Your Highness."

She eyed him suspiciously. "You're late."

"I had to go back to my room after dinner, remember?" Daniel replied.

"You brought it?" Luciana asked eagerly, jumping up from the piano bench.

In response, Daniel pulled out his journal and held it out to show her. Luciana took the book gently, but the wide smile on her face betrayed her true excitement.

"It's so worn," Luciana said, examining the cracked spine and folded corners of the cover.

"It's been through a lot," Daniel said.

"What do you generally write? Poetry? Or do you do more in-depth descriptions of what you've done that day?" Luciana asked, hardly taking any breaths between her questions.

"If you'd hand me the book you'll find out," Daniel said. Luciana looked hesitant to part with the journal. "Unless you plan on reading to me instead?"

"I do think it would be more effective coming from you." Luciana sighed and handed the book back. Their hands touched as she passed off the journal, a fleeting sensation, but Daniel's breath caught in his throat.

Luciana flopped onto the bench. "Well, let's get into it! Take a seat!"

"Where do you want to start?" Daniel asked, ripples of anxiety starting to course through his veins as he sat. He'd never shared his writing with anyone. There were bound to be errors. Improper grammar, sentences that didn't make sense. What if his descriptions weren't vivid enough? Would Luciana laugh at him?

"You should start at the beginning," said Luciana.

Daniel had been hoping she would request something a bit later in the book. He had no doubt that he'd look back on his first entry and cringe. But he opened the journal to the first page and cleared his throat, trying to get rid of his nerves.

"Year 735, Day 1 of Spring," he began. "Today I have left the palazzo for the adventure of a lifetime."

Luciana listened intently, showing no signs of boredom as he read. If she was judging his writing ability, she hid it well. And although Daniel knew she could hide her displeasure at something if she so chose, her guard was down. She would be honest with him.

Daniel read about ten journal entries aloud, chronicling his journey to military training, his first days in service, and even the beginnings of his friendship with Capitano Quirino, who at the time had been just a Tenente. Quirino had thought it was funny that he ranked higher than the Principe himself, even as a

Junior Officer. But after a while, his voice grew tired and his mouth dried out from all the talking. Daniel closed the book gently.

"That's all for tonight. I don't think I could read anymore," Daniel said. Luciana looked almost disappointed, and Daniel fought back a smile knowing that she was so invested.

There was a sparkle in Luciana's eyes that made his heart flutter. He shouldn't be looking at her like this, regarding her as if they were really courting. Daniel knew that his heart was going to do what it wanted, but he also knew that Luciana would never return any affections he gave her. Daniel stood, dusting off his jacket and heading toward the small door. If he couldn't handle himself around her right now, he would have to go.

"Leaving so soon?" Luciana asked.

"I'm tired," Daniel said simply. He tried to keep his eyes off of her lips as he got ready to depart, but it proved difficult. She was so beautiful in the candlelight that all he wanted to do was pull her close, run his fingers through her hair and... no. He couldn't think like this.

"I'll see you here again tomorrow, right?" said Luciana hopefully.

Daniel nodded. "I'll be here."

8

Day 22 of Summer

$\mathcal{E}$smeralda looked strangely vulnerable without Camila by her side. Luciana hadn't realized how much time they spent together until they were suddenly apart, almost like they didn't trust themselves to be in close quarters anymore. Not that they had changed too much else. They still giggled amongst themselves at breakfast. But this afternoon, it had been surprisingly easy to get Esmeralda alone.

Esmeralda tucked a lock of her short brown hair behind her ear and took a small sip of sparkling wine. "I was surprised you wanted to see me today. Do you have more questions for me about your sister?"

"Yes," Luciana lied, glancing around to make sure there were no servants around to hear their conversation. She needed Esmeralda to do what she did best. Talk.

Spending time with Daniel had made Luciana lose track of what was truly important—becoming Reina. Each day as she glanced at the flute that contained the rolled-up letter from Nicolas's daughter, it seemed to grow heavier, weighing on Luciana until she couldn't stand it anymore. If anyone would have intel on this lost Princesa, it would be Esmeralda. But Luciana couldn't just come right out and ask, so she figured she'd ease her way into it.

"Has there ever been a time when you felt jealous of Camila's future husband?" Luciana asked.

"What do you mean by that?" Esmeralda asked in reply, leaning back and looking out the window.

"I mean, did either of you explore the possibility of just remaining unmarried? So you could be faithful to one another?"

Esmeralda's face scrunched up. "It was a short-lived idea but yes." Luciana gestured for her to continue, and Esmeralda sighed. "It was right at the beginning of our relationship, after we realized what we had was more than something fleeting."

Luciana thought back to the balls Camila had attended, wandering around the ballroom with a sea of admirers trailing behind but never letting any of them close enough to court her. It made much more sense now.

Esmeralda continued, "Camila decided she didn't care about the rules. She would just marry me, royal line and Ambassador of the Sun be damned."

Luciana's eyes widened. She'd never heard anyone dismiss a title like the Ambassador of the Sun so flippantly. Esmeralda must really trust Luciana to say something like that, for if she'd said it in lesser company she could have been ostracized.

"What made her change her mind?" Luciana asked.

"Me," Esmeralda admitted. "Loving someone means wanting what's best for them, even if it isn't what you want. She and I agreed that we would respect tradition, and there aren't any laws requiring Reinas to be faithful to their husbands. It's a dreadful thing to do, of course, but she could never lose her throne over it."

Of course, Camila and Esmeralda had a plan. They were clever. Luciana's heart sank a bit at that. She should have seen it coming. Even though Camila might not know much about politics, she did know how to protect herself. But as interesting as this was, it wasn't why she'd met with Esmeralda. She had to steer the conversation towards Nicolas.

"I wonder if there has ever been a Rey or Reina who never got caught breaking the rules?" Luciana asked.

Esmeralda tilted her head thoughtfully. "Perhaps."

"I don't know. I just find it hard to believe that a law as strict as that one has lasted without fail."

"I suppose we'll never know, will we?" said Esmeralda.

"I mean," Luciana prompted, "my uncle could have skeletons in the closet that we know nothing about."

"He could," Esmeralda mused. "But he seems like a very straight-laced man. I doubt it."

Luciana gritted her teeth. Esmeralda was no help. She'd have to dig deeper. If anyone knew anything, it would be Esmeralda and Luciana didn't want to give up just yet.

"There could have always been someone he met in passing, maybe someone he thought was worth breaking his vows for," Luciana said.

Esmeralda just shrugged. "It would have to have been a servant or a craftsman. Anyone with a title surely would have exposed him, especially if their union resulted in a child. A person of noble birth would have the power to ensure that baby ended up in the line of succession."

Now she was getting somewhere. The mysterious daughter's mother didn't have money. That, on top of Nicolas's status as an Ambassador of the Sun, would be reason enough for him not to claim his love child. It didn't make it right, but it was understandable. Luciana would need to look at the letter from Nicolas's daughter tonight before Daniel arrived in the music room.

A gentle knock sounded on the door, and Luciana, startled, turned to look for the source of the sound. Camila smiled brightly as she opened the door and entered.

"I'm sorry to interrupt," she said gently.

"Oh!" Esmeralda stood quickly. "I forgot about our ride, didn't I?"

"It's alright," Camila said, taking Esmeralda's hand. "We still have plenty of time if we leave now."

"I apologize, Luciana," Esmeralda said.

"Go enjoy your ride," Luciana said brightly. "Thank you for your company this afternoon."

Esmeralda nodded politely, then looked at Camila. Both of them blushed, then they turned to the door and left together.

"What's on the agenda tonight?" Daniel asked, sinking into what had become his chair in the music room.

"Why are you asking me?" Luciana countered, lighting a candle as the sun set outside. "You're the one who insisted on these meetings."

"It's the deal."

"The almighty deal," Luciana said, rolling her eyes.

"What? Do you want out?" Daniel teased, arching an eyebrow challengingly. "We could always stick with the engagement plans."

Luciana took a deep breath. "No."

Daniel smirked, but part of him couldn't help but wonder what he would have done if she'd agreed. Would he still break off the engagement or would he go through with it? If they didn't have this chance to get out of the match, if escape was never an option, could Daniel have been happy with Luciana?

"Well, you've only got two days to change your mind," Daniel joked.

"Two days. It's hard to believe," Luciana remarked.

"Then you'll finally be free of me," Daniel said, throwing himself across his chair.

Luciana leaned forward and smiled mischievously. "That was always the goal."

"You wound me," Daniel said.

"Has it been hard being away from home?" Luciana asked, sitting down across from him, and scooting in close.

Daniel thought back to his journal entries and how harsh he'd been about Askaña in the beginning. Now, his daily writings seemed to be more inquisitive—and more about Luciana. He didn't want to admit it to anyone and he'd since hidden his journal away in his chamber so Luciana couldn't read what else he'd written, but every time he put a quill to paper, he only saw her face.

He described her as truthfully as he could when he wrote. He'd hoped that by writing everything out it would let him feel some peace, but instead, it only made him notice more details about her. Of course, he'd written about her striking features. Her eyes were the color of an ocean wave and her hair fell in perfect brown ringlets, so dark they almost looked black in the candlelight. But he'd noticed smaller things about her, too. When she felt nervous, she twisted the gold ring on her finger. When she was proud of her musical performances she would run her hands over the folds of her skirt.

He wasn't sure what to make of any of it.

"I thought I would miss Osmain much more than I do," Daniel admitted.

"You like Askaña?"

"I like the people," he said.

Luciana smiled slightly. Daniel's eyes flickered down to her hand, where she slowly twisted her ring. He looked back up at her eyes. Her lips were slightly parted and she drew in a breath as their gazes met. Daniel's pulse quickened as he took in her face, the candle between them casting shadows on her features.

"Osmain is different from Askaña," Daniel said, his

voice cracking as he broke the moment between them. "We have some hills back at home but no mountains like you have here. It's also warmer."

"Doesn't it snow?" Luciana asked.

"Not really. Maybe once a year in the northern regions. I've only seen snow once myself, and it wasn't even in Osmain."

"Only once?" Luciana laughed disbelievingly.

"While I was serving in the military. And it wasn't much. Maybe an inch if that."

"You should see the winters here. That would be a change for you," Luciana said.

"I think I might freeze to death," Daniel joked.

"You might," Luciana agreed. Daniel searched her face for any hint that she was joking, but he couldn't find one.

"Why don't you play something for me?" Daniel asked, disturbed by the thought of dying in a brutal winter. "An Askanese song I might not have heard before."

Luciana leaned back and sighed. "I suppose I can do that."

"Try a different instrument this time," Daniel smiled. "I'd like to see what else you can do."

Luciana frowned at the room. "Which one?"

Daniel glanced around. Not the cello. He'd have to give up his beloved chair for her to play that one. Not piano. He'd heard that one before. His eyes found a shiny silver flute in the corner. That was different. He hadn't noticed her only wind instrument before. He knew that Luciana could play any number of string instruments, but the flute would be an interesting change.

"How about the flute?"

Luciana looked taken aback. "I... well. You don't want to hear me play that one."

"Why not?" Daniel asked, getting up to fetch the flute from the shelf.

"I'm not very good at it. I started my study just recently, you see." Luciana twisted her ring.

"That's okay," Daniel said reassuringly. "I don't mind. I'd actually like to see proof that you're not good at everything."

"You want proof? You got it! Let's look at my embroidery," she cried out in rising desperation.

Daniel had to admit he was curious about her embroidery failures, but he was more interested in the flute. She couldn't possibly be that bad, and her objections had begun to make him even more curious.

Luciana tried blocking his path, but Daniel was swift and he snatched the instrument off its small shelf.

"No!" Luciana exclaimed, reaching for her flute.

"Okay, okay," Daniel said, putting his hands up in exasperation. "I get it. You don't want to play." He held out the instrument to Luciana. She reached out to reclaim her property. As she did, Daniel noticed something sticking out slightly from the end of the flute as he handed it over. It almost looked like rolled parchment.

"Wait," Daniel said, pulling his hand back. He pried the paper out by the exposed corner.

"Daniel, stop," Luciana commanded.

Daniel obliged and looked at Luciana. She stood there shaking in a way he'd never seen from her before. This was beyond nerves. This was terror.

"What is this, Luciana?" he asked calmly, more curious than anything.

Luciana pursed her lips, thinking of something to say. Obviously, she saw this as a huge invasion of her privacy. It wasn't Daniel's business and as much as he wanted to know what the parchment said, he was a man of honor.

He put a hand on Luciana's shoulder and held the letter out to her. She calmed under his touch. "Here. I didn't mean to upset you. I want you to know that you can trust me. If you ever want to tell me—"

"You should read it," Luciana said softly, meeting his gaze and gently pushing the letter back to him.

"What?" Daniel asked, dumbfounded. "I thought you just said—"

"I know what I said." Luciana twisted her ring. "But you say I can trust you, right? Prove it."

Daniel unrolled the parchment, his eyes growing wider as he scanned each word. At the end of the letter, Daniel handed the letter back to Luciana. He was stunned to silence.

"Who is she?" Daniel finally asked.

Luciana shook her head. "I don't know."

"But she wants the throne of Askaña."

"I guess. This letter was written a long time ago. Things might have changed since then," Luciana explained.

"Who else knows about this?" Daniel asked.

"I'm not sure," Luciana admitted. "Only my uncle, as far as I'm aware."

"He's a religious figure, right? He's made a vow of chastity?"

"An Ambassador of the Sun, yes," Luciana said. "If this note were to become public, it could ruin him. Or it could upset the line of succession."

"You need to find this woman before she finds you," Daniel said, and Luciana nodded. She stumbled to her piano bench, sat, and buried her face in her hands.

"What is it?" Daniel asked after a moment of silence.

Luciana took a deep breath, in and out. Her voice shook as she said, "Can I trust you with something?"

"Something else?" Daniel aked.

"Yes."

Daniel shrugged. "Sure."

Luciana glared at him threateningly. "That is not enough. I am about to confide something to you that I have never told another living soul. If this were to be found out, I could be disowned or even killed for treason."

Daniel's mouth dropped open. Luciana, treason? His head was swimming, and he could hardly concentrate as he stuttered, "I-I promise. I won't tell a soul."

Luciana smiled, satisfied. "Good," she said. "Because I could use your help." Daniel could not imagine what she could be hiding that would be considered treasonous, much less something that Daniel needed to be involved in. Daniel wasn't sure he liked what he'd gotten himself into. Treason wasn't something to be taken lightly. It could even start wars if he was discovered to be a part of it. He opened his mouth to back out, but before he could retract his promise, Luciana simply said, "I want to be Reina."

Daniel did not know how to react. He sat there and considered what she had said. It did make sense. Her violent opposition to their engagement—which would have removed her from the Askanese line of succession, the way she carried herself in public, even her unusual ability to speak multiple languages. She had been grooming herself for the role. He was surprised that no one else had seen it.

Luciana fidgeted with her ring nervously, unable to

sit still now that she had told him her big secret. "Please say something. I feel silly," she said.

"It's not silly," Daniel said. "It makes sense."

"It does?"

"It seems you've positioned yourself to be the ideal candidate for Reina."

Luciana blushed. "I would like to think so."

Daniel considered the situation. Why had she told him this? Daniel had no more political sway in Askaña than Luciana did. He could maybe write to his father about it, who could write to Rey Nicolas, but that seemed too convoluted.

"It seems to me," Daniel said, "that you're wasting your time." Luciana shrank back, a hurt expression on her face. Daniel had to backtrack fast or he was going to lose her. "That came out wrong. What I meant to say was if you want to rule so badly, why not just marry me? You'd be my Imperatrice. You'd have a country to rule without any of the risk." It was forward, he had to admit. But there was a part of him that still wanted her to want him.

Luciana considered his suggestion for a moment, but she shook her head. "I don't know. I don't know Osmain the way I know Askaña."

Daniel nodded. He could not imagine leaving Osmain forever. He could only imagine how she must have felt receiving the news of their engagement—

learning that she'd have to leave everything behind. As much as Daniel complained about the engagement, he couldn't deny her situation had much higher stakes. If the marriage were to happen, the worst case for Daniel would be to come home with a woman he didn't know if he liked. "So, what is it you need from me, exactly?" Daniel asked.

Luciana shrugged. "Your secrecy. And your ideas."

"What do you mean?"

"Well, the most straightforward way to the throne would be to kill Camila, but I refuse to do that, for obvious reasons."

"I'd be a little worried if you considered that a legitimate option."

"The other choice that stands out would be to convince Camila to choose to become an Ambassador of the Sun, and then see to it that her purity was destroyed."

"You mean, have someone… violate her?"

"You see why I'm having trouble. Neither of these are viable options."

"What would happen if Camila were to break her vow of chastity on her own?"

Luciana's brow knit as she took his question seriously. "She would be cast from the royal family. She'd likely be exiled from Askaña."

Daniel sighed. "Is there a third way to become Reina?"

"Precisely."

Daniel considered the situation. He didn't know Askanese law nearly as well as Luciana did. "What about Rey Nicolas and his mysterious daughter? If Nicolas claimed her as his heir, then it would prove he had broken his own vows. Could she even become Reina if your uncle was cast out because of it?" Daniel asked.

"I'm not sure," Luciana replied. "I can't seem to find any precedent for this situation."

Daniel thought for a moment. Helping Luciana was a risk, but he was coming to like her. If her plan succeeded, they would both rule their own kingdoms one day. An alliance with her could be advantageous. He said, "Well, she's either been paid off and gone away or she's dead. It's possible all she wanted was some money and not the throne. If she's still alive, we could find her and make sure that she isn't a threat. Then use her and the letter against your uncle—convince him that he would either have to make you Reina instead of Camila or be exposed."

Luciana gaped at him for a moment, then started rambling. "That could work. But there would be a million things to figure out, assuming we could even find her. There isn't much to be learned from the letter, and what if she is dead? How could we prove that?"

"You know the castillo better than anyone. If your uncle were to have more evidence of his daughter, where would it be hidden?"

She sighed. "We aren't likely to find anything hidden anywhere other than his study."

"Great," said Daniel. "Then we start there."

Luciana shook her head. "It's forbidden."

"The study?"

"Yes. He's made it very clear that no one is to enter without his express permission. I've never been invited inside."

"Have you been inside at all?"

"Once." Luciana shivered. "I've never seen him so angry. I thought he might hit me, but there's nothing Nicolas values more than appearances. He probably didn't want to explain a bruise to the court."

"That's terrible," Daniel said. His father could have a temper sometimes, but Daniel had never felt threatened by his presence.

"We shouldn't look in there," Luciana said. "It's too risky."

"So, blackmail is totally fine but sneaking around is off the table. Got it."

"You go in there, then! There's a door to the study from these tunnels. I can take you to it and you can search for yourself."

Daniel laughed. "Oh, no. This is not my problem to solve. You're coming with me."

"But—"

"What time would your uncle be least likely to be in his study?"

Luciana shrugged. "I don't know. Dinner. But we have to be at the table with him. His meeting times vary depending on the day, so it's not safe to plan around those. Besides the middle of the night there really isn't any guarantee—"

"So 'tomorrow night' is what I'm hearing you say."

"What?"

"Tomorrow night. You and I will meet here after the rest of the castillo has gone to bed. Then you will show me the tunnels, and I will help you search your uncle's study for evidence of your missing cousin."

"Are you crazy?" Luciana hissed.

Daniel flashed her a lopsided smile. "Maybe a little bit."

9

Day 23 of Summer

*L*uciana had barely been able to sleep. She'd spent the entire night tossing and turning, thinking about her plan with Daniel. When Alora had thrown her shades open the next morning, sending rays of sunshine onto Luciana's eyelids, she was just as tired as she had been when she'd gone to bed.

Luciana had to pull herself together and act like nothing had changed. Despite the past few days, she still had to act as though she and Daniel were friendly if she was going to get out of the marriage. She could never let on the depth of their plans. The one person she wanted to talk to was Camila, who certainly couldn't know about the plan. It left Luciana feeling twisted inside, like she could explode from her secrets at any moment.

As Luciana sat across from Daniel and ate her breakfast, she tried not to act suspicious. He avoided looking at her, and Luciana was grateful for it. Every once in a while he would make a harmless remark about the weather or some such, and Luciana would answer politely. He seemed to have taken to the plan quite well, and he was playing his part excellently.

Luciana also treaded lightly with her uncle. She didn't want him sensing anything off about her mannerisms. He sat at the head of the table, brooding and watchful.

"Uncle," Luciana said.

"What is it?" he grumbled.

"I was wondering if I might join you for your meetings today?"

"Luciana, we've been over this." Nicolas frowned. "I don't need the help of you or anyone else. Why don't you mind your own business?"

Luciana sighed. She was disappointed, as usual, but the only way to ensure he didn't notice anything wrong was to bother him about his meetings. She made the mistake of looking at Camila, whose expression of pity made Luciana's stomach churn. She couldn't stand it when people looked at her like she was a kicked puppy.

One by one, the other occupants left the table until only Daniel and Luciana remained. A few servants milled about, clearing plates and waiting to tend to any requests, so when she and Daniel spoke, they did so quietly.

"How did you sleep last night, Your Highness?" Daniel asked.

"Not well, I'm afraid." Luciana replied truthfully.

"That's alright," Daniel said, winking at her. "I am sure tonight you will sleep well indeed."

Luciana blushed. She hoped Esmeralda was out of earshot, otherwise the whole castillo would be abuzz with gossip that she and the Principe were flirting. Luciana had to remind herself that he was only hinting at their plans for raiding the study tonight. But then again, he'd been speaking so softly the servants probably couldn't even hear. Could Daniel's teasing mean something more?

With that, Daniel stood and left the table. Luciana didn't know what to make of him. How had he gone from her enemy to her friend so quickly? And what game was he playing at with his flirting? He couldn't be actually interested in her. That would be ridiculous. Still, if anyone had heard him, that would have been a problem. Daniel was playing with fire, but Luciana was still happy she had him as her partner in crime.

Luciana finished her breakfast then went to go about her morning duties. She stopped by Camila's study to read the briefing papers, but this time she waited until she was sure Camila and Esmeralda were elsewhere before she entered. After she'd finished in the study, she walked down the hallway past the throne room. The door was ajar and Luciana heard a voice from inside.

She found herself stepping toward the door out of curiosity. When Luciana glanced inside the large room, she saw her uncle sitting rigidly on his golden throne. He was glaring at a small woman who wore a modest gray frock.

"I have been sent on behalf of my village," the woman said. "We beg for your assistance."

"With?" Nicolas said tersely.

"I have been a shopkeeper for many years," the woman explained. "I've lived through my fair share of trials, but I've never seen anything like this. Your people are starving and dying. There is not enough food to go around. Your lack of action has left many of us, me included, feeling as if you don't care about us."

Nicolas snorted. "If you're all so concerned about your crops, why are the fields that remain fertile getting burned down by the rebels?"

"While I think it is wasteful, Your Majesty, I believe they are trying to get your attention. The wealthy are the only ones able to afford the food that is grown on those farms. There isn't enough for everyone. They believe if you go hungry, you might understand how they feel."

"That's ridiculous," Nicolas said, waving his hand at

the woman dismissively. "Your lives are just fine. You're ungrateful is all."

"Please, Your Majesty. Your people are starving. We work hard, but there is only so much we can do for ourselves when almost all of our income is taken for taxes. I beg of you, please take care of us," the woman said, going down on one knee and bowing before Nicolas.

"Who are you to speak so brazenly to your Rey?" Nicolas said, standing. He motioned to his guards. "Take this woman away. Throw her in the prison where she belongs."

"No, please! I only—"

"I take care of you. If you can't accept the help I give, then you can reflect on your choices from behind bars."

The woman held her head high as guards flanked her on either side. She said, "If you're so rattled by a woman with a simple request, I look forward to hearing about what happens when the rebels finally reach you."

The guards began to pull the woman towards the door. Luciana gasped, unwilling to believe what she'd just seen. Askaña was in trouble and her uncle refused to help. Nicolas turned his head to face the door, and Luciana ducked out of the doorframe just in time to avoid being seen. She practically ran down the hallway, putting as much distance between herself and the throne room as possible.

When she reached her bedroom, Luciana closed the door behind her, breathing heavily. If Nicolas refused her help and wouldn't listen to the requests of his own subjects, Luciana would have to go over his head. She would have to find more evidence of Nicolas's daughter and use it against him somehow. The future of Askaña depended on it.

LUCIANA AWOKE WITH A START. It was still dark outside. Good. She had decided to retire early after dinner to avoid her uncle and given her poor night of sleep the day before, she had deserved a nap. She'd closed her eyes just as the sun was setting, and now it was pitch-black outside of her window. Was she already late?

In a panic, Luciana threw back her blanket and slipped on her quietest shoes. She ran her hands through her hair to smooth the knots that had formed while she slept. Luciana quietly slipped out of her room, still in her night dress. If anyone caught her out of her room this late at night, she wanted to be able to give insomnia as an excuse.

Luciana practically ran down the stairs. It was several flights down from her tower bedroom to the tunnel system, the entrances to which were only on the lower levels of the castillo. She could have used the servants' stairs, but she would have stuck out if anyone saw her using them. Luciana didn't want to linger in a common area any longer than necessary, and so she moved quickly.

As Luciana neared the tunnels, she saw a shadow. It approached her slowly, but her stomach flipped in a panic. Luciana ducked into an adjoining corridor, flattening herself against the wall to avoid being seen. Her heart beat in her chest as the shadow neared. She mentally rehearsed what she would say if she was discovered.

Good evening. I'm having the hardest time falling asleep tonight. Yes, I'll let you know if I need anything.

As the shadow moved past her hiding place, Luciana peeked out to see a servant carrying a tray with a pitcher of orange juice, heading down the hallway toward the stairs. Someone must have ordered the drink, but who? Luciana would need to be more careful.

Once she was certain that the servant was gone, Luciana snuck back to the entrance of the tunnels. She glanced around again, making sure she wasn't being followed. The coast appeared to be clear, so Luciana gently opened the secret door. She wove through the cavernous hallways until she reached her music room.

She'd spent hours of her childhood wandering around the tunnels, lost, and it had taken years to master their twists and turns. Luciana hadn't dared make any kind of map or key to them. She had been surprised to see Daniel in the music room every night, without him getting turned around or lost.

Luciana swung the door open. The only light inside was a single candle, which sat on a table next to the chair where Daniel was asleep. She shut the door, expecting to wake him with the noise. But instead, he let out a small snore. Luciana scoffed.

She moved to wake him, but as she reached out for his shoulder to shake him, she paused. He really did look quite comfortable. He'd been there for a little while, judging by the small pool of wax gathering around his candle. The flame illuminated the warm brown of his hair, making his curls appear almost like a rich chocolate, and gave his skin an ethereal golden glow.

If things were different, Luciana supposed that he would have been the type of man who would have caught her eye. If Daniel had been born Askanese, Luciana might have been tempted to court him. Now that she knew he had a good heart as well as good looks, she would have been a fool not to. Yet here she was, plotting to get out of their marriage. The irony wasn't lost on her.

Luciana sighed. She couldn't help but hate herself a bit. There was a familiar sharp and melancholy pang in her chest as she looked at him. With a start, Luciana realized she knew the feeling. It was longing. Usually, she felt it when she thought about becoming Reina, but this was different. She'd never felt it toward something —someone—so within reach. Daniel was right there, sitting in front of her. If she wanted to, she could reverse the deal and insist upon marrying him.

What was she thinking? Luciana shook her head. She needed to wake up. There was no use mourning what could never be. She forced herself to prod Daniel, and as soon as his eyelids fluttered open, she yanked her hand back, embarrassed that he might have seen her so close to him. It was strange to touch him, and she didn't want to know if she'd like it or not.

"Huh?" he mumbled, yawning.

"I'm here," said Luciana. "Let's go."

"You're late," Daniel said with a dramatic stretch of his arms.

Luciana decided not to dignify his statement with a response, so she stood there in silence as Daniel slowly woke and pulled himself out of the chair. He grabbed the candle from the table and said, "Let's go."

Luciana nodded, and they slowly crept into the tunnels. Sneaking around like this was risky. If someone found them in her uncle's study, they could be treated as criminals. Luciana had been warned before not to sneak in, as the consequences for being caught would be severe. The last time she'd been inside, she'd been just a child, and Nicolas had ordered the servants not to serve her meals for three days. Now that she was grown, she would probably be tried for treason. But desperate times called for desperate measures, and to become Reina she would have to risk it.

Luciana led Daniel through the maze-like tunnels. She knew where the study's door was, despite never having used it. The corridor was tight and dark, and Daniel had to follow behind her since the space wasn't wide enough for them to walk side by side. They rounded corners, walked up levels, then back down again a few turns later.

Finally, they reached a small door. Luciana crouched down and pushed it open only a few inches. She glanced inside but didn't see anyone or hear anything coming from the study. It was also remarkably dark inside. Unless Nicolas was asleep at his desk, there was likely no one inside. It was a fairly large room, with a bookcase along one wall and a desk on another. There were plenty of drawers and spaces to hide things in. Luciana doubted they would be able to find too much tonight. Perhaps she would have to come back on her own another time.

Seeing that the coast was clear Luciana crawled into the room, brushing dust off of herself as she stood. Daniel wasn't far behind.

"Where should we start?" he whispered.

"I'm not sure. Maybe the desk?"

Daniel nodded, and together they went through each drawer of the desk, careful not to move more than they needed to. In the first drawer there was only a quill and some paper. Luciana flipped through every page, hoping she would find something, anything. But alas, they were all blank.

The next drawer contained the exact same royal posts that were delivered to Camila daily. Once again, Luciana searched through them, looking for any clues about Nicolas's daughter. The news had become genuinely disturbing as of late. The rebellion continued to move toward the castillo, slaughtering more high-ranking officials along their path, burning down their homes and spilling their blood. Luciana could hardly bear to read the briefings anymore, because they got her thinking about her own safety. She set the news aside. There was nothing helpful to her current mission hidden in those papers.

One drawer after another, it was more of the same. Tax records, royal decrees, reports, and statistics. No mention of a daughter anywhere. The desk was useless. Luciana didn't know why she was surprised. The letter hadn't been in a file cabinet. Perhaps there were more clues in her uncle's books.

"Let's move over here," said Luciana, moving to the bookcase, though she didn't really know where to start. Look at every page of every book, like she had before?

She picked up a few books and tried just that, but none of them seemed to have any pages glued together, like the one in which she'd found the first letter.

Next, she tried pulling books off of the shelf, hoping for some kind of latch for a hidden door. She did about two shelves of this before Daniel finally picked up a book. He opened it, only to discover that the pages had been hollowed out in the middle, hiding a secret box inside.

He smiled. "I think I found it."

A rush of excitement coursed through Luciana's veins. This might be the answer she had been looking for. Carefully, Luciana lifted the lid of the box. Inside was another folded letter and a silver ring. Luciana pulled it out to get a closer look.

"Look at the jewel on this ring," she said. "It's Esmarish blue."

Esmar was the kingdom that bordered Askaña to the west. They were known throughout the realm for their vast supplies of silver. Almost all of the jewelry in Esmar was silver, and if it wasn't, it was usually a fine sky-blue stone.

"Do you think it's hers?" Daniel asked.

"Why else would we have something Esmarish hidden away like this?"

"I'm not sure. A gift maybe?"

Luciana shook her head. "Then it would be with the

rest of the royal jewels. Maybe this ring is connected to Nicolas's daughter. Perhaps it was the way that she proved her legitimacy."

"She must be Esmarish then. Or at least her mother is. Read the letter next!"

Luciana pulled out the folded paper that had been with the ring, and uncrumpled it. She whispered its contents aloud to Daniel.

"Day 30 of Spring, Year 730

Father,

I'd thank you for your assistance if it wasn't so long over-due. I will remain out of your way for now, but rest assured, should you cross me or my mother again, I will find a way to bring you and everything you love to the ground."

"Did she sign her name?" Daniel asked.

Luciana squinted at the parchment, but again she couldn't make out any specific letters in the squiggled signature. She sighed. "Not really."

"That's okay," Daniel said. "We found some excellent clues. She's Esmarish, she's probably alive, and she got paid off. She's not after your throne."

"For now," Luciana gulped. But what about after Nicolas died? What would stop this woman from making a claim on the throne?

"It's interesting that Nicolas didn't cover his tracks better than this," Daniel mused. "Destroy the evidence, you know?"

"As much as he'd deny it, he probably can't bear to do it," Luciana replied, shrugging.

Luciana carefully replaced the letter and the ring, then handed the box to Daniel. She put the fake book back on the shelf empty, making sure nothing looked out of place. Luciana could only hope that her uncle didn't check the book often.

The sound of keys jingling outside the door snapped Daniel and Luciana to attention. They looked at each other as if to say, *Move*. Without saying a word, they both dove for the door to the tunnels. Daniel went in first, snuffing his candle, and Luciana followed closely behind, just pulling her skirts in and nearly closing the secret door before the real study door opened. Luciana left a small crack rather than pull the trap door closed, just enough to see what was happening. Her uncle burst into the room, followed by her mother. Luciana narrowed her eyes. What were the two of them doing awake at this hour?

Natalia closed the door lightly behind her.

"What do you want, Nicolas?" Natalia crossed her arms.

"I've received some disturbing news," said Nicolas, his brow furrowing.

"News that couldn't wait until the morning?"

"I'm afraid not. I received a letter tonight."

"Riveting," Natalia yawned. Luciana almost never

saw her mother in such a state. Usually, Natalia was the perfect picture of grace and poise, even around her own family. Luciana supposed that the lateness of the night and being in the presence of her brother had made her more relaxed.

"It was from the head of the rebel army."

At the mention of the rebels, Natalia snapped to attention. "What did they want?" she asked. Luciana tried to place the tone she heard in her mother's voice. Could it be fear?

"They have officially declared their intentions to invade the castillo and overthrow my rule. They say I am unfit to rule Askaña and must be removed from my position. It's ridiculous," said Nicolas.

Natalia scoffed. "That is hardly news. They declare war on us every other week."

This was true. Most of the time, when a rebel group declared war, the militia would swoop in quickly and end it before it even began. While this had worked in the past, Luciana wasn't so sure this one would be crushed quite as easily. If the visits from the Barón and the shopkeeper were any indication, the threat posed by the rebels seemed to be growing.

"I cannot allow them to undermine my authority any longer!" Nicolas was clearly disturbed, his voice rising as he spoke.

"I understand. Perhaps you could just appease them?

Give them tax cuts, make sure the poor have enough to eat." Natalia took a seat and closed her eyes. "Make them feel seen?"

"And allow them to think they can push me around? I think not."

Natalia sighed impatiently. "What do you want to do then? We cannot carry on like this forever. They're invading our cities. Killing off members of our court. They're weakening us."

Nicolas paused dramatically, then said, "We will give them what they want. A war."

His tone was so deathly serious that Luciana had to hold back a gasp. In her shock, she lost her balance and fell backwards. Daniel caught her soundlessly and held her steady as she continued to listen. Her uncle couldn't seriously be considering killing off his own subjects. Hardworking people who just wanted to see their country flourish? The rebels were technically traitors, but so was Luciana at the moment. She hardly found it fair to judge them for wanting change. And they were right to want it. Living conditions in poor communities along their borders were terrible. Winters saw people starving or freezing to death, and the poor often had nothing to their names but the clothes on their backs.

Social reform would be the very first thing on her list to do when she became Reina.

"You can't be serious," Natalia laughed. "You cannot wage a war on your own country!"

"I can and I will," Nicolas said grimly. "It is the only way to preserve both the country and my authority."

"Just send out the militia like usual," Natalia suggested. "Enforce a curfew and gently remind them who's in charge."

"What do you think I've been doing?" said Nicolas. "It hasn't been working. In fact, the rioting has only gotten worse."

"So, what are you going to do? Kill innocent people by the thousands? Murder everyone you're supposed to be taking care of?"

"I will start with villages that are known rebel bases," Nicolas explained. "Arrest who I can and make examples of them. Burn down the villages, execute the traitors. Until my subjects stop undermining my position as their Rey, I will do what I must."

Luciana's fists clenched. This was awful news. The last thing Askaña needed was more unrest. This was the worst possible decision Nicolas could make. The rebels had been using similar tactics, it was true, but they had wanted to reason with Nicolas. He'd refused to negotiate, yet here he was fighting fire with more fire.

"That is disgusting," Natalia said, and Luciana silently agreed.

"My men have been given their orders. They will begin tomorrow morning," Nicolas said.

"So why did you ask my opinion if you have already decided on war?"

"I do not recall asking for your opinion," Nicolas snapped. "I simply meant to inform you of coming events."

Natalia stood, head held high. "I have no part in ruling this country, Nicolas. As long as you persist in reminding me of that fact, I will stay out of your affairs. I'm going back to bed. Have fun with your war. I will have no part of it."

Natalia stormed from the room, leaving Nicolas alone. He sat at his desk and slammed his hands on the rich wood in anger. Luciana watched a few minutes more, but it was clear he wasn't going to do anything else of note. So, she gently closed the panel, and her thoughts began to swarm.

Not only was Nicolas a traitor to the crown by breaking his sacred vow of chastity, but he was a monster. He would rather kill his own citizens than listen to their grievances. Luciana's hands trembled as she sank to sit with her back against the wall. Daniel held up the candle and looked at her as if to ask if she was okay.

Letting out a shaky breath, she gathered up the two letters and the Esmarish ring. Luciana knew what she had to do. The ball was tomorrow, and desperate times called for desperate measures. Blackmailing Nicolas was low, lower than she'd expected to stoop. But to get him off of the throne and save her people from bloodshed, it might be worth it.

10

Day 24 of Summer

*L*uciana gripped her bedpost with a strength that would have made even Askaña's finest mountain climbers jealous. Alora had pulled in so much on the strings of Luciana's corset that faint beads of sweat were beginning to appear on Alora's forehead.

Askanese high fashion was intricate enough when it came to daily wear that Luciana's ball gown was not much more elaborate than her usual costume, but today would be a big day for her. If everything went according to plan, she would be declared Reina by the end of the night. She wanted to look somehow more perfect than perfect when that time came.

After a few more minutes of pulling and struggling,

Alora finally tied the stays, wiping her forehead in defeat. Luciana let go of the bedpost and adjusted herself, getting ready for the next layer of clothing.

"You will be the jewel of the ball once I am through," said Alora.

Luciana smiled. "I should hope so. This could be my engagement ball, after all."

The ball to announce Luciana's engagement had apparently been planned months ago, yet no one had bothered to tell Luciana until Daniel arrived in Askaña. If all went according to her uncle's plan for the evening, Daniel and Luciana would formally announce their engagement. No one, not even Alora, needed to know about their intentions to call off the marriage. Better for everyone to think she looked forward to having a ball thrown in her honor.

"I heard there is to be nobility from every kingdom in the realm in attendance tonight," Alora said excitedly.

Luciana had heard similar rumors, although she had yet to see a formal guest list. Many noblemen were staying at a manor adjacent to the castillo, and some had added visits to friends or family to make their journeys worth it. She hoped she could remember the languages of the realm properly or that would be very embarrassing. She hadn't asked, but she had a feeling that Daniel only spoke Askanese and Osmainian. Most people of her station didn't take the time to learn more than one or two. And if there was truly to be nobility from every nation in attendance, Luciana could take advantage of the opportunity to start making diplomatic agreements of her own.

Luciana smiled at Alora as she pulled her gown over her head. "I hope so. I would like to say hello to everyone."

Alora began working diligently on Luciana's gown, fluffing out her skirts and tying everything into place. She said, "You've always been so adept with people and politics."

"Why, thank you, Alora," Luciana said, blushing slightly. It was true, of course, but Luciana was so rarely recognized for it that the compliment left her flustered.

"Do you remember several years ago when the Tatrians visited and you learned how Tatrians play marbles just to play with their young Tsarevna?" Alora asked.

Luciana nodded. She had been fifteen and Tatria's heir, Tsarevna Azura, had been only eight. The little girl had been so shy and nervous that Luciana had stayed up all night with a book of Tatrian culture, hoping to learn something that might help the poor girl. It had worked, too. Azura and Luciana had become friends after that simple game of marbles, and Azura had been in such good spirits for the rest of the visit that her father, the

Tsar, had renewed the trade agreement between their two countries.

"Even as young as you were, you were able to help our kingdom prosper," Alora said. "Think of what you could do now at the side of a Principe."

Luciana found she didn't have a good rebuttal for that. Something as simple as a game of marbles had helped feed her people. Could marrying Daniel help her people just as much as if she were Reina herself? Could she do similar good from the throne of Osmain?

Luciana stopped that thought before it went too far. As much as she could help her people from Osmain, she could do much more from the throne of Askaña. Osmain seemed to be a country with very little turmoil. Their people, from what Luciana had heard, were hard-working, well-off, and liked their Imperatore… and Askaña would still be firmly under Nicolas's thumb. Luciana had to go forward with her plan.

Alora finished getting Luciana ready in relative silence, detangling her curls, and placing a traditional Askanese crown on her head. The gold of the crown shot out from Luciana's head like the rays of the sun. While not as large as the crowns Nicolas or Camila would be wearing, it was still exquisitely beautiful. Luciana couldn't help but feel a surge of confidence as she caught a glimpse of herself in the mirror.

Luciana thanked Alora and made her way to the ballroom, stopping briefly by the music room so she could grab the first letter from Nicolas's daughter. She tucked it into her corset. Who knew when she might need it?

THE PARTY WAS in full swing by the time Luciana arrived. Scanning the crowd, she saw no sign of Daniel. This was good. It meant things were going according to plan. He would be absent for much of the evening, and then when he arrived he would regretfully inform Nicolas that he would not be marrying Luciana. Then Luciana could put into action the second part of her scheme.

Also absent from the party were Camila and Esmeralda. Luciana wondered if they were together. Besides that, it seemed that Alora was right. Scanning the crowded ballroom, Luciana was able to pick out guests wearing the signature colors of each nation. The Esmarish wore their blue and silver, the Tatrians white and gold. Not in attendance, it seemed, was Tsarevna Azura. Luciana's heart sank a bit, as she'd hoped to catch up with her after so many years.

Luciana's name was announced and many of her guests turned to face her, some even curtsying or bowing. Luciana smiled her brightest smile and descended the stairs to the dance floor.

As she eyed her guests, Luciana couldn't help but

linger on the Esmarish guests. Perhaps one of the women in attendance tonight was her long-lost cousin. If so, that could ruin everything. Luciana hoped with every fiber of her being that Nicolas's daughter had been paid off so well that she would never show her face in Askaña again.

One Esmarish guest in particular stood out to her, as he spoke with Nicolas on the other side of the room. The Duc de Étoiles was a long-time friend of her uncle's. The Duc and Nicolas had met long before she was born, and given that the man lived so far away, Luciana could count on one hand the number of times she'd seen him over the years.

The Duc met Luciana's eyes from across the room and his cold, penetrating gaze sent shivers down her spine. She couldn't quite place why, but he'd always made her feel uneasy. Perhaps it was his tall stature. Or maybe it was the perpetual scowl on his face. But something about men like that always reminded Luciana to watch her back.

Luciana felt a tap on her shoulder. She reflexively turned around, startled, to see Prince Wes of Randera. Luciana and Wes had always gotten along, as they were exactly the same age, but Luciana had not seen him in three years, since the last time the Randerans had visited Askaña.

Wes was a tall, athletic man. He had beautiful skin

even darker than Luciana's and muscles so defined that women swooned at the very sight of him. While he had something of a reputation as a flirt, Luciana had always found him to be very engaging in conversation, even if she had to speak Randeran to communicate with him.

"Wes!" Luciana exclaimed.

"Good evening, Your Highness," he said, kissing Luciana's hand. "You look lovely this evening."

Luciana smiled. "Why, thank you. If I had known you were coming I would have arrived at the ball much sooner. How is Randera?"

"Evergreen, as usual," said Wes. Randera was full of lush forests, and as long as the trees were green, it usually meant a good harvest on the farmlands as well. Randerans had fertile soil that was good for growing many different types of fruits and vegetables, and they exported their commodities throughout the realm.

"I'm glad to hear it," said Luciana.

"And how is Askaña faring?"

"Same as always," Luciana said with a smile. What else could she say? *Actually, Wes, our people hate us, and my uncle is waging a war on them to keep them in line.*

"I've heard rumors," Wes said, raising an eyebrow.

"About what?" Luciana asked. She hoped he hadn't heard of the rebellion. Nicolas would have done his best to keep any sign of cracks well contained.

"Is it true you're to marry the Principe of Osmain?"

Wes asked. Luciana let out a breath, relieved at hearing a question she was prepared to answer tonight.

Luciana shrugged. "That is up to the Principe, I'd imagine. He has yet to officially ask for my hand." It was strange to refer to Daniel by his official title. When had she stopped calling him the Principe to herself?

Wes shook his head. "Only a fool would throw away a match with you."

"Really?" Luciana laughed.

"Of course," Wes said, smiling flirtatiously. It had never bothered Luciana that Wes liked to tease her. She knew it was all only in good fun.

"Why haven't you offered to marry me, then?" Luciana asked, half-kidding and half-curious.

"I don't think I'm quite ready for marriage," Wes said.

"And I am?" Luciana laughed.

Wes looked into her eyes, searching her gaze. Luciana shivered as he said, "I believe you might be. You've always been more mature of the two of us. Besides, as long as my father sits on his throne, I'm in no hurry."

"There's truly no one who's caught your eye?"

"Oh, plenty of women have caught my eye," Wes said. "But when I meet the woman who will become my wife, I think I'll know."

Luciana laughed. "You think it will be that easy?"

Wes shrugged. "Why not?"

"Because," Luciana said seriously, "I don't think love is ever simple."

"Perhaps you're right. Maybe I'll be a bachelor forever." Wes held out his hand to Luciana. "Care to dance?"

Luciana took his hand, and he led her to the floor. The band played an upbeat tune, and Wes gently led Luciana through the dance, her feet moving to the rise and fall of the beat. Candlelight swirled around Luciana as she stepped through her dance, painting her world in shades of red and gold. She was vaguely aware of eyes following her as her shadow crossed the floor, but she didn't care. And as the song played on, Luciana let herself forget for a single splendid moment everything to do with her uncle, his daughter, and the approaching rebellion.

Too soon, the music made its final crescendo and Luciana twirled on the floor, ending the dance in Wes's arms as he dipped her low.

Luciana couldn't help but beam. "Thank you for the dance," she said.

"You are the loveliest dancer in the whole realm," Wes said, kissing Luciana's hand.

Luciana went to thank Wes, but before she could, she heard a voice behind her. "May I have a dance, Your Highness?" Luciana cringed.

Daniel.

~

Daniel had meant to stick to the plan. Truly, he had. All evening, he had forced himself to stay away from the ball, hiding in his room. He kept staring at the clock, hoping that it would move far enough into the evening that he could finally go downstairs.

He'd thought about just going to the ball anyway and trying to avoid her, but he knew that if he saw Luciana, he would not be able to stay silent. So, he'd obeyed her instructions and sat in silence, trying in vain to write anything in his journal.

Except that every time he'd picked up his quill, he'd pictured her. This wasn't exactly new. She seemed to permeate most of his thoughts these days. Still, it disturbed him that every time that his quill touched paper, he'd write a few sentences, then realize with a start that he had been describing Luciana. He'd somehow managed to write an entire paragraph about just the blue of her eyes without realizing he'd done it.

So, he'd been forced to set down his journal and stare out the window at all of the guests arriving. The only kingdom without anyone in attendance was Osmain, but Daniel presumed that he was to be the representative.

This ball was truly a cruel twist of fate. In fact, the whole engagement had been cruel. There weren't many women out there like Luciana. Every time he tried to think about letting her go, his chest got tight, and he couldn't pull himself back to focus.

Daniel knew enough about romance to know that Luciana was not his only option. He believed in true love, sure, but he also believed that love was what you made it. Despite the fact that he'd thought about it, he'd never dared to make any sort of advance toward Luciana. It seemed like a waste of time to do so when she would never return his affections. He needed to focus his attention to other options. There would be a lovely woman waiting for him in Osmain, he was sure.

One day, he'd look back on everything that had happened in Askaña and laugh. But today was not that day.

For now, Daniel could not stop thinking about the fact that tonight he would be actively setting Luciana free, right as he'd gotten to know her. He didn't know what was happening to him. He couldn't figure out if he was disappointed because she was beautiful or because some small, secret part of him hoped that the arranged marriage would have worked out. It would have been easy—too easy—for Luciana to have been his perfect match.

What if she had been? What if his father's plan had worked?

He'd known Luciana for only ten days, but he knew

enough of her to know that he wasn't ready to say good-bye. How could he now give away his chance at a perfect happy ending?

Not to mention the political unrest in Askaña. He didn't know the extent of the country's problems, but from what Luciana had told him and the little he'd over-heard, it seemed like Luciana and her family could be in real danger. Nicolas would wage war on his own subjects, and suddenly, he and the entire Askanese royal family could be headed for the chopping block. Daniel had read enough history to know what a rebellion meant for a royal family. Even if Nicolas succeeded in quelling it, there would always be a level of distrust between him and his people. And that was the best-case scenario.

While Daniel didn't care what happened to Askaña, he did care what happened to Luciana. Even if her plan worked and she somehow became Reina, how could she fix the glaring problems in Askaña before the rebels caught up to her and killed her? If Daniel went home to Osmain and Luciana was killed, he didn't know if he could forgive himself. He'd known men in the military who died in the field, and he'd seen enough bodies of men he cared about to last a lifetime.

Without knowing what he was doing, Daniel found himself pacing around his room, steps moving faster and faster as his mind whirled. If Luciana didn't care about him, that was one thing. But staying in Askaña would be a death wish. Screw the plan. This was bigger than both of them. If all he could do was save her, then it was what he had to do.

Luciana would hate him for this. But he would rather destroy every chance they had than see her dead.

He would have to go to the ball. He would dance with her. He would propose in front of everyone, and he would cement her fate as Imperatrice of Osmain. She would return home with him, out of the rebels' path and to safety.

Daniel entered the ballroom without pausing for any kind of ceremony. He headed past the herald without pausing, making his way to the floor, searching through the crowd for Luciana. Then he saw her.

Luciana was dancing with a man whom Daniel recognized as Prince Wes of Randera. While he'd never met the Prince, he had met his father, King Oliver, and recognized the rich green cape.

Randera and Osmain weren't on the best of terms. There hadn't been bloodshed between the two nations for many years, but war with the Randerans had been responsible for the end of the previous Osmainian dynasty and a transgression that egregious was not easily forgotten. Daniel tried to put aside his personal distrust of Randera and focus on Luciana. Wes swept

Luciana around the floor, and Luciana absolutely glowed as they stepped in time to the music.

Of course, Luciana would be the best dancer on the floor. He wasn't surprised, just amazed. She moved with an unmatched grace and beauty. Daniel didn't know if she was turning heads or not, as he could not bring himself to look away from Luciana as she swirled across the ballroom. She deserved to be seen. Her curls bounced as she twirled, her skirt sweeping behind her. But the most impressive thing he noticed was her smile. She looked happy, like she was home.

Guests twirled around Daniel, but he didn't care. He didn't even care if he was staring. Until the dance was over, he would not be able to look away. She was radiant, plain and simple. Luciana, on the other hand, didn't see him. She didn't even seem to notice Wes. She was in her own little world, just like she had been that first time he'd seen her play the piano.

Every fiber of his being wished he could be Wes in this moment. Daniel could hardly breathe at the thought of pressing his body against hers while they danced.

Daniel watched until her partner dipped her, and the music stopped. Once it was clear that Luciana had come back to reality, Daniel found himself moving toward her. He cleared his throat nervously as he approached.

"May I have a dance, Your Highness?" he asked, hoping he sounded charming.

Luciana turned to him, and while she smiled, her eyes narrowed. "Of course," she said.

She then turned back to Prince Wes and said something to him in Randeran—which, of course, she spoke—and the man in green kissed her hand, leaving with a devilish grin.

"What are you doing?" Luciana hissed as she took Daniel's hand. She'd accepted his dance. No backing out now.

"Dancing with you," said Daniel, hoping she wouldn't ask any more questions. But it was Luciana, so he was not surprised when she continued.

"I thought we'd agreed you wouldn't appear until the end of the ball?" she said under her breath, trying not to let anyone else hear.

"I changed my mind," Daniel said, shrugging.

Luciana scowled at him, no doubt plotting how to get around this complication. She might not like it, but he had to protect her.

From there, they danced in silence. Luciana said nothing else, and sensing her anger, Daniel kept quiet. He knew Luciana would never lash out at him in public, but he didn't want to hear any false politeness. He would rather just wait until he had her alone to discuss his decision.

While her dancing was still technically perfect, the light that had been coming from inside her seemed to be gone. She was back to her cold and calculating self and knowing that change was all his fault was crushing.

When the song finally ended, Luciana simply nodded at Daniel and walked out of the ballroom, prim and proper as ever.

Without thinking, Daniel found himself running after her. What did she think she was doing? Clearly, she was not happy with his decision to change their plans, so he wouldn't have to be tactful any longer. He just had to find her.

As he left the crowd behind, Daniel saw the fabric of Luciana's train swish around a corner. He followed after her, but once he got there, she was already gone. Predictably. She must have ducked into the tunnels. Daniel ran to the one tunnel entrance he knew and climbed inside. He ran as fast as he could, trying not to trip on the uneven stone floors. All he could do was hope that she would be in the music room when he arrived.

Daniel pushed open the door, and sure enough, there she was. She sat at her piano, fingers on the keys but unmoving. She stared straight into space, not crying, not even frowning. She just seemed to be shocked.

The sound of the door closing perked her up, and she whirled to face him. "What do you think you were doing back there?" she seethed.

"Please just let me—"

"You've done enough." Luciana turned back to her piano and said softly, "I can't believe I trusted you."

There was a pain in Daniel's chest. He wanted to be trustworthy for her. But he had to be sensible first. "Luciana," Daniel said, inching forward. "Please listen to me. This is the only way to keep you safe."

Luciana groaned and turned back to him. "I don't need you to keep me safe."

"Yes, you do!" Daniel insisted. "You heard what your uncle said last night. It's only a matter of time before the rebels knock down your door and your whole family winds up dead."

Luciana stood now, defensive. "You think I don't know that? I need to become Reina soon if I'm to save myself and my country."

"How will you do that?" Daniel asked, genuinely curious.

"I have a plan," Luciana spat. "And I certainly don't need you following me around the castillo to tell me what I want."

Daniel almost laughed. "I know what you want," he said.

Luciana crossed her arms. "Then why are you still in my way?"

"Because you could die!" Daniel exclaimed.

Luciana stepped closer. "It is my duty to die for Askaña, just as you should be ready to do for Osmain."

"There won't be an Askaña left to defend when the rebels take over!"

"You mean if," Luciana said. "*If* the rebels take over. I can still fix this, Daniel."

Daniel deflated a bit. She would never understand what he was trying to do, not until it was too late. He looked at her in the moonlight. She was angry but powerful. Her brows knit tightly and her lips pursed in frustration, but Daniel couldn't help but stare. He was surprised at how much he *wanted* to kiss her.

"Daniel?" Luciana said, waving a hand in front of his face. The movement snapped him out of his trance.

Distracted, Daniel had forgotten what they'd been talking about. "Um, yes."

"Now you're not even listening to me. Lovely," Luciana complained, rolling her eyes, and turning away.

"I am, I promise," he said, grabbing her hand in desperation. "I know you want to do what is best for your kingdom, and I know you're perfectly capable of doing whatever you set your mind to. If you wish to stay behind, I won't stop you. But I cannot stand idly by and let you be hurt. I just want to protect you. Please come with me."

"You want to protect me?" Luciana said, leaning in closer to Daniel than she ever had before, her face mere inches away. Daniel weakened as her eyes flickered to his lips for a split second, then back up to stare directly into his soul. "How are you going to do that?"

The bubble of hope Daniel had been carrying burst. She wasn't going to go with him. "I don't understand why you don't want this, why you don't want *me*," Daniel said. "I'm offering marriage. Companionship. Political alliance. A crown."

Luciana sighed. "Please don't make this harder than it already is."

"Luciana, I will never forgive myself if you get killed."

"And I will never forgive myself if I'm not there for my people in their greatest hour of need. I have to make things right for all the Askanese, the rebels included."

As she spoke, Daniel could feel his heart beginning to break.

For the first time, he saw cracks in Luciana's perfect façade. Her lips pulled tightly shut and her hands curled into fists at her sides, but her shoulders slumped. She was more defeated than she was letting on.

Summoning all of his strength, Daniel said, "I'm not ready to say goodbye."

Luciana shook her head. "Neither am I. But it must be done." She brushed past him to the door, then looked back. "Don't bother returning to the ball. If I see you again, I will run."

Daniel reached for her, but she pulled away. He

sighed in defeat. "If you change your mind, please come to me. I will always be your friend, Luciana."

He'd only seen her look so cold at their first meeting. All of the emotion in her face was gone, and she looked like an empty shell of the woman Daniel had come to know. Her voice didn't waver once or betray any emotion as she spoke one last time. "Goodbye, Daniel."

11

Day 24 of Summer

*L*uciana took longer than she'd wanted to recover from her falling out with Daniel. She'd ran to her chamber and tried to calm herself, waiting for tears to come, for her anger to explode. But nothing happened. Instead, she'd sat in the silent darkness, unable to do anything but think of his face, his eyes, the way he'd begged her to leave for Osmain with him.

Luciana wanted to hate him for what he'd tried to do, but she couldn't. Her heart ached for him, despite what she wanted to tell herself. He seemed to care for her and he didn't judge her for her ambitions, and on top of everything else, he was unusually handsome. It was difficult to leave a man like Daniel behind. But she'd only known him for ten days, and despite their connection, ten days couldn't outweigh the ten years she'd spent wishing to be Reina.

So, she stared at herself in the mirror, waiting until she could breathe normally again. Where once she'd seen the confident future Reina of Askaña staring back at her, she now saw a woman who knew heartache. A woman who knew the cost of earning a crown. How had these ten days managed to change her so much?

Once she was sure she looked as perfect as she had before, Luciana left her room and slowly descended the several flights of stairs that led to the ballroom. Once there, Luciana scanned the crowd. Camila still hadn't made an appearance and Daniel hadn't come back either. Good. That would make things easier.

Luciana spotted Nicolas observing the festivities from his throne, but as she tried to make it to the other side of the room, a nobleman asked Luciana to dance. Fighting against her very nature, she declined. She couldn't stop for pleasantries. There was no time. As guilty as she felt for breaking etiquette, if she was going to become Reina, this was her chance. So, she excused herself, making her way to the throne. She nervously curtsied before her uncle, who simply nodded in return.

"Your Majesty, may I have a word?" Luciana fought to keep her voice steady. This conversation would either end with her becoming Reina or outcast as a traitor to the crown.

"Certainly," said Nicolas, motioning for her to continue.

Luciana cleared her throat and whispered, "Not here, uncle. It's a matter of great political importance, and I'd hate for anyone to overhear."

Nicolas rolled his eyes impatiently. "Spit it out!"

"Accompany me to the hallway."

"I won't be leaving the ball," Nicolas said sternly. "You know how I despise you trying to get involved in affairs of state. Besides, you have an engagement to announce soon."

"Actually, I needed to speak with you about the engagement. It's urgent," Luciana said.

"And you can't just speak to me out here?"

"I'm afraid not."

Nicolas scowled, but he hoisted himself up and held out an arm to Luciana. "Let's get on with it," he grumbled.

Luciana took his arm and nodded. They slipped out behind the throne to a small hallway, which led to many common areas in the castillo. Luciana quickly confirmed the hallway was empty.

"What is so important?" Nicolas asked, his proper demeanor dropping immediately. He towered over Luciana, crossing his arms and scowling.

Luciana took a deep breath and reminded herself of her position. She was in control. She had the upper hand. "It is the Principe. He has called off our engagement," Luciana began.

"What?" Nicolas roared. "What did you do?"

"He wants to marry for love, and he does not love me," Luciana said plainly. But Daniel's desperate face flashed in her mind, making her feel emptier inside than she liked.

Nicolas looked like he might explode at the news. His face grew red, and he almost looked sick. "You could not make him love you? Did you even try to seduce him? What will we tell the guests? They expected this to be an engagement ball!"

Luciana blinked in surprise. She'd known he wouldn't be happy at her news, but this seemed... desperate. Could it be that the rebellion was more imminent than she'd thought? A new alliance with the Osmainians could help him crush the rebels with the additional military power. Or was he just so concerned with appearances that he would get angry at the first sign of trouble?

"It is of no consequence, uncle. I have a solution," Luciana said, forcing her tone to stay even.

"What's that? You'll go after him and beg for his hand?"

Now was the time. She had to do this now or she

could lose her chance to be Reina forever. She had to take the leap for her people. She didn't know how much longer they could last under her uncle's rule. She'd never intended to demand a crown immediately, just that he remove Camila from the line of succession. But given what she'd learned of his plans to attack his own subjects, Luciana had to unseat him quickly. Luciana took a deep breath, while Nicolas eyed her expectantly.

"No," Luciana said, squaring her shoulders and mustering all of her confidence. "I will not beg him. You will make me Reina."

There was a pause, and Luciana tried to read Nicolas's expression. She'd laid her cards on the table—almost all of them, anyway.

Nicolas's face contorted into a smile, and he let out a hearty laugh. "You have lost your mind! Why would I ever do that?"

The heat of anger rose in Luciana's chest and up into her cheeks, leaving her speechless. She'd worked so hard for so long to be the best at everything. She'd spent late nights in the library studying law, early mornings catching up on current events, all of her days begging for a seat at the table, just to be laughed off? It was almost comical that Nicolas would laugh at her suggestion when he was so bad at running the country that his *own people* wanted him dead.

Luciana resisted the urge to lash out at him. She had

to be tactful for this to work. "In case you haven't noticed, uncle," she said calmly, "I am perfectly capable of leading our people. I am qualified in every way. Name one quality that a Reina should possess that I do not."

Nicolas shrugged thoughtfully, then finally said, "You are not the firstborn. That is reason enough."

One dismissal she'd expected. Two refusals? She'd honestly expected that as well. She'd hoped Nicolas would immediately relent to her demand, but she'd known in her heart that he would never even consider the possibility of naming her Reina without more significant persuasion.

Luciana's stare became as hard as stone as she stared into her uncle's unfeeling eyes. If he wanted to do this the hard way, so be it. She reached into her corset, earning her a shocked stare from Nicolas, and pulled out the letter. She held it just out of his reach but close enough that he could see exactly what it was.

"Camila is also not the first born," Luciana said.

She had to force down the corners of her lips, which were tempted to curl into a satisfied smile at her uncle's expression. A brief moment of recognition passed across his face, then panic, and then he was back to his stone-cold stare.

"I don't know where you got that, but I've never seen it before," said Nicolas.

A third dismissal. Luciana was, again, disappointed. But not surprised. "Apparently, it's from your daughter."

"I don't have a daughter," said Nicolas.

Nicolas's poor child. That girl had grown up in Esmar without her father, a man who did not want her and would not even acknowledge her existence. No wonder she had tried to get her revenge. Luciana might not want her anywhere near the throne, but she couldn't help but pity the girl.

"Who is she?" Luciana asked. She hadn't meant to. It wasn't important. But she wanted to know. Nicolas didn't answer her question, but he looked less angry now and sullener. The topic seemed to have added about ten years to his appearance.

"How did you get that?" Nicolas finally asked.

"So, you do have a daughter then?"

"I never said—"

"I think you just did." More silence. Luciana decided to press forward. "If she doesn't exist, why don't I go read the letter to the ballroom out there? Or perhaps show them the little box you'd hidden with her second letter? Then you can explain to them yourself that it isn't true."

Nicolas's head whipped up quickly. "No," he conceded. "It would ruin me."

"Then give me what I want."

Nicolas's façade was melting. Luciana saw more

desperation on his face now than she had in the rest of her years combined. If she kept pressing, she could walk away the winner.

Nicolas shook his head. "I should have expected this from you. I've always suspected you wanted to become Reina."

This took Luciana aback for a moment. If he'd known about her goal all this time, why hadn't he helped her? She was certainly a more qualified and dedicated candidate than Camila. Or if he didn't want her as Reina, why hadn't he exposed her as trying to steal Camila's title? Luciana shook herself back to reality. She didn't have time to question her uncle's decisions, not when she was this close to making her dream come true.

"I'm glad you didn't," Luciana said, trying to sound smug to hide the fact that she was a bit shaken. "You made becoming Reina easy."

Nicolas let out a laugh. "*Becoming* Reina is the easy part. They're going to eat you alive."

Despite the insult, Luciana couldn't help but be intrigued. She'd never seen him so sincere. "What is that supposed to mean?" Luciana asked, arching her brow.

"You could give these people everything they could ever ask for and they would still be ungrateful."

"Maybe if you made sure they could eat, that wouldn't be a problem," Luciana said. "I can still fix the situation before it becomes a full-out war. Let me take over while there is still time."

"How do you know so much about the insurrection?"

"You'll find that I know everything about my country, uncle. The good, the bad, and"—Luciana pointed to Nicolas—"the ugly."

Nicolas scowled.

"So, what will it be? Shall we go out together and pretend like the ball was meant to be your abdication announcement all along? You can keep the protection of the castillo. Or I can go out there instead and present this letter, dooming you to shame and what is sure to be a short life on the streets. After all, there's sure to be a price on your head."

Nicolas snarled. "Nice try, but I will inform my advisors of your treason and—"

"I wouldn't do that," Luciana interrupted. "After all, you have no proof that this conversation happened, while I have multiple letters proving you violated your vow of chastity. If you turn me in, I will say that all I wanted to do was speak to you about the treason you committed and you made up a story to slander and exile me."

The two of them stood in silence as Nicolas's eyes darted around like a cornered animal. Then, he reached for the letter. Luciana jerked her hand away, but Nicolas grabbed her wrist instead and he tried desperately to get to the letter.

Nicolas was much stronger than he looked, and Luciana had never been very strong. She tried her hardest to escape his grasp, but she wasn't able to wrench her wrist from his iron grip. Nicolas pulled her towards him as he swiped for the letter, which Luciana was keeping from him by mere inches. Luciana would have to outsmart him or it would all be for nothing.

Luciana had worked so hard for the chance to become Reina. In the final hour she would not be thwarted by an old man.

She dropped the letter.

It fluttered to the ground, and by the time Nicolas realized what had happened, it was too late. It had already fallen out of his reach. Nicolas let go of Luciana and dove to the ground to retrieve the letter, and as he bent over, Luciana swiftly raised her skirts and kicked him square in the groin.

Nicolas doubled over in pain, collapsing to the ground in shock. Luciana reached down and retrieved the letter, tucking it back in her corset. She leaned down and said, "If you try to have me arrested, they'll find the letter in my corset and you'll go down with me."

"You… little… bitch," he finally ground out. Luciana simply smiled.

"Is that any way to talk to your Reina?"

"You're dead, Luciana! I'll have you—"

"You could be arrested for threatening me, you know," Luciana chuckled. Nicolas tried to stand, but in his weakened state she was able to hold him down with her foot.

"Fine. I'll move you to next in line," Nicolas grumbled.

"I think I made my terms quite clear. You are to abdicate immediately."

"But—"

"Have it your way." Luciana shrugged, her hand moving to her corset. Luciana worried for a moment that he'd try to fight her again, but he gritted his teeth and glared at her.

"The throne is yours," Nicolas said, his face red with anger and his teeth bared. But Luciana didn't care. She'd won.

A MERE TEN MINUTES LATER, Nicolas and Luciana entered the ballroom arm in arm. To the party guests, they seemed perfectly content. Nicolas looked no more stern than usual to those who didn't know him, although Luciana was sure that her family—who, it seemed, had finally decided to attend the ball—would be able to tell that something was off. He had an air of silent fury about him, almost as if he radiated wrath.

Luciana, on the other hand, appeared perfectly placid. Years and years of forcing herself to swallow her tears had been perfect training for this moment.

Half of her soul was singing. Her ten years of scheming, planning, and work had finally paid off. But on the inside, Luciana's heart was torn. She had undoubtedly given up everything to achieve this one singular goal. She'd burned bridges, first with Daniel and now her uncle.

And so, they entered the ballroom together. Nicolas held up his hand to silence the crowd and the music slowed to a halt. The guests stared at Nicolas with expectation. Luciana spotted Prince Wes from across the ballroom, and she stood up a bit taller knowing that one day she would be a true equal to her friend.

"Friends, thank you all for attending tonight," Nicolas said cheerfully. It was amazing how well he was hiding his anger. But perhaps hiding emotions simply ran in the family. Luciana was a master and so, apparently, was Camila. If no one had caught on to her affair with Esmeralda yet despite the obvious clues she doubted they ever would.

Camila! Luciana found her and Esmeralda in the crowd. They'd arrived just in time. This was the perfect opportunity for them—now that Luciana was bound for the throne, Camila and Esmeralda could be together. Camila would lose the throne, sure, but she'd never really taken an interest in running the kingdom. And now she could have something much more important.

Luciana could not wait to see Camila and Esmeralda walking into a ball together, or attend their wedding, or even just to see the joy on their faces as Nicolas made his announcement. Camila smiled at Luciana. She could tell the gesture was mostly out of pity, but there was an honest bit of reassurance in her eyes that showed Luciana that her sister had her back. Camila probably thought this was a marriage announcement. Her night was about to get much better than that.

"I have something very important to announce," said Nicolas. He looked at Luciana, and she saw an angry flame in his eyes. She would have to regard him as an enemy from now on. She had no doubt that he would plot behind her back. Still, he smiled to the masses.

"As many of you know, I have occasionally expressed my desire to lead a quiet life," he continued. Luciana nearly rolled her eyes at the lie. No one knew this, he'd never done any such thing, even in private. But who would dare to challenge the Rey?

"I know the decision is unorthodox, but I have made the decision to step away from the throne," Nicolas said. Luciana swore she heard his voice crack a bit near the end of his statement, but she couldn't be sure.

A hush fell over the crowd, then gasps of shock and small whispers behind gloved hands. Luciana looked at Camila, who looked exceptionally pale. Almost sick. *Good*, thought Luciana. Now she knew for sure that Camila did not want the responsibility. Her sister would feel nothing but relief, and Luciana could assume her throne without guilt.

Nicolas held up his hand again and the whispers faded back into silence. Luciana took in a shaky breath. This was it. So why didn't it feel quite right?

"Taking my place as the leader of Askaña will be my very own niece, Princesa Luciana," said Nicolas, gesturing to Luciana. Luciana simply nodded her head, then the ballroom erupted into chaos.

Some cheered. Luciana saw Prince Wes clapping for her from across the room as his translator relayed the news. Some guests immediately turned and started gossiping with their neighbors. Luciana looked at her mother, who had found herself at the center of a million questions. And some were stunned into silence.

One look at Camila's blank stare and tear-filled eyes, and Luciana's heart sank. Camila stared at Luciana, and a single tear fell down her cheek. Then she fled the ballroom. And that's when Luciana knew.

She had made an irreversible mistake.

12

Day 25 of Summer

*L*uciana yawned, trying not to fall back asleep as she read the daily briefing in what had been Camila's study but was now hers. Once it was time for her official coronation, she would take her uncle's study. But for the time being, the only thing keeping her awake was the news of the rebellion. The situation had become even more dire, as Luciana had heard word that the Barón of Heilo had been attacked. Despite the additional security Nicolas had provided, he'd been murdered in his own home. Not by the horde of rebels headed his way, but by his own people. Luciana had already begun thinking about what she would do to combat the problems plaguing Askaña. She had to stop the oncoming revolt before it killed anyone else. She tried coming up with solid plans of how to proceed, but she couldn't focus after the events of the night before.

After the announcement at the ball, everyone seemed to have questions or congratulations for her. It was her obligation to greet everyone, but she only wanted to speak to two people. And one of them would be leaving Askaña soon, probably the next morning. It had been well into the night by the time the ball had begun to wind down and Luciana was able to excuse herself. She had searched everywhere in the castillo she could think of but couldn't find either Camila or Daniel anywhere. She finally decided that Camila would wait. She would still be there the next day, but this was her last chance to see Daniel.

She knew it was ridiculous, but she wanted to say goodbye to him. Civilly. And she wanted to tell him that he had been right. That she should have gone with him. There was nothing to be done about it now, but Luciana wanted some kind of closure.

So, she looked all over for him until finally she came across Alora in the hallway. Luciana pulled her maid to the side.

"Where is Daniel?" Luciana whispered.

Alora looked at her, confused. Luciana could have kicked herself. Alora didn't know him by his name, only his title, and how embarrassing that Luciana had used it accidentally, even if it was just in front of her maid.

"I mean the Principe," Luciana clarified.

Alora cleared her throat. "He left, Your Highness," she said nervously. She must have sensed Luciana's rising panic. And truly, nothing could have prepared her for that news. Luciana felt sick.

He couldn't have left.

"It's the middle of the night!" Luciana exclaimed.

"I know. That's what I told him, but he insisted—"

"Tell me he is just out for a ride."

"I'm afraid not," Alora said.

Luciana trembled. No. She had to tell him. He had to know…

"He seemed to be in such a hurry, and I called for a carriage. He left more than three hours ago," Alora continued.

Three hours. There was no way for Luciana to find him now. In the dark on horseback, she would never catch up with him.

Luciana fell back against the wall, biting her lip to keep herself from shedding any tears. Even then, she would not cry. She'd made her bed and now she must lie in it.

And now the next day, she still hadn't seen Camila. She'd meant to find her after reading the post, but her restless night and lack of sleep had left her in a haze, and she'd been in the study much longer than she had intended. Knowing she wouldn't be able to focus, she pushed away from the desk and went to find her sister.

Luciana searched the gardens, the stables, and even knocked on Camila's bedroom door, but she was nowhere to be seen.

As a last resort, Luciana decided to search out her mother. She, unlike Camila, was very easy to find.

Natalia sat in the drawing room with a piece of cloth, embroidering. When Luciana entered, she looked up, startled.

"Have you seen Camila?" Luciana asked.

"Not today," said Natalia with a flick of her wrist.

"Where could she be?"

"Darling, I've been in here all morning. How should I know?" While Natalia focused on her embroidery, Luciana could tell that she was upset.

"Mother, I am worried that Camila is angry with me." Luciana was planning on easing her way into the conversation, but there hardly seemed to be a point.

"I see why," Natalia said. "The poor girl wasn't even given a warning."

Luciana sighed and sat down with her mother. "I'm sorry you weren't told in advance. It was sprung on me at the very last second as well," Luciana lied. She hated lying, no matter how much she had to do it.

"I felt rather silly," Natalia said, finally looking up to acknowledge her daughter.

"I know. That was unfair," Luciana said. And she meant it. If she'd been less selfish or if she'd had more time, perhaps she could have spoken with her family about the announcement. "I must speak with Camila as well. I must make sure she is able to see the good in the change."

"What good is there for her in any of this?" Natalia shrugged. "I know she's never had an affinity toward the crown but still. Given what I heard last night, rumors are already circulating."

"Rumors like what?" Luciana asked, curious. She'd been so busy at the ball that she hadn't had time to consider what the guests might think about her sister.

"Crazy things. They think there must be some kind of breach of the vow of chastity," Natalia explained.

"For Uncle Nicolas," Luciana said, nodding.

"What? No!" Natalia said. "For Camila."

Luciana's brow furrowed. How could that be? "But Camila hasn't made a vow of chastity," she said.

"Well, yes. But she is"—Natalia cleared her throat—"*was* next in line for the throne. So, her sudden demotion can only mean one thing. That she is no longer pure and that she has refused to marry a gentleman."

Luciana almost choked on air. How had the gossips figured out the truth so fast when no one had suspected a thing before? Still, she had promised Camila that she would not tell anyone about her affair. She would keep to her word, even now. "What?" was all Luciana could manage to croak out.

"The amount of time Camila spends with Condesa Esmeralda has begun to raise some flags," said Natalia.

"If they were together, hypothetically, wouldn't that be a good thing?" Luciana asked hopefully.

"Of course, dear. You know I only wish for what's best for the two of you. But others may not see it that way. If the rumors of her love affair are true, it would be shame Camila. They'll say that no good Reina puts her own feelings above the needs of her country."

Luciana almost sunk into herself. Without even saying anything, she'd somehow announced her sister's secret. And how could she judge Camila for putting Esmeralda above Askaña when she herself had been distracted by Daniel? It would have been almost admirable if Camila had decided to follow her heart. Luciana wished she could be that lucky.

"So, what is to be done then?" asked Luciana.

"Nothing on your part. You've already picked up your burden. Unfortunately, Condesa Esmeralda will not get off so easily," said Natalia.

"What is to happen to her, Mother?" Luciana asked fearfully.

"Nothing horrendous, but she will leave the castillo. I'd imagine she's already gone."

With that, Natalia continued working where she'd left off on her embroidery. But Luciana wasn't done.

"Where will she go?" Luciana said, realizing her voice was rising more with every question she asked.

"To Osmain, I'm sure, to her cousin. And it's only temporary. After your coronation and the gossip dies down, I'm sure she will return. She does have an estate to manage as Condesa, after all."

Luciana nodded. This was unfortunate, but Esmeralda's exile had to be done to save Camila. Still, it was no wonder that Camila was angry. She probably thought Luciana had told Nicolas about the affair without even considering that Nicolas also made a sudden departure. Next time she saw Camila she would have to explain everything.

Luciana must have been sitting in silence for too long, as Natalia asked, "Do you have any other questions?"

Luciana simply sighed again. "Should I give her space?" she finally asked.

Natalia nodded. "I think so. She will come around when she is ready." Natalia took Luciana's hands in her own, and Luciana was suddenly aware of how small her own hands were, how childlike she was. Lost in a world that was too big to comprehend.

For the first time since her father died, Luciana leaned forward and gave Natalia a hug. In turn, Luciana was wrapped tight in her mother's reassuring embrace. "I know this must be a lot for you," Natalia said. "I'm sure you will become a great Reina."

A swell of pride rose in Luciana's chest. Her mother was right. She would serve her country well.

13

Day 31 of Summer

Daniel's trip back to Osmain had gone by in a haze. He'd spent his days staring aimlessly out of the carriage windows, feeling a strange sort of emptiness. He hadn't even been tempted to break out his journal to write, telling himself that he was sure to spill his ink thanks to the rocky Askanese roads. But he knew the truth. Every word he wrote would be about Luciana. He couldn't stop thinking about how she'd looked when he'd seen her last—so devoid of emotion, so heartless. How had things gone so wrong so quickly?

By the time Daniel reached the palazzo, he hardly knew what it was like to feel like himself anymore. As he gazed upon the spires of his home, he didn't feel the relief that he'd expected. Instead, there was a numbness in its place.

Daniel spent most of his first day back doing absolutely nothing. He'd told the servants to give him time alone, saying he merely needed time to get settled back in. It was all a lie, of course. Once he made it back to his bedroom, he spent nearly all the daylight hours staring out of his window.

Osmain was famous for the water that ran throughout its cities. The palazzo was built right next to the canals which also ran throughout the seaside towns of Osmain. Watching the boats sailing past his window filled with travelers and tradespeople was a reasonable enough way to pass the time. By the time the sun was starting to set, however, Daniel's stomach was grumbling with hunger. Despite not being interested in engaging with his father, he figured he should probably attend dinner. Hopefully there wouldn't be a lecture waiting for him about Luciana.

Daniel was the first one to reach the table, and grateful for the few minutes of extra silence, he enjoyed his meal. He'd always preferred Osmainian food to any other cuisine, and tonight was no exception.

Unfortunately for Daniel, his silent dinner didn't last long. Antonio strode into the room with confidence and didn't seem fazed at the sight of his son. Someone must have informed him of his arrival earlier in the day.

"Good evening, son," said Antonio.

"Father," Daniel said simply.

Antonio sat at the head of the table. "I trust your journey was pleasant?"

"Quite," said Daniel. What was wrong with himself? Daniel was not usually one to shy away from good conversation, and until recently, Daniel had always gotten along well with his father. Somewhere among all the marriage negotiations, their relationship had turned sour.

The pair sat in silence for a moment until Antonio cleared his throat and said, "You came home quickly, didn't you?"

Daniel expected this, but still he resisted the urge to roll his eyes. "I suppose so. The Princesa and I were not meant to be."

"That's too bad," Antonio said, almost too knowingly. Could he tell that the ending of the engagement had been Luciana's choice? If he did, he didn't say anything as the two resumed their dinner. Daniel kept eyeing his father, who was eating his food quite contentedly. What was Antonio playing at?

Finally, Daniel set down his fork a little too forcefully. The plate made a loud clanking noise, and Antonio glanced up from his meal.

"What are you doing?" Daniel demanded.

"I am eating dinner, son," Antonio said condescendingly.

"No. I mean, why did you drop the subject so easily?"

"You clearly did not want to marry her. It's alright."

Daniel grunted in frustration, then said, "But why is it alright? I expected a lecture from you! What kind of father lets his son call off a marriage to the Princesa of a large kingdom and does not make a fuss?"

Antonio shrugged. "I can give you a lecture if you'd prefer."

Daniel seethed with anger. What was going on?

Daniel must have been quiet for too long because Antonio continued, "Would you like a lecture, son?"

"No," Daniel snapped.

"I hardly see the point in admonishing you. I still expect you to be married before the year is out. You've had enough time to dawdle. If you haven't chosen a bride by then, I'll choose you one myself and there will be no getting out of the engagement."

At that moment, a woman ran into the room. "So sorry I'm late," she said. She looked to be about Daniel's age, and she stood so straight and poised that it seemed as though even the slightest draft coming through might risk snapping her in half.

She was pretty, he supposed, with clear porcelain skin and blue eyes almost as striking as Luciana's. Almost. Based on the blond shade of her hair and her thick accent, Daniel assumed that she was probably Esmarish.

It was then that Daniel noticed. There was a third plate set at the table. He had been so deep in his own head that he'd failed to notice what was right in front of him. Who was this expected guest?

"There you are," said Antonio cheerfully. "Take a seat. Make yourself comfortable."

"Thank you, Your Majesty," the woman said.

Daniel glanced around, looking for some kind of answer. It was as if his entire life had shifted while he'd been in Askaña. Suddenly his father didn't want to lecture him, and there was a strange woman eating dinner with the royal family.

The stranger smiled at Daniel, then sat down. At the place set right next to Daniel. Daniel fought the urge to glare at his father. Did Antonio think he was stupid? He knew his father, and he knew the games he liked to play. He imagined Antonio's plan went something like this. Tell Daniel that it's fine that he turned away Luciana, then present a new woman to try and make him fall in love with yet another stranger.

If Daniel's blood hadn't already been boiling, it was now. How could Antonio throw someone at him immediately after what had happened in Askaña? Of course, Antonio would have no way of knowing the circumstances in which Daniel and Luciana had parted, but it was inconsiderate at the very least.

"Daniel," Antonio announced, "this is Mademoiselle Sibella Bellerose of Esmar."

Mademoiselle Bellerose flashed a dazzling smile that would certainly melt the heart of any man in the realm. Any man except for Daniel. She was stunning, certainly, but Daniel was still trying to figure out what his life had become. He wasn't exactly keen on falling head over heels for the first pretty face he saw.

"And Mademoiselle Bellerose, this is my son, Principe Daniel Leonardo Gabriel DiAngelo of Osmain," Antonio said, gesturing to Daniel, who could only nod in response. It was strange to be introduced by his full name at an informal family dinner, and he resisted the urge to cringe.

"It's very nice to make your acquaintance, Your Highness. I've heard much about you," Mademoiselle Bellerose finally said.

Daniel cleared his throat. "Um, yes. It's nice to meet you as well."

The room fell into silence. Everyone seemed to be looking at Daniel, waiting for some further response, but he truly had nothing to say. If this was his father's plan, then so be it, but he shouldn't be expected to forget about Luciana like nothing had happened between them. He felt a crushing sadness at that thought as he realized that nothing had happened. Not really. Despite his heartbreak, he had no good excuse to turn Mademoiselle Bellerose away.

Finally, Antonio broke the silence. "What part of Esmar are you from again, Mademoiselle?"

Mademoiselle Bellerose perked up. "I grew up in Céleste."

"Near the royal château."

"I was raised in the country just outside of the city, yes."

Daniel fought the urge to yawn. He did not care where she was from. If Antonio was trying to push them together, he would much rather learn something about her personality. He felt terrible for tuning them out as they continued to chat, but the line of conversation only led to Mademoiselle Bellerose describing the desert climate of western Esmar. Truly, who could find that interesting?

Daniel finished his dinner and sat in silence, waiting for a chance to excuse himself. He must have sat there for five minutes half listening before Mademoiselle Bellerose turned to him.

"Which is your favorite method of travel for arid regions, Your Highness?" she asked.

Daniel blinked in surprise. He'd never traveled in an arid region. How should he know?

"I, uh… carriage?" Daniel said pathetically.

"Same here!" Mademoiselle Bellerose said excitedly. "I find nothing compares."

Daniel nodded. How many methods of desert transportation were there? He made a mental note to visit Esmar again and actually visit the desert regions to find out.

Mademoiselle Bellerose and Antonio then continued to prattle on, leaving Daniel feeling silly sitting at the table with an empty plate. But every time he made a gesture towards leaving, Mademoiselle Bellerose would ask him something to keep him rooted at the table a while longer. His favorite color, his favorite type of wine, how he liked the recent weather.

After far too much time, Mademoiselle Bellerose stood and excused herself, gliding from the room with impossible grace.

"Father," Daniel said, crossing his arms.

"Yes, son," Antonio replied.

"Who is that?"

"That's Mademoiselle Bellerose. I already introduced you."

"No, I mean, why is she here?"

"She is our guest," Antonio said, taking the last few bites of what must have been a very cold dish at this point.

"I know that," Daniel growled.

"Then why ask?" Antonio said. If Daniel was any less

composed, he would have lunged across the table at his father to strangle him. The endless talking in circles was driving him insane. He didn't want to come out and accuse Antonio of playing matchmaker. He would much rather his father tell him directly, but if his father wouldn't admit it then Daniel would do what had to be done.

"Did you invite her here as a potential bride for me?" Daniel asked.

"Why, son, you think so lowly of me," Antonio said, putting a dramatic hand over his heart.

"So, you didn't ask her to come here to court me?"

"No, you're right. I did."

Daniel stood up to leave. This was ridiculous. Was it too much to ask to be able to choose his own bride? Besides that, the fact that Mademoiselle Bellerose was already in residence meant that she'd been invited while Daniel was still in Askaña. Reports of their disinterest toward one another must have reached Antonio's ears somehow. It wouldn't be surprising to learn that Antonio had instructed Daniel's staff to write him reports. Antonio had such little faith in Daniel marrying Luciana that he'd brought in a spare. It was insulting.

"Daniel, wait," said Antonio.

"What?"

"Just hear me out. I know you want to marry for love and I respect that."

"Then why—"

Antonio held up a hand to silence Daniel. "I will not force you to marry Mademoiselle Bellerose. But you must marry by the end of the year. I've had enough of you avoiding your responsibility to this country. The remainder of the summer and the autumn is plenty of time to find a suitable bride."

Ah. There it was. The deal. Antonio always seemed to have one at the ready.

"Fine," Daniel ground out. It would be easier to just agree with him than fight. He would never win anyway. He just didn't want to try. He'd already found the woman he wanted to marry, but she was out of reach. Marriage seemed pointless if it couldn't be with Luciana.

"I will spend some time with Mademoiselle Bellerose, but I make no promises," Daniel said.

"Very well," Antonio nodded.

Daniel swept himself out of the dining hall. If he was to be married, so be it. But he would do so on his terms.

14

Day 62 of Summer

"Introducing Her Royal Majesty, Reina Luciana Marqueza of Askaña!"

Every head in the crowd turned to the balcony. Luciana swept into the ballroom with all the grace the new Reina of Askaña should have. She wore the golden sunburst crown with a pride and radiance that would have put any other Reina to shame. She'd even had a special gown made for the occasion, a traditional coronation gown colored pure gold that matched the sparkling dust swept gently over her lips and eyelids.

Luciana's subjects bowed as she stood over them, regal and proud. This was the moment she'd been waiting for. Her entire life had led up to this, and here she was—basking in the glory and respect of her entire nation. Her heart swelled with pride at the scene before her. She'd done it. While she had much work to attend to, she would not miss her first ball as Reina.

Besides, this would be her last night of fun for a while. Not that she could let her guard down at the ball even if she wanted to. Now that she was Reina there would be expectations. She'd have to marry soon to continue the line since Camila and Esmeralda's relationship ensured becoming an Ambassador of the Sun was out of the question. A ball seemed a natural place to find a potential husband. While she knew of several Duques who would happily wed her, she found it hard to believe that any would be suitable matches. The nobility would surely only want her for her title and resources. That was only to be expected, but it did not make her excited to marry. And aside from avoiding the risk of fortune-hunters, she didn't think she could stop thinking about Daniel long enough to get to know any of them.

It felt like it had been forever since Daniel had left for Osmain, but she still thought about him more than she'd like to admit. Every once in a while she'd sit by her piano and feel a stab of pain that he wasn't there to play for. Or she'd think about Osmain and what he might be doing at that moment. Perhaps he had already moved on.

The band began to play, snapping Luciana from her thoughts. She gathered her skirts and descended the grand staircase that led to the dance floor, unable to contain her smile as she heard hushed appreciative murmurs from the guests in attendance. She was aware that every eye in the room was trained on her, so she glanced around the ballroom. It looked like all of Askaña's nobility were in attendance.

As soon as Luciana reached the floor, the predictable and new frenzy of gentlemen appeared. It was strange, in a way, to be their focus. Luciana had never been the sister to whom men flocked. Camila was sunny. Camila was personable. And besides that, she was the heir. Every young man with a title would have been a fool not to take his chances with the future Reina. They had left Luciana alone for years, which was exactly the way she had preferred it.

The first man to reach her she knew to be a Conde, but she could not for the life of her remember his name. Could it be Samuel? Santiago? No, neither of those sounded right.

"Your Majesty," the young man bowed. "Would you care to dance?"

Luciana gave him a polite smile. "Of course."

Luciana took the Conde's hand as he led her to the floor. His palm was sweaty, she noted. The poor thing must have been so nervous. Poor... poor... she still couldn't remember his name.

He led her through the dance rather unceremoniously. He was not an exquisite dancer by any means, but he didn't step on Luciana's toes, so it could have been much worse. At least that's what she thought until he opened his mouth.

"Your Majesty—may I call you Luciana?" he began.

Luciana was taken aback. It was almost funny how quickly he'd dropped her title. She resisted the urge to laugh in his face. This could be her future husband, after all. Luciana cleared her throat. "Um, no. You may not."

"Why not?"

Luciana could only bring herself to blink in response. What could she possibly say to that? She didn't want to belittle him.

"I see you have no response," the unnamed gentleman said.

"So, you are a Conde, correct?" Luciana blurted, trying to change the subject.

"As of now. But I would be more than happy to pass my title along to my next sibling if I were to advance," he said, pulling Luciana in close. So close, in fact, that she could feel his damp breath on her cheek.

Luciana stepped back, making the gesture appear as part of the dance.

"So, you are a Conde then. How are things in..." Luciana trailed off, hoping he would fill in the gaps of her memory.

"In?" he asked.

"In…" Luciana said again, hoping he would catch her hint.

"In what?" the Conde asked.

Luciana ground her teeth. How could anyone possibly be this clueless? Did he want her to come right out and admit she didn't know or care who he was?

"Where you live," Luciana said slowly.

"Oh! They are fine, thank you for your concern," he replied.

Luciana was going to pull her hair out. Was this what flirting was like? This was horribly painful.

They danced in an awkward silence until the song concluded. The Conde bowed to her once again. "When can I see you again?" he asked.

"I'm not sure," Luciana said. Truthfully, she hoped he would realize he wasn't meant for her and leave her to meet the other bachelors at the ball.

The Conde grabbed her hand. "But Luciana—"

Luciana ripped her hand away from him. "Your Majesty," she hissed.

The Conde broke into an irritatingly cocky smile. "You're already calling me Your Majesty!"

Luciana once again was only able to blink. She was fairly certain her mouth was hanging open. When she finally spoke, all that she could manage was a squeaky "what?"

"I didn't think you'd already be seeing me as your husband so early in our courtship," he explained.

"Our courtship?" She was stunned. One dance did not qualify as a courtship, did it? No. If it did, she'd be courting Daniel. Or even Prince Wes for that matter. Never mind the fact that the Conde would never be anything more than *Your Highness*. Luciana's husband would never rule Askaña. He would simply be Luciana's consort—a means to get an heir.

"I really feel like we have a connection," he said.

Luciana practically growled, "I don't even know your name."

He opened his mouth to speak, but Luciana turned on her heel and left him standing alone. Not five seconds later she was pulled back onto the dance floor by another gentleman, and the cycle began again.

She danced for hours or at least what felt like hours. Each man was the same—looking for a fortune, looking for a title, looking to rule. Truly, it was disgusting. When she'd finished dancing with the last gentleman, some others came rushing up to her to ask for a second chance. But seeing Camila out of the corner of her eye, Luciana excused herself.

Despite her best efforts to explain everything, she'd hardly seen Camila in the days following Esmeralda's departure. It was to be expected. Luciana had been busy and Camila had been angry. But they were still sisters, and even though they didn't spend much time together anymore, Camila was still friendly and talkative when Luciana saw her for meals. Surely if anyone understood the pressures of finding a husband among these idiots, it would be her. So, Luciana snuck off to the corner where Camila stood, arms crossed, observing the ball.

"Let's take a walk," Luciana said.

"Why?" Camila asked.

"I need an excuse to walk with my sister?" Luciana retorted, and before Camila could object, Luciana grabbed her sister's arm and pulled her into the hallway. Stares followed them as they left the ballroom, but no one dared to say anything. The party quieted for a moment but then returned to its usual volume. The sisters walked at a slow pace, and Luciana let her heart slow back down to its normal rate after all the dancing before she spoke.

"It was a bit stuffy in there," Luciana said.

"I suppose so," Camila agreed.

"All the dancing wore me out. I don't think I've ever been so requested at a ball."

Camila shrugged. "I suppose not."

Luciana took a sideways glance at her sister. She was acting strangely, but it was to be expected. After all, Luciana still hadn't had a chance to explain what had happened at the engagement ball.

"Have you heard from Esmeralda?" Luciana asked, trying to steer the conversation away from herself.

Camila nodded. "I received a letter just yesterday."

More silence.

"And?" Luciana prompted. "What did it say?"

Camila shrugged. "Nothing important."

Luciana grinned and grabbed her sister's arm playfully. "Come on now! There must be something! When is she planning to return?"

"I don't know, alright?" Camila snapped, shrugging Luciana off of her. Apparently, Esmeralda was still a sore subject.

They walked in silence some more. Luciana's mind was swirling with possible conversational topics. She'd burned so many bridges to become Reina, she would not allow Camila to go up in smoke, too.

"How did you do it?" Luciana finally asked.

"What?" asked Camila.

"Deal with all of those noblemen?"

Camila sighed. "Same way as you're doing now, I suppose."

The words were simple and if they'd been said more jovially, Luciana could have laughed along with Camila. But there were daggers in Camila's eyes, and Luciana stopped walking, stunned. "Camila, please. I'm asking for advice. One of those men is to be my husband."

Camila crossed her arms. "The great Reina of Askaña asks a humble Princesa for advice?"

Now Camila was just being difficult. Luciana rolled her eyes. "Camila! This is my future!"

"No. It's mine," Camila said, facing Luciana and looking into her eyes with an intensity that made Luciana's heart skip a beat.

"What?" said Luciana.

"Becoming Reina was *my* birthright," Camila seethed.

"You didn't want it!" Luciana argued.

Camila's face went red with anger. "Who said that I did not want it? I was perfectly prepared to marry a stranger and run Askaña, and you took that from me!"

Luciana couldn't help but laugh. "Perfectly prepared? Tell me, Camila, how many languages do you speak?"

Camila stayed silent, not wanting to dignify her with a response.

"How much do you know about current events or of law?" Luciana continued. "I've read and studied and learned all I could about history, about culture, about everything that a Reina needs to know, while you were busy sleeping with Esmeralda!"

"How dare you!" Camila screamed. "I knew it! You did tell uncle about Esmeralda and me!"

Luciana stepped back. How could she not have predicted this? Of course, Camila thought she'd broken her promise. That's why she was angry with her. She'd meant to clear the air, but with everything else going on, she'd not had the chance.

"Camila, I never—"

"I trusted you!"

"I never told him about your relationship!" Luciana had to shout over Camila to be heard, but it worked. Camila shut her mouth, still visibly steaming.

"Do you honestly think so low of me? Of course, I would never betray your trust like that. Uncle stepped down himself." So yes, she lied just a bit. She didn't feel great about it, but the important thing was to ensure that Camila knew that her trust was never broken.

"It does not matter," Camila said.

"What do you mean?" Asked Luciana.

"You are still to blame."

Luciana's stomach flipped. Was it possible that Camila knew about the blackmail? Would Nicolas have told her anything?

"What do you mean?" Luciana asked again.

"I mean," Camila said, "you took the throne by force."

Without knowing how much Camila knew, she wasn't about to admit anything directly. Luciana stood in the hallway sputtering, trying to think of something to say.

"I don't know how I didn't see it sooner," Camila continued, the truth dawning on her face. "You were always trying to better yourself. Trying to be the best in school, the best with manners, the best at everything. Do you know how much I wished to be like you?"

Luciana was shocked at her sister's words. Did Camila really envy her? After so many years of wishing to be Camila, the irony wasn't lost on her. She had the urge to wrap her arms around her sister and cry and make it all okay. But she didn't. She stood there, silent and stupid.

"You were the perfect golden child. The darling. And I… I was the heir. That was all I had," Camila continued.

"That's not true!" Luciana exclaimed. No, Camila was so much more than just the heir. She was electric. She could wrap a room around her finger with just a few words.

"Well, I hope you're right," said Camila. "Because now I have nothing. No crown. No Esmeralda. No purpose. The rest of my life will be spent living in your shadow, staring up at my perfect little sister. Truly, I don't know how you managed to convince uncle to switch our places in the order of succession. I believe that you didn't expose Esmeralda and me, but rest assured, I will find out what you did. And I will destroy you for it. The very same way you have destroyed me."

Luciana's heart dropped. She could barely breathe, panic setting in. "Camila, please! We can work this out together!"

"Until you understand what you have done to me, I

will never forgive you," Camila said. It was cold. It was simple. She did not scream or yell. She said it in such a calm and even tone that it sent a shiver down Luciana's spine. Then she turned away and went back to the ballroom, leaving Luciana alone in the hallway.

She had wanted to be Reina her entire life. She'd envied Camila for having that thing Luciana craved so badly handed to her on a silver platter. But now that she was here, now that she had what she wanted, it wasn't everything she'd hoped it would be. Luciana ran to her music room and sat at the piano, needing a moment to calm down.

Everything was heavy, like she was carrying the weight of the world on her shoulders. And in a way, she was.

She'd gotten her crown, but at what cost?

She'd destroyed her relationship with Camila. She'd stooped to blackmailing her uncle, who might not deserve to rule, but blackmail was a low blow. And she'd turned away Daniel, who had been better matched with her than any other suitor she'd met.

Luciana didn't know how long she'd been in the music room by the time she calmed herself down. Thirty minutes? An hour? Finally, she took a deep breath and stood. She'd made her bed. Now she would have to lie in it.

She headed into the tunnels, navigating through the

passageways until she reached her exit, this one in the hallway outside of the ballroom. As she inched the secret door open, she heard a large crashing noise coming from the ballroom itself.

Luciana sighed. Someone must have accidentally knocked over one of the refreshment tables. She emerged into the hallway and was brushing dust off her gold dress when she heard a scream. Perhaps one of the more sensitive ladies had been cut by a glass. But as she got closer to the doors, it became clear that what was happening was much more sinister.

One scream turned into two, which turned into ten, and by the time Luciana entered the room, everything was in chaos.

The beautiful stained-glass window in the ballroom had been smashed, leaving shards of glass all over the floor. Men and women wearing all black were stalking through the ballroom, grabbing anyone they could find and impaling them on swords.

The rebels. It had to be.

Luciana had known they were on their way to the castillo. She'd just wanted more time. Luciana fought the urge to empty the contents of her stomach as the nobles were slain one at a time. Men and women she'd known since her childhood were dying before her, and even as their Reina there was nothing she could do to stop it. She backed away from the carnage to remain out of sight, but she could not look away. She knew she should charge into the battle, but without a weapon she would certainly be killed immediately, ensuring the rebels' victory. No, she had to stay alive, at least for now.

This was all her fault. If she'd just been faster getting the crown. If she'd not held this ball…

Then she spotted her sister. Camila was hiding behind a potted plant in the corner of the room, shaking with fear. She looked around frantically, searching for an escape route. Luciana had the urge to run to her sister, to pull her out of danger, but she was frozen with fear. Her feet could not move. She stood paralyzed as Nicolas and her mother were dragged to the center of the room by a group of rebels and another group found Camila.

Luciana tried to scream, but her voice would not work. She could not run away and she couldn't run to save them. Her heart beat faster and faster in her chest, pounding and pounding until Luciana fell against the wall in shock. Her countrymen were dying left and right, and all she could do was stand there, useless.

Camila thrashed and begged for help as she was pulled to the center of the ballroom. The remaining nobility watched, eyes wide with fear, no one willing to risk their own lives to save her. One of the rebels kicked Camila down and others held her in place.

A large man who appeared to be the leader of the

rebels stepped forward. He held a large sword, blood dripping down the blade from the others he'd slain. He started with Nicolas, hacking away at him until his head rolled across the floor in a gory mess. Next was Natalia, then finally Camila. Camila screamed and fought them, but there was no escape. The blade struck her, and her screams died away.

There was blood. There was so much blood. Luciana's head swam as she tried to keep down the contents of her stomach. This had to be a nightmare. There was no way this was real. She must have fallen asleep in the music room.

But no. The panic in her soul told her all she needed to know. This was real. And unless she got out fast, she was going to die along with her family.

Finally, Luciana forced her legs to move away from the ballroom and down the hall.

She did not move quickly. She was shaking so much that her run turned to more of a light jog. Every once in a while she would glance behind her, and from the glimpses of them that she got, it seemed that the rebels were making their way out of the ballroom. No doubt to search the rest of the castillo.

Luciana didn't know where she was running to. She couldn't leave the castillo. The rebels would certainly have people stationed at all exits to pick off any stragglers. She was going to have to hide inside, at least for now.

Luciana ran as fast as she could to the tunnel entrance. She bit her lip as she put her shaky hand to the panel. The door opened and she tasted blood as she tumbled through the small door. When she went to close it behind her, her heart dropped.

A small girl of no more than ten stood in the hall right where she'd just been. She had skin as white as a ghost, and red hair that almost looked like flames in the candlelight. And she looked directly at Luciana.

Luciana trembled. The girl wore all black. She was with the rebellion. The girl even carried a small dagger to defend herself. She must have been told to stay away from the ballroom.

Luciana's hand shook as she raised a finger to her lips. Her intent was clear. *Please don't tell anyone you saw me.*

The girl cocked her head, eyes wide as she took in the tunnel and the woman inside it. Then the girl flashed a mischievous grin and nodded.

Luciana mouthed, *Thank you.* And then she closed the door.

15

Day 63 of Summer

The dawn was an important time of day for the Askanese. It symbolized renewal, a fresh start. But as Luciana hid in her music room, crouched under her piano, this new day hardly felt like a good omen. She'd spent the night sleeplessly curled up on the floor, lying in a puddle of her own silent tears.

The commotion outside had gone on for hours, crashes sounding outside the window and loud footsteps thundering on the floor above her. The noise was a constant reminder of what was going on, and while she was still in shock, the reality of her situation was starting to settle in.

She was no longer Reina.

The position she'd held for less than a day was now gone, possibly forever. Who knew what the new leader of Askaña would do to the political system, with the majority of the aristocracy dead?

Bile rose in Luciana's throat at the thought. She'd run before she could see anything else, but as ruthless as the rebels had already been, she found it hard to believe that there were any survivors. And if there were, they had likely already fled the country and denounced their former titles and holdings. Luciana couldn't help but feel a bit envious at the prospect. The rebels would likely hunt her down no matter where she went, because as long as she lived, any other claims to the throne could be considered treasonous and illegitimate.

But what could she do? Her allies were all dead. The rebels had won. It would be nearly suicidal to try and gather an army from the remaining loyalists in the militia. And as much as she'd like to think she'd have a chance to truly wear the crown, deep in her heart she knew it was impossible. Unless... she did know someone with an army strong enough to give her a fighting chance to reclaim her crown.

She'd survived the night, but with the new day came new problems. How would she escape the castillo? And if she couldn't, how would she care for herself while trapped in the secret passages? She was just grateful she hadn't been found yet. The odds of that lasting were not in her favor.

It did seem that, at least for the time being, her location had stayed secret. The little girl she'd seen at the tunnel entrance last night hadn't sent the dogs after her, and she was grateful. Perhaps she had an ally. Maybe if she found the little girl again, she could help Luciana escape.

Luciana pushed herself to her feet slowly. Her muscles ached from a night spent on the floor and her limbs were stiffer than usual. Between her sore joints and the haunting image of her family's blood spilt on the cold tiles of the ballroom, it was all she could do to stand.

Still, she forced herself to go to the tunnel entrance, careful to stay out of view of the window just in case patrols were outside looking for her. She dropped her crown and some of her more cumbersome garments in the corner, giving her more freedom of movement and less recognizability. She pushed the door to the tunnels open. Where would a little girl be at this time of day? Without knowing who she was, Luciana had no sense of where to try first. She could check the servant's quarters. Perhaps she was here to be a lady's maid in the new regime.

So, Luciana began to slowly traverse the tunnels. She walked slowly, careful not to make any noise. Maybe she was being paranoid, but she couldn't afford to make any mistakes at a time like this.

The servant's quarters were on the other end of the tunnels and as they were isolated from the rest of the castillo, it took Luciana several minutes to reach it. As she neared the exit she wanted, she noticed something on the ground and her heart stopped. In the dim light she could barely make out the shape of a person curled into a ball. Shocked, Luciana gasped and tumbled backwards. She tripped on the hem of her dirty coronation gown, landing on the ground with a thud.

The person looked up at her, then stood and came closer in the dark. Luciana's heartbeat like thunder in her ears. It was impossible to determine the identity of the figure in the shadows, and fear coursed through every fiber of her being. This had to be a rebel, someone the girl had told about the tunnels, who was now guarding the exit. Luciana tried to shuffle backwards, but she got caught in her billowing skirts and fell back to the floor.

As the person neared her, Luciana noticed that she wore the dress of a castillo servant. The stranger held out a hand to Luciana, and without thinking, Luciana took it. When she regained her balance, she found herself face to face with Alora. Relief flooded her and it took Luciana a moment to calm herself after the scare and shock, but as her heart rate slowed, tears began to prick at her eyes.

Wordlessly, Luciana embraced her friend, Alora breathing shakily against her shoulder. She was not alone. She might not have Camila or her mother anymore, but the rebels hadn't taken everyone.

Luciana let go of Alora, then grabbed her hand and pulled her back to the music room. The tunnels were as safe a place as any, but they had an echo. It would be much safer to hide in the relatively soundproof music room. While it would be possible for someone outside the window to hear if she played an instrument loudly, a quiet conversation would likely go undetected.

They traveled in silence, and upon reaching the music room, the two women hid together behind the piano. Luciana looked at Alora. Her black hair was a mess and her dark skin and homely dress were streaked with blood. While Luciana was only covered in dust and dirt from the tunnels, it was clear Alora had made a narrower escape.

"You're alive," Luciana said, keeping her voice low.

"As are you. It's a relief to see you well, Your Majesty," Alora replied.

Luciana fought back tears. She forced out a sharp breath and said, "Just Luciana, please."

"But—"

"I think it's clear that I am no longer titled. Until I am restored as Reina, you may call me Luciana."

Alora frowned, a mixture of sadness and understanding so clear in her eyes. "Very well."

Luciana nodded. "Tell me what happened."

Alora took a deep breath. "I was in the servant's quarters during the ball. By the time I realized what was happening, it was too late. The rebels had begun sweeping through the servants as well. They were ruthless, and the only way to escape was to swear allegiance to the new rule," she explained.

"Did you?" Luciana asked.

Alora shook her head. "I was able to run. I got to the tunnels right before they would have gotten to me."

Luciana almost smiled. Who could have known that night years ago, bringing the piano through the tunnels with Alora, would save her life one day? At the time Luciana had just wanted a partner in crime and it paid dividends when Alora was able to attend to her much more quickly than any other servant. But this... this was the best possible use of the tunnels. The thought warmed Luciana for a moment until her heart sank. How could she have been so selfish as to not tell her family about the escape route?

"I'm glad you're here," said Luciana weakly.

"What are we going to do?"

Luciana sighed. "I don't know. I saw someone last

night… a little girl. She saw me go into the tunnel, but I don't think she told anyone I was here. I was hoping I might find her."

"What did she look like?" Alora asked. "If you trust her, then I will go look for her. You must remain here to protect yourself."

"No," said Luciana. "I can't let you die, too."

"But—"

"I know this tunnel system better than anyone. I'll have the best chance of finding her without being spotted."

Alora's eyes widened, her mouth agape. "You're sure?"

"Positive. I can do this."

Alora still seemed to be in shock, but she slowly nodded. "If anyone can get us out of this, it's you. Good luck."

IT TOOK Luciana several hours to find the girl. She was limited by the reach of the tunnels, which only spanned a few floors of the castillo, and she had to stay behind the door in each room she scanned to stay out of sight. She looked in the servant's quarters, the library, and the kitchens, but the girl had yet to make an appearance. There was an immense amount of destruction from the night before, and servants buzzed all around, repairing windows, repainting walls, and sweeping the corridors. But none of the servants she saw was the person she was looking for.

Finally, Luciana cracked open the secret door to the Rey's study. It was a long shot, but she'd looked everywhere else. And sure enough, sitting in the Rey's chair was the small girl from the night before. She was petite, wearing a simple dress, but there she was as though she belonged in the study.

Also, in the room stood a huge man, tall and muscular, and Luciana shut the door as much as possible to avoid being seen. She recognized him instantly as the man who had executed her family the night before. Luciana was torn between fear and anger. Part of her wanted to run away and never look back, and the other wanted to hurt him as badly as he'd hurt her. Ultimately, Luciana did nothing. She crouched in the tunnels, a fist clenched in silence as she watched him pace. He didn't stomp, but the floor still creaked as if he did. This was the kind of man who could rip her apart with his bare hands.

He spoke to the little girl, and Luciana listened. "You were so brave last night," the man said.

"Thank you, Papa," the girl replied.

"Are you ready to be Princesa?"

Luciana's stomach dropped out beneath her.

Somehow this was the salt in her wound she hadn't expected. The rage overwhelmed her so much it was almost physically painful, and she had to let go of the door as her hands shook.

How dare these people invade her home? How dare they murder her family and then move in, acting as if nothing was wrong? How dare Askanese life continue on without her?

The girl smiled. "Will I still go to school with my friends?"

The large man laughed, and the sound sent shivers down Luciana's spine. "Heavens no! But if you wish to have your friends here, it will be so. I will arrange for them to be your lady's maids."

"Maids?"

"Of course! You can't go to school with commoners, Sapphire. You will have private tutors now."

The girl—Sapphire—grimaced. "They are my friends, Papa! They could not possibly—"

"I will send for them immediately."

"But Papa—"

"Which of your friends would you like to bring into your employ?" When Sapphire didn't reply, the man continued. "How about Jade and Aurora? They're nice enough girls. They'll make for loyal servants."

Sapphire considered for a moment. "I suppose if I had to pick, I would choose them."

"You will be cared for here," the man said, stooping down to meet her at eye level. "I will see to it that you will never want for anything ever again. I promise."

Sapphire looked at the ground. "Yes, Papa."

"Very well. Now I have many urgent matters to attend to. I will see you in a little while," the man said, then he barged out of the study. His footsteps fell so heavily that the walls nearly shook.

Once Luciana was positive the man was gone, she let out an unsteady breath and pushed the door open. This was risky. Sapphire had every reason in the world to turn her in. Yet something told Luciana to trust her.

Sapphire was quick to see the door swing open, and she flung herself from the chair, dashing toward the entrance. Sapphire opened her mouth as if to greet her loudly, but Luciana quickly held a finger up to her lips, and Sapphire nodded.

Sapphire whispered, "Hello!"

"I need your help," Luciana said.

Sapphire smiled a wicked grin and dove into the tunnels after Luciana, and then the two were off. They reached the music room in no time, thanks to Sapphire's excitement. She kept running ahead of Luciana, forcing her to run to catch up.

When they opened the door to the music room, Sapphire finally gasped. "These tunnels are incredible! You must tell me where each door goes!"

Luciana shook her head. "I'm afraid I don't have the time." She gestured to Alora, who was still hidden behind the piano. "My friend and I need to escape."

Sapphire cocked her head. "Hmm. I'm sure I can assist. What's in it for me?"

"What do you mean, 'what's in it for you?'" Luciana hissed. Luciana didn't have much experience with children, but Sapphire couldn't have been older than ten and Luciana was fairly certain bribery was something usually reserved for adults.

"What do I get for helping you?"

"You get… the tunnels."

Sapphire shook her head. "Nah. See, that was my reward for the first time I saved you. What do I get now?"

Luciana had nothing to really offer. She shrugged. "You get the satisfaction of helping someone?"

Sapphire crossed her arms and pouted, but when Luciana raised her eyebrows sternly, the young girl groaned. "Ugh, fine," Sapphire said. "I've heard things. They're looking for you. You are Reina Luciana, yes?"

Reina Luciana. What a joke. But still, she nodded.

"I thought so. They're starting to look in the woods. You'd have to go at night and get out fast to get past them," Sapphire explained.

"We will leave tonight then. Can you help us gather supplies?"

Sapphire shrugged. "That depends on what you need."

Luciana thought for a moment. She couldn't take much, only the bare essentials so that they could move quickly. "Rations that will last us a few days. New outfits that won't draw any attention. And you'll need to prepare a few horses. Can you do that?"

Sapphire nodded. "That's easy."

"Thank you."

"Luciana," Alora piped up, "this is a fine plan and all, but where will we go? We haven't exactly got anyone left who could take us in."

Luciana's breath caught in her throat. The thought had been in the back of her mind, but she'd been too afraid to say it out loud. It was a long journey, and it would be dangerous. But Luciana could only think of one person in the realm who might be willing to help.

Luciana and Alora hid under the cover of night as they made their escape. Luciana felt a bit better about leaving Askaña knowing that Sapphire was next in line for the throne. She had been tremendously helpful, gathering food and a bit of money for their journey. She'd even readied horses for them, but she'd had to leave them in the forest surrounding the castillo. They would surely be spotted if they rode away from the stables on horseback, so they would have to make their way off the castillo grounds on foot.

As Luciana raised the hood on the cloak Sapphire had brought her and made her final trek through the tunnels, she felt a pang of sadness. She'd had to leave all of her instruments behind, all of her clothes, and worse, any memento of her family. The only thing she had of any value was her lost cousin's ring and letters. Despite this, nothing was worse than saying goodbye to her homeland. Knowing that this might be the last time she saw the Askanese castillo, Luciana tried to capture every final moment.

She ran her hands along the cold stone walls of the tunnels, savoring its earthy feel one last time. When they reached the door that would bring them outside, Alora put a reassuring hand on her shoulder, and Luciana silently wrapped her maid in a hug. Alora was all Luciana had left from Askaña, and she wasn't going to let her go.

After they broke away, Luciana pushed the small door to the outside open. This was the only tunnel door that led to the outside of the castillo, and Luciana was grateful for it. There was no way they could have made it out from inside otherwise. It was dark on the other side of the door, and the warm summer air filled Luciana's lungs. She glanced around. It was hard to tell in the darkness, but she was fairly sure that there was no one around to see them escape.

Luciana stepped out cautiously and Alora followed. After they shut the door behind them, they bolted for the cover of the trees. As they reached the forest, Luciana turned to look back. There was a patrol walking by where they'd just been. They'd managed to avoid being spotted but just narrowly.

Pushing down her fear, Luciana stepped through the trees, careful not to step on anything that would make a loud noise. Alora followed suit, and the two of them made their way to where Sapphire had promised their horses would be.

Sure enough, as they entered the small clearing, there were two horses tied to the trees, their saddle bags full of supplies for the journey. Luciana moved to untie her horse when she heard the snap of a twig behind her.

Luciana whipped around to see a boy of no more than sixteen step into the clearing. She squinted to make out his features in the moonlight. He had an athletic build, with long dark locks framing his face. But the most striking thing about him was that he wore all black. Luciana instinctively pushed Alora behind her, fear coursing through her body.

If this boy yelled, he could attract a swarm of rebels that would descend upon Luciana and Alora in minutes.

Luciana eyed the small dagger in his hand, which he kept tightly gripped at his side.

Luciana took a shaky breath and said in the smallest voice she could manage, "I mean no harm."

The boy took a step closer, and Luciana tensed. He said, "I know who you are."

Luciana nodded. "I know."

"My orders are to kill you," he said.

"I only want to escape," Luciana said. She still held out a small bit of hope that one day she might return, but it didn't seem likely.

"Of course you do," the boy said. "So you can come back with an army and make all of our lives worse."

Luciana tilted her head in curiosity. "I wouldn't want to make anyone's life worse."

"Really?" the boy asked. "Because it seems like you royals only care about yourselves."

Luciana looked at this boy. She could tell from his timid expression that he didn't really want to hurt her. He was too young to be fighting in a war like this, yet here he was. If Nicolas had only listened to his people and made changes for the better, perhaps this boy wouldn't have lost his childhood so soon. There was a sadness in his eyes but also innocent hope. Luciana felt the crushing weight of everything her family had done. Despite the horrors that the rebels had committed, she couldn't take the hope of a brighter future away from the boy.

Luciana slowly took her lost cousin's ring off of her finger, holding it out for the boy to take. He approached her slowly, eyeing the blue jewel with curiosity.

"Take it," Luciana urged. "Use it to buy you and your family a better life."

The boy stepped forward and gingerly took the ring.

"I'm truly sorry that my uncle failed you. I hope the new regime treats you better," Luciana said. She was surprised to find that she meant it. If she was going to die that night at her own people's hand, she still wanted Askaña to prosper.

She met the boy's eyes, and his hardened expression melted. He said, "You should go before someone else finds you. You'll need to move quickly. And don't come back. They're never going to stop looking for you."

Luciana nodded solemnly. "I understand. Thank you."

The boy didn't say another word as Luciana and Alora untied and mounted their horses. As Luciana prepared herself for the long road ahead, several voices cut through the silence, growing closer.

"Cedric!" one of them called.

"They're coming! Go, now!" the boy said urgently.

Luciana nodded, then looked over to Alora, who offered a nervous smile.

"Cedric!" said another voice, even closer than the last.

"I'm here!" the boy responded. "Give me a moment, I'll come to you."

Without another word, he disappeared into the brush, and Luciana and Alora took off into the unknown.

16

Day 70 of Summer

The waves crashed gracefully onto the Osmainian shores as Daniel rode along the coastline. The day was sweltering hot, and Daniel would have loved to jump into the clear ocean water to cool off. Unfortunately for him, he was accompanied by Mademoiselle Bellerose, who was certainly not made for swimming.

He'd tried his best to get to know her since returning to Osmain. He could not deny that she was beautiful, but she seemed just a bit too agreeable, a bit too restrained. As if she was trying to be the person she thought he wanted.

She would never be what he wanted. Even after all this time, he couldn't get Luciana out of his head.

Luciana had been bold and unexpected. Mademoiselle Bellerose never had a unique opinion. There was no discourse, no chemistry. And it was boring.

He glanced over to where she sat on her horse. She sat primly and properly, never going faster than a light trot to keep from knocking the wispy sand of the beach onto her gown. Daniel was surprised that Mademoiselle Bellerose could ride a horse at all, given how tightly she held onto her parasol.

Her clear skin was the color of a porcelain doll and she had sunny blond hair to match. For someone as fair as she was, he supposed the relentless Osmainian sun would cause some concern. But between her light complexion and ghostly white dress, she was so bright in the daylight that he could hardly look at her without squinting.

"What do you think of the beach?" he finally asked.

"It's lovely," replied Mademoiselle Bellerose.

Silence.

"It's a bit warm today, but the beach is perfect in the autumn," Daniel prompted.

"You will have to bring me back once the summer ends then."

Silence.

"What else would you like to see during your stay here?"

"Whatever you think I should see."

More silence. This was infuriating.

Mademoiselle Bellerose simply flashed him a smile that should have made his heart flutter, but instead he just wanted to ride away and leave her to make small talk with the seagulls.

Unfortunately, Daniel knew his options were slim. Time was ticking, and unless he found someone he liked better, Mademoiselle Bellerose was his best option. She might not excite him like Luciana had, but he supposed it was better to be bored than unhappy. At least a marriage to Mademoiselle Bellerose would allow him to focus on being a better Imperatore when the time came.

"Thank you for showing me around Osmain. I truly do like it here," Mademoiselle Bellerose said.

"It's been my pleasure," Daniel replied. It had been a pleasure to see his kingdom again, at the very least.

"I do hope to have many happy years here."

Daniel was glad his horse didn't require constant direction as he was shocked into stillness for a moment. Was this Mademoiselle Bellerose's way of reminding him that she was here to be married to him? Somehow it sounded much more formal coming from her.

After a silence that was just slightly too long, Daniel said, "Won't you be missed in Esmar?"

Mademoiselle Bellerose paused, contemplating her answer. Finally, she said, "No, I don't think I will."

Something in the tone of her voice begged him not to press further, so he didn't. Instead, he changed the subject. "Shall we go back to the palazzo?"

She nodded. "Of course."

The palazzo was perhaps a mile off the coast, but it was surrounded by the water of the canals which ran through the coastal towns of Osmain. It took them a while to ride along the canals before they finally reached the only land entrance to the palazzo. Besides a bit of small talk, the two didn't converse at all the entire ride. Daniel wondered if she'd been cast out from Esmar. She obviously didn't have much of a connection to anyone there and her desire to marry him seemed purely for personal advantage.

As Daniel neared the gate to the palazzo, he spotted an altercation taking place between several guards and a hooded figure, wearing a cloak the deep color of blood. He held out his arm, signaling for Mademoiselle Bellerose to stop. Then he noticed a second figure in a cloak that matched the first.

The figures weren't being violent, and Daniel had seen no signs of them wielding weapons. Still, he turned to Mademoiselle Bellerose. "Stay here."

"Are they dangerous? You could be hurt!" Mademoiselle Bellerose protested.

Could they be dangerous? Possibly. He could stay

back and allow his guards to sort it out. But there was no leaving the military. Once he had become a soldier, there was no going back. He shook his head and said, "As a soldier in my father's army, it is my job to protect Osmain."

Before Mademoiselle Bellerose could protest again, he spurred his horse to ride ahead, leaving her behind. As he neared the scene, he wondered who these newcomers could be. Their cloaks were of high quality, but they were smudged with dirt and grime. The sign of a thief.

"What is going on here?" Daniel asked as he dismounted his horse. He kept one hand on his dagger, which was safely sheathed at his waist. For now.

His guard, a man he'd only met in passing, called out to him. "Your Highness! I caught these thieves attempting to break into the palazzo! They demanded to speak to you, but they're lowly criminals!"

The first figure turned to him and lowered their hood. It was a young woman, with kind eyes and skin as black as night. Certainly not the look he'd imagined for a thief but a con artist… possibly. The woman gestured to the second hooded figure and pointed to Daniel.

The guard continued to ramble on. "They said they needed help, that you were their last hope, that if you didn't help them they'd certainly die…"

Daniel couldn't hear the guard anymore. Time

seemed to slow to a stop as the second hooded figure turned to face him. He knew it was her before she lowered her hood. He'd sensed her, somehow, known her presence.

Luciana's lip quivered. Her eyes had bags under them, her eyes red and puffy. Tear stains ran down her cheeks, leaving streaks in the thin layer of grime that covered her face. Her curly hair was tangled and wild, and she no longer wore a crown.

Luciana took a shaky deep breath. "Hello, Daniel."

He couldn't believe it. Luciana was here. She was real, and she had come to him. He could have jumped for joy if it hadn't been for her ragged state. Daniel was taken aback by how vulnerable she looked. If Luciana was here without royal guard, without regal gowns, without fanfare, she wasn't here as Reina. She was here as a fugitive.

IT HAD BEEN a rough few days for Luciana. No, scratch that. A rough summer. But the seven-day trip to Osmain certainly hadn't made things any easier.

The roads had started out rough as Luciana and Alora navigated the harsh terrain. For the first few nights they couldn't risk staying at an inn. Many of the villages they traveled through were known to be rebel territories, so they hid in the woods, sleeping under the pine trees and the night sky.

Alora slept, anyway. Luciana was much more hesitant knowing that the new Rey would be after her. As much as she'd longed for rest, she couldn't, and her body had begun to ache from the stress. By the time they reached the Osmainian border she'd nearly passed out from exhaustion, and even then she'd slept only lightly.

Daniel must have seen the fatigue on her face, as he looked at her with an air of concern and maybe even pity. Usually, she'd resent someone looking down on her like that, but today she didn't care. She had always thought that she would fight for Askaña until the end. But when the time had come to spill her blood for her people, she'd faltered. Dying had felt like a useless sacrifice, and as awful as it was, the only way to protect her family's line was to run away.

"I'm so sorry, Daniel," she said softly. "I'm sorry for everything I said to you. I know I don't deserve your forgiveness or even your charity, but I need your help."

Finally, as if shaking himself out of a daze, Daniel ran to her and wrapped her in a tight embrace. Tears pricked at Luciana's eyes, but she blinked them away. She had made it. Daniel was with her now, and he would protect her. She melted into his arms, the heat from his body warming her heart.

Daniel said nothing. He must have known what had

happened based on the sight of her alone, even if news of the coup hadn't yet spread to Osmain. She was grateful for his silence. Luciana didn't think she could bear recounting everything she'd experienced just yet.

Her knees buckled beneath her, fatigue finally catching up to her. She'd spent her last bit of energy begging the guard to let them inside. Now she didn't even feel like she could stand.

Daniel put his arm around her and helped her walk inside. As they passed staring servants, he would call out orders. "Bartolo, prepare hot soup and bring it to the guest room at the base of the south tower! Gabriella, run ahead and prepare the room and a bath. Mia, see to it that our guests have something sensible to wear."

The servants each bowed and scurried off to fulfill Daniel's requests.

Luciana then remembered Alora, who was following closely behind. "Two rooms," said Luciana.

"Of course," Daniel said. "As soon as you're settled, I'll take care of your friend."

At their slow pace, it took them much longer than it should have to reach the south tower. Gabriella was waiting at the door when they arrived, and Daniel helped Luciana shift her weight onto her new maid.

"Take care of her, Gabriella," he said. "Let me know when she's ready for visitors."

Luciana looked back and Daniel was still there watching her, concern in his honey-brown eyes.

"Thank you," she whispered, as she was led away. Daniel, if he heard, he didn't respond. He just watched her until she was out of sight.

THE DOOR to the bedroom closed. While Daniel knew it was for the best, it was difficult to watch anything, however small, come between himself and Luciana again. He wanted to be with her while she recovered from what must have been a hard journey. To feed her soup and fluff her pillows and—his cheeks got hot at the thought—help her wash off all the dirt from the road.

His heart ached to be with her, but he was the last thing she needed. For now, he needed to inform his father they had new guests. Then he heard a voice behind him that snapped him out of his thoughts. "You should let me take care of her, Your Highness."

Daniel turned to face Luciana's companion. She had been so quiet that he'd almost forgotten she was there. He smiled at her. "Thank you very much for your help, but we can take it from here. You should rest."

"But—"

"I insist, Miss. I will show you to your room."

"My room?"

"Yes."

"That is very generous of you but hardly necessary. The servants' quarters will suffice."

Daniel stopped in his tracks, and the young woman stopped in turn. "What is your name?" he asked.

"I—uh, Alora, Your Highness." She curtsied respectfully.

"Alora, do you feel well?"

"I am a bit weary, but I am well enough."

"Well enough to tell the Imperatore what happened in Askaña?"

Alora seemed shocked and almost shrank in on herself, but she nodded.

"Good," Daniel said. "We will inform my father of what has happened, and then I will show you to your room."

"But—"

"If you wish to remain in service to her Highness Luciana, you may. But seeing as you helped keep her alive, I think you deserve a better place to sleep than a cot by the kitchen."

Alora bowed her head. "Thank you, Your Highness."

Daniel led Alora to the throne room, where Antonio would certainly be at this time of day and barged in without waiting to be announced. Antonio was there and looked up in shock, almost dropping the block of cheese he was holding. If Daniel had been anyone else, he would have been embarrassed for interrupting the Imperatore during his lunch. But he wasn't anyone else.

"Father, something has happened."

Unbothered, Antonio waved Daniel off. "Not now."

"This is important!"

Antonio sighed and laid the cheese back on the tray in front of him. "What is it, son?" Antonio leaned back on his golden throne, visibly tired.

"It's Askaña."

"What about it?"

"It's been destroyed."

Antonio sat up. "What?"

"Well, it might as well have been, anyway," Daniel clarified.

"Was it the Randerans? I knew they were no good—"

"No, Father. Listen. I've brought a survivor here to tell you her account." Daniel gestured to Alora, who stepped out from behind him. "This is Alora, a servant to Reina Luciana. She knows much more than I do." Daniel then turned to Alora and whispered gently in Askanese, "Tell him everything. And don't be afraid. I'm here."

Alora cautiously stepped forward, curtsying before the Imperatore. The room filled with silence as Alora waited for permission to speak. Daniel gave her a nudge. "You may speak," he said. He'd almost forgotten that servants in Askaña were much more formally trained than in Osmain.

Alora cleared her throat. "Your Majesty, I-I'm humbled to be in your presence."

"Wasting valuable time," Antonio bellowed, switching from speaking Osmainian to Askanese. "Tell me why you're here."

"Uh, yes. Well, it's Askaña, Your Majesty."

"So I've gathered."

"It hasn't been destroyed exactly but overthrown."

"By whom?" Antonio prompted.

"Askaña has been in political turmoil for some time, you see. The poor felt unseen and unheard, and Rey Nicolas met their peaceful protests with violence. The rebellion eventually caught up to us, and... well... they're all dead."

"All?"

"All who attended the coronation. The noble families, the loyal servants, the royal family. All except myself and Reina Luciana."

Antonio huffed, concerned. "Delightful. And I presume your Reina is in my home as well?"

"Yes, Your Majesty."

"And what do you hope to gain by staying here?"

"We didn't know where else to go, Your Majesty. We mean you no harm. We were only searching for somewhere safe to stay where their hunters can't reach us. I believe Reina Luciana would like to discuss with you the possibility of assistance in taking back her throne, but I cannot speak for her."

Antonio sat in silence for a moment, stroking his dark beard as he considered the news. Finally, Antonio waved his hand at Alora. "You may go."

Alora nodded quickly and practically ran from the room, closing the heavy marble door behind her. As soon as the door latched shut, Antonio stood.

"Bringing fugitives into our palazzo? Are you suicidal?" Antonio hissed, his words echoing in the otherwise empty chamber. Daniel recoiled, taken aback. His father hadn't been this upset with him in years, not even when Daniel had resisted the arranged marriage.

Daniel couldn't think of anything to say, but it didn't matter. Antonio kept going. "These girls could ruin us! The last thing we need right now is to make an enemy of the Askanese, and an alliance with the new Rey could be important."

"We could help her take back her crown," Daniel protested. "We have plenty of troops."

"That isn't an option, Daniel. I'm not sacrificing our men for a shaky alliance with the Reina of a kingdom that's falling apart. I don't even want them to stay here. The servant girl likely won't be tracked here but Reina Luciana? Do you know how many people probably want her dead? Her presence here is a risk that I'm not willing to take."

Daniel knew the risks. It wouldn't be easy keeping her safe, considering the assassins and bounty hunters certainly on her trail. But Osmain was a well-off country and their military was a force to be reckoned with. The turnover of the Askanese government meant they weren't likely to attack soon, anyway. They'd be too busy fixing their own kingdom for a while, but it would only be a matter of time until the Askanese became strong enough to attack. If they found out that Osmain was sheltering Luciana, it would make Osmain their enemy going forward. Antonio was right. It was a terrible idea to keep Luciana in the palazzo.

But he had to do it. For many agonizing days he'd spent every waking moment thinking of her. Now that he'd been given a second chance, he wasn't ever going to let her go again. Especially not now, when her life depended on him.

Daniel approached his father's throne slowly and knelt before Antonio. "I am begging you, as your subject, please let them stay. We are their only hope of survival."

"They would be just as safe in some remote village without endangering us," Antonio protested.

"That's not true. They need our resources. Please."

"The Askanese could wage war on Osmain. What will you do with that blood on your hands?"

"I won't allow it to come to that."

Antonio huffed. "You can hardly promise that."

Daniel stood, looking his father directly in the eye. "Not so long ago you wanted this woman to bear your grandchildren. Now you don't care if she dies?"

Antonio shook his head. "Things have changed since then, Daniel."

Daniel saw red. "You might see her as just a political pawn, a means of gaining alliances, but she's a person. If you don't let her stay here, then I will be leaving with her."

Antonio stared at Daniel, and Daniel stared right back, challenging his father, seeing who would blink first, who would break. Perhaps he'd gone too far, but Daniel didn't regret his threat. Sometimes that was the only way to reason with someone as stubborn as Antonio.

Antonio blinked and looked away. "What about Mademoiselle Bellerose?"

Daniel shrugged. "What about her?" He hadn't thought about her since Luciana arrived. Hopefully she'd been seen safely to the stables.

"What will you tell her?"

"The truth. That Askaña was overthrown." With that, Daniel turned to leave. He sighed. He'd bought himself some time.

As he reached the door, Antonio said stiffly, "You're

swimming in deep waters, Daniel. You'd better figure this out soon... before you make enemies of both Askaña and Esmar."

Daniel paused but didn't bother to turn around as he left the throne room. He knew what his father meant. To win his happy ending with Luciana, he'd have to woo her, get the Askanese off her trail, and reject Mademoiselle Bellerose without causing trouble with Esmar. All by the end of the year.

17

Day 71 of Summer

Luciana woke to the soft sound of knocking on her door. She groaned and tried to roll out of the bed, but her muscles, still sore from the long and desperate journey, didn't move fast enough for her to get up before the door creaked open. Daniel peeked inside.

"Good morning," he whispered.

Luciana tried to respond, but all she managed to get out was a whiny grunt.

"I hope I didn't wake you," Daniel continued. This time Luciana didn't even try to reply. "I just thought I'd check in. Gabriella told me last night you were exhausted, so I figured I'd wait to see you until today."

Luciana yawned and instinctively pulled the thick purple blanket up to her chin. "What time is it?"

"Early afternoon."

Afternoon? She really had been tired. Luciana was used to making the most of the light in Askaña, happily waking up with the sunrise.

Luciana must have made a nasty face because Daniel quickly said, "Hey, don't worry. You needed to recover."

Luciana fell back onto her pillows. This was humiliating. She was still in the night clothes Gabriella had provided! Heat rose into Luciana's cheeks, and she pulled a pillow over her face to hide her blush. No man had ever seen her like this before, so weak and vulnerable. She didn't have her jewels or glittering ball gowns to hide behind now, and for the first time, she could be seen like a peacock without feathers.

"I just wanted to check in," Daniel repeated himself. "Make sure you're settling in alright."

"Fine, thanks," said Luciana, her voice muffled through the fluff of her pillow.

"May I come in?" Daniel asked cautiously.

Luciana wanted to tell him to get lost, but instead she chucked her pillow off the bed and said, "Might I dress properly first?"

Daniel blushed even deeper than Luciana. His tanned cheeks turned crimson as he nodded. "Oh. Yes, of course. Sorry. I will call for Gabriella to come assist you. I'll return once you're ready."

Without saying anything else, Daniel backed away and closed the door. Luciana pulled herself out of bed and stumbled over to the vanity. She still hardly recognized the girl in the mirror. All the scrubbing, hair brushing, and rest hadn't made her look any less bedraggled. Her frizzy hair shot out in a million directions, and the bags under her eyes hadn't faded.

Luciana slouched onto the plush vanity stool and glanced around her chamber. Osmain was different than she had anticipated. Her bed here was much plusher than a bed in Askaña would be. There were curtains over the window blocking some of the sunlight, which would have never been allowed in Askaña. Instead of the miscellaneous golden trinkets that had lined her shelves at home, a collection of seashells sat in its place.

Luciana sighed. She'd hardly had time to mourn everything she'd lost, let alone learn a new culture. She was safe and all things considered, she was living quite well. But she couldn't stop the stab of pain in her heart as she remembered the life she'd left behind.

Her mother. Camila. The throne. The only home she'd ever known.

She knew she should cry, let out her feelings or whatever people usually suggested, but all she could feel was a dull throbbing in her chest and a never-ending numbness.

Luciana gingerly lifted the hairbrush that was sitting before her. Gabriella would be in soon to dress her for the day, but seeing as she was no longer royalty, she felt like an imposter having someone else care for her. Besides, if anyone was going to care for her, she would prefer it to be Alora.

Gabriella was a fine lady-in-waiting, but she lacked the history and friendship that Alora had provided for all those years. On top of that, there was the language barrier. Luciana knew Osmainian, but she only knew the royal dialect. Gabriella's accent was thick and improper, and Luciana struggled to keep up with her.

So, Luciana brushed her own hair, gently caressing her curls until they settled into something a little more normal. When Gabriella finally arrived, she helped Luciana into a much simpler dress than those she was used to. There was no train, no hoops, nothing. It was clearly well-made and probably the height of fashion in Osmain, but Luciana felt strange wearing it.

Gabriella dressed Luciana in silence. While it made getting ready feel much longer, Luciana was grateful for the quiet. She preferred that to stumbling over a language she didn't know nearly well enough.

When Gabriella finished dressing Luciana, she mumbled a goodbye and left swiftly. Luciana gave herself a once-over in the mirror. Her head felt bare without a crown—or even a tiara—on it, but she supposed she'd have to get used to the sensation.

Luciana paced the room a few more minutes, but she soon discovered that being alone allowed space for her grief to creep in. The weight of her regrets began to drag her down, and she decided she couldn't wait for Daniel any longer. She threw open the door to her chamber only to find Daniel on the other side, hand poised as though he'd been interrupted about to knock.

"Oh!" Luciana said, taken aback.

"You're ready," Daniel said, more of a comment than a question.

"Yes," Luciana replied. Daniel held out his arm to her and she slowly took it, surprised at how sturdy his muscles were under her hand.

"Have you been settling in alright?" Daniel asked.

"Very well, thank you," Luciana said. She couldn't tell if she was just grieving her losses or if she simply hadn't gotten used to Osmain yet, but she knew as soon as she said it that it wasn't true. But she couldn't tell Daniel that, not after he'd been so gracious to her.

"I thought I might show you the palazzo today," said Daniel. "Since you'll be here for the foreseeable future, you might as well learn your way around."

The foreseeable future. He was right, of course. She didn't have any money, any station, anything. She'd have to stay here until she was able to figure something out. Until things in Askaña blew over. Not that she had any idea what she'd do after she left the palazzo. Up until now she'd only been concerned with escape.

"Thank you for your generosity," Luciana said earnestly. "You've been more than helpful already."

Daniel stopped walking and looked deep into Luciana's eyes. She fought to keep herself from shivering under his gaze. "No need to thank me," he said. "I'm just glad you're safe. And I intend to keep you that way."

"Thank you," Luciana said instinctively, then bit her lip. "Actually, I do have one more favor to ask."

"Anything," Daniel said, tucking a loose strand of hair behind her ear. Luciana melted under his gentle gesture.

"Do you know where Condesa Esmeralda is staying?" Luciana finally asked.

Daniel's eyes widened. "She escaped Askaña?"

"She… well… she left a while ago. I believe she came here," Luciana said, shifting her eyes to the floor so as to not give away the truth. That she was ashamed of what she'd done.

"I see," Daniel said hesitantly. "If she's in Osmain, I'd imagine she'd be with her family."

Luciana nodded. That made sense. Esmeralda had

been proud of her well-connected family. "Do they live far from here?"

"She only mentioned one family member to me, Capitano Quirino. There could be more, I suppose, but if she's staying with him that should only be a few hours' carriage ride."

"Do you think," Luciana said, looking into his eyes pleadingly, "that you might show me the palazzo another day? I will be here for the foreseeable future, after all. I need to find Condesa Esmeralda and tell her what's happened. I must warn her not to go home."

"That's right. She'd be in danger as well," Daniel said, then cracked a devilishly handsome smile. "I suppose that would be a bit more important than walking around the palazzo, wouldn't it? Come with me. We'll arrange for a carriage."

As Daniel led her through the palazzo, Luciana tried her best to remember each twist and turn of the passages that led to the stables. But each archway they passed under looked eerily similar, and it didn't take long for her to lose her way.

Once they reached the stables, the carriage was made ready quickly. Daniel's servants were incredibly efficient, and before she knew it, Luciana and Daniel were driving through the narrow streets of Osmain.

Through the window Luciana could see open markets bustling with activity. They passed squares with live musicians playing their instruments in front of restaurants, some passersby even stopping to listen or dance along. She'd never seen such a lively town. But then again, she'd never left the grounds of the castillo back in Askaña. Was this how the people of Askaña lived? Or were their conditions much, much worse?

As they left the dense village, Luciana realized that the streets were narrow for a reason. On either side of the carriage was water. Small boats navigated the canals, carrying passengers or cargo as they slowly floated along. When the roads got especially narrow, Luciana noticed that there would sometimes be people standing at the edge of the path, waving up at the royal carriage. There seemed to be no one else on the road and Luciana figured they must be driving on the walking path.

As they found themselves traveling farther inland, the canals that had once surrounded the carriage began to vanish. The only view for miles and miles was gently rolling fields lined with neatly planted crops.

"You have a beautiful country," said Luciana.

Daniel smiled proudly from his seat across the carriage. "Osmain is known for its beauty. I'll have to take you to the beach soon."

"It must be nice," Luciana said wistfully, "to know your country so well."

"You didn't know Askaña?"

Luciana considered her words carefully. "I knew

everything on paper," she finally said. "But I never actually experienced it firsthand."

Daniel leaned forward in his seat with a mischievous look in his eye. She could feel the intoxicating heat of his body as he got closer to her. The carriage was small, and he was so close to her that she could feel his breath on her cheek. Luciana looked into his eyes but quickly averted her gaze as heat rose to her cheeks.

After what felt like an eternity of silent longing, Daniel finally said, "Lucky for you, you've got the best tour guide Osmain has to offer."

Then he leaned back in his seat.

With the moment broken, Luciana let out a disappointed breath. She hadn't realized exactly how much she wanted him until now. It was too late to turn back time though, as Daniel began to tell her about the history of Osmain, and Luciana listened intently for the rest of the carriage ride. There was something about the way Daniel spoke that was enchanting. He was calming, and for those few hours Luciana let herself forget about the mess that her life had become. He had a way with words. His journal was more polished, but it was obvious that he had a writer's mind.

"The farm to your right is one of the oldest in Osmain, first established in the year 409. The Ajello family has been cultivating grain there ever since," Daniel said as they passed rolling green pastures.

A while later, Daniel pointed out a small stone temple. "That building to the left was originally built as a shrine to Imperatore Marco Alessandro Giovanni Cattanio. A long name, I'm aware. He was the last of the Cattanio line, at least as far as our historians can tell. He was slain in battle against the Randerans in the year 296 before he'd been able to father a child. His younger sister took the throne and became the third Imperatrice of Osmain. She had already been married and changed her name before taking the throne, so the Cattanio dynasty became the DiAngelos."

Daniel continued to tell her stories as they drove, until they reached an isolated estate in what seemed like the middle of nowhere. Luciana stepped out of the carriage and gazed up at the beautiful home, and the butterflies in her stomach came racing back. The searing pain of regret filled her. Esmeralda had lost so much already and now she was going to learn she'd lost even more. That was assuming Esmeralda didn't have her removed from the premises on sight.

Daniel offered Luciana his arm again, and she gladly took it. She knew she should face Esmeralda alone to break the news, but every second until then she'd need Daniel's support. He gave her an encouraging smile as they reached the door.

They were whisked inside by a servant and led to the main drawing room. A few minutes later, a dashing man who had to be a few years older than Daniel appeared in the doorway. He was tall, with tanned skin and dark hair, and looked eerily similar to Esmeralda. He wore the expensive clothing of a man who was well-off, but he proudly displayed the Osmainian royal crest at his lapel, distinguishing him as a member of their military.

Daniel stood excitedly. "Quirino!" he exclaimed, wrapping his fellow soldier in a hug.

"Daniel! What a surprise! How are you, my friend?" Quirino asked, smiling broadly.

"I am well. You?"

"Well enough," Quirino laughed. It was an infectious sound, and Luciana saw why Daniel liked him. "What brings you to my humble abode today?"

Daniel dropped his voice very seriously. "Is your cousin here?"

"You mean Esmeralda?" asked Quirino.

"Yes," Daniel nodded.

"She is. I didn't know you knew her, but that makes sense. You were up in Askaña for a while, right?"

"Not long," Daniel clarified, "but long enough to make her acquaintance."

"She should be down in just a moment," Quirino said happily. Then he turned to Luciana, who had been sitting quietly, not wanting to interrupt their happy reunion. "Who is this?"

"She, uh…" Daniel trailed off for a moment, remembering the grim reason for his visit. "She is the one who actually needs to speak with your cousin."

"I see," said Quirino jovially, taking a seat. "Nice to meet you."

"You as well," said Luciana. She was grateful that Daniel hadn't actually introduced her. Of course, *he* didn't know why Esmeralda would have cause to hate Luciana, but Quirino surely would. The last thing she needed was to be tossed onto the street before she could even see the Condesa.

"How do you know my cousin?" Quirino asked.

"She and I are old acquaintances. We knew each other through Princesa Camila," Luciana said, trying not to get choked up as she said her sister's name.

"Any friend of Esmeralda's is a friend of mine." Quirino smiled. "And how do you and Daniel know each other?"

Luciana was surprised that Quirino dropped Daniel's title so flippantly, but she supposed the brotherly bond they shared was deep enough to not bother with such formalities. At the same time, she wasn't sure how to answer that question without giving herself away. Luckily, she wouldn't have to, as Esmeralda appeared in the doorway. She let out a shriek of surprise upon seeing Luciana, then quickly scowled. Esmeralda's eyes darted back to the hallway, debating whether or not to run, but she looked at Quirino instead.

"What is she doing here?" Esmeralda sneered, her voice dripping with disdain.

"She needed to speak with you," Quirino said simply.

This time Esmeralda looked directly at Luciana and sneered, "I have nothing to say to you, Your Majesty."

Quirino looked back at Luciana questioningly. "Your Majesty?"

"Quirino," Daniel interjected, "this is Reina Luciana of Askaña."

Quirino's face turned from confused to angry. His jaw clenched and he stood, fists at his sides. "I think you should both leave," he hissed.

"What?" Daniel asked.

"That woman is not welcome here," Quirino said.

Daniel stood as well. "Why is that?" he demanded.

Luciana fought to keep herself calm despite their confrontation. She'd expected some hard feelings, of course, and she'd even imagined them telling her to leave. But that didn't mean she was any less rattled now that the actual argument had started.

"She ruined my cousin's life!" Quirino exclaimed.

"What?" Daniel asked.

Luciana's breathing came faster now, as she continued to fight a losing battle with her nerves. Her thoughts raced out of control. Quirino was about to tell Daniel everything. Daniel would kick her out of the palazzo. She and Alora would be on their own. The

Askanese would find them. Their bodies would be dumped in a sparkling Osmainian canal, but their heads would be brought back to the new Rey as proof of their demise.

"She didn't tell you, did she?" Quirino said, almost pityingly.

"Typical," Esmeralda muttered, loud enough for everyone to hear.

"Didn't tell me what?" Daniel asked.

"I expected better from you, Your Highness," Quirino said, shaking his head. "You don't even know the company you keep."

Quirino turned to Esmeralda, whose face was still pale with surprise in stark contrast to Quirino, who was red with rage. "Should I tell him what she did or would you like to? Considering it's your secret."

"I would really rather prefer not to tell anyone at all," Esmeralda said. "Especially not someone apparently close to *her*."

Luciana was invisible in the room, and she couldn't decide if that was good or not. Still, if she didn't defend herself, no one else would. "Please, if I may—"

"No, you may not." Quirino interrupted. "I think you've done quite enough already."

"I've come with important news, if you'd just—"

"You think we'd believe anything you say?" Esmeralda scoffed.

And suddenly everyone was talking over one another. Luciana could barely make out who was speaking. The pressure in her chest built and built as their volume increased, making Luciana's head spin until she thought she might explode at any moment.

"How dare you speak to her like that!"

"You are on my property, and I can speak to her however I'd like."

"Please listen!"

"And to think I trusted you!"

"Luciana is my guest, and you'd do well to remember that."

"She is no guest on my land."

"Camila is dead!" Luciana screamed. She stood suddenly, and the room quieted, everyone staring at her. She couldn't take it anymore. If Esmeralda was going to kick her out, she could at least deliver her message first.

"What?" Esmeralda said quietly.

"Esmeralda, I know you hate me. And you should. But I need to talk to you. Alone," Luciana said firmly.

Daniel moved to leave and Quirino followed. But before leaving entirely, he said, "We'll be right outside, Esmeralda. If she makes you feel uncomfortable, you can leave. I don't care if she is royalty." Then he slammed the door behind him.

Silence.

"Esmeralda, I know this might be a bit of a shock—"

"You're lying!" Esmeralda yelled. "Tell me you're lying!"

Luciana couldn't even form words. What could she say?

"I wish I was," she whispered. "I wish I had more to prove to you that what I say is true, but you have to understand—"

"This is just another trick!"

"Look at me, Esmeralda! I have no crown on my head, and I'm wearing an Osmainian gown. Why do you think that is?"

"Because you…" Luciana could tell Esmeralda was wearing down. "Because you're trying to convince me."

"Really?" Luciana mused. "That seems like a lot of effort."

Esmeralda's lip quivered, but she didn't say anything.

"Let me explain everything. Then you will understand. If after all of this you still think I'm lying, then I can't help you. But believe me, I'm here to make amends and to warn you not to return to Askaña," Luciana said.

"What happened?" Esmeralda asked, her voice shaking.

"The rebels attacked the castillo. She was killed," Luciana explained. With every word, Esmeralda shook more with sobs. "They overthrew the country, Esmeralda. They killed them all. The servants, the nobles, everyone there. The only survivors I know of were you, me, and my lady-in-waiting."

Esmeralda stumbled back as if she'd been struck. She held her hand to her heart, tears flooding her eyes. Esmeralda shook her head in disbelief, harsh breaths turning into cries which turned into sobs. She fell to the floor, unable to keep herself standing.

"No. No, this can't be true!" Esmeralda cried. Luciana found herself with a lump in her throat.

"I'm so sorry," Luciana said, descending to sit on the floor with Esmeralda.

Esmeralda let out a raw, guttural cry that shook Luciana to her core, a sound closer to a scream. Her cry spoke of more suffering than Luciana had ever seen in another human being.

"How did it happen?" Esmeralda wailed.

"I wasn't in the room at first," Luciana tried to explain, but when she did, all she could see was the blood on the ballroom floor. She tried to maintain her cool exterior, but it was starting to fail as tears welled in her eyes.

"Did you see it?" Esmeralda asked, holding tightly onto Luciana's arm.

Luciana paused. It hurt to say out loud. "Yes," she said. Even after everything that had happened over the course of the summer, she'd managed to keep her emotions in check, yet here she was, about to lose control.

"What happened?" Esmeralda said. She looked into Luciana's eyes, and a shiver ran down her spine.

"It was a sword," Luciana tried to say, but the more she spoke, the more tears escaped. It was almost just as painful to keep the tears in to let them out, and Luciana didn't think she could keep everything inside forever.

"He brought it down on her... in the ballroom... and..." Luciana lost her words. She couldn't continue. Esmeralda looked like she'd heard enough, anyway. She fell on her hands and knees, weeping so violently that Luciana would have stopped to help if she'd been able to.

But Luciana was also lost. She didn't know how long she cried with Esmeralda. She'd been fighting down her feelings for so long just to survive. She was long overdue to let herself feel something.

When they both had calmed enough, Luciana said, "I'm sorry."

Esmeralda didn't reply, so Luciana continued. "I want you to know that I never revealed your relationship to anyone. I am many things. Many bad things. But I am not a liar. I told Camila I wouldn't tell anyone, and I didn't."

Esmeralda shook her head. "I don't believe you."

"I thought you might say that." Luciana sighed and

reached into her corset where she'd kept the letter from Nicolas's daughter. She'd grabbed it from the music room before she left Askaña, and now she was glad she had.

Luciana handed the letter to Esmeralda, who wiped tears out of her eyes to read the letter. Her eyes widened as she scanned the page. "Is this…?"

"It is."

"But how?"

"I don't know, but Nicolas had it hidden pretty well. I found it and saw it as my way to the crown. I shouldn't have acted on it, but this is what I used to blackmail him into making me Reina." Luciana hung her head in shame. It felt so dirty to admit out loud.

Esmeralda shook her head. "Thank you," she said and reached forward to give Luciana a hug.

"Esmeralda?" Luciana said, taken aback.

"Camila never wanted to be Reina, Luciana."

"Are you sure? She seemed so angry. We had a fight about it right before—" Luciana cut herself off. She didn't want to start crying again.

"Believe me, I know"—Esmeralda took a deep breath —"*knew* your sister. Camila was mostly upset that you did it all behind her back. She still loved you."

Luciana hadn't known how much she needed to hear that. The unbearable weight of guilt for her fight with Camila lifted off of her shoulders.

Esmeralda continued, "We could have worked better as a team, but I'm just so relieved that you never betrayed us."

"I don't break promises."

Esmeralda smiled. "I know."

"We'll both have to be careful going forward," Luciana said. "The new government will be after us."

"What do we do then?" Esmeralda asked.

Luciana sighed. "I've considered every angle. We aren't likely to find another kingdom willing to wage war on Askaña to help me get back on the throne. All of our resources back home are gone. The nobles are all dead, and I assume the loyal militia members are, too."

She faltered, almost unable to continue. It felt physically painful to admit, but her dream of becoming Reina was dead. She said, "You'll have to abandon your title. So will I."

"But my people..." Esmeralda shook her head.

"I'm sure they'll be alright. They already appointed their new Rey. They probably have plans for every rank of nobility."

Esmeralda sighed. "I hate to admit it, but I think you're right. Our days in Askaña are over."

Luciana shook her head sadly. "I always said I was willing to die for my kingdom, yet here I am, giving up on my people. I feel like a traitor."

"That's not true," Esmeralda said. "Your people gave

up on you, not the other way around. You need to stay alive. You owe it to yourself and you owe it to Camila."

Luciana nodded, Esmeralda's encouraging words comforting her.

"I'm sorry about your title, Esmeralda," Luciana said.

Esmeralda shrugged. "I'm related to a wealthy family here. I'll be just fine."

Luciana hadn't thought about it that way. Esmeralda was nobility in two different countries. When she was ready, she'd probably be able to easily find herself a wife with a title, and her life would go on.

"What about you?" Esmeralda asked.

"Right now, I'm staying at the palazzo, but I'll have to start lying low. Maybe I'll become a governess or something," said Luciana.

"That's why you had the Principe with you?"

"Yes, he's been very generous."

"Hmm," Esmeralda mused.

"What?"

"He knows the danger you're putting him in, I assume?"

Luciana shrugged. "I suppose."

"Hmm."

"What?"

"When is the wedding?"

Luciana almost laughed, but the only thing she could think to say was "What?"

"The arranged marriage," Esmeralda prompted.

"We're not engaged."

Esmeralda looked genuinely surprised, then shrugged. "You should be."

"Pardon?"

"He's risking war with the new Askanese regime for you? This man is either crazy or crazy in love," Esmeralda explained.

"It's not like that," Luciana tried to say, but she found it was pointless. A part of her wished he would be in love with her because, truth be told, a little part of her was in love with him.

Esmeralda seemed to see straight through Luciana anyway because she just let out a small, amused noise again. Unsure how to respond, Luciana just shrugged.

Esmeralda sighed and stood, extending a hand to Luciana. "Let's go check on the gentlemen. Make sure they aren't tearing each other apart."

DANIEL HADN'T REALIZED the visit to Quirino and Esmeralda might not go smoothly. Of course, how could he have known? It seemed no one told him anything. After Luciana had finally managed to get Esmeralda alone, Daniel and Quirino stood outside the door, unsure how long the conversation would take. Quirino, who was usually very talkative, stood in silence, which was unsettling. Conversation had always come easy to them.

After a few minutes, Daniel cleared his throat. Quirino didn't even bat an eye in Daniel's direction.

"Quirino, are you alright?" Daniel asked.

"Fine," Quirino snapped.

"It's just that you're acting strangely…"

"I'm sorry, Your Highness," Quirino said in a mocking tone, "I'm trying to make sure my cousin doesn't get hurt any further by your little friend."

"What happened?" Daniel asked. He knew Luciana was ambitious and she would certainly use people's weaknesses to push herself further, but what had she done to Esmeralda?

Quirino huffed. "None of your business."

"Not my business?" Daniel said. "Given the circumstances, I'd say this is my business. I'm keeping Luciana in my home now that hers has been destroyed."

"What?" Quirino asked, turning to face Daniel for the first time since they'd entered the hall.

"Askaña was overthrown by rebels."

Quirino thought for a moment, then shrugged. "Serves her right."

Daniel was shocked by Quirino's flippant attitude. "Lots of innocent people died, Quirino."

"That woman is a liar, Daniel," Quirino said, looking

into Daniel's eyes with an intensity that nearly made him shudder. "She broke her word. Because of that, Esmeralda had to leave Askaña."

Daniel shook his head in disbelief. "Luciana would never break a promise."

"Then you don't know her," Quirino said simply.

This sparked something in Daniel. Quirino hadn't even known what Luciana looked like earlier. Now he claimed to know her better. Daniel grabbed Quirino's shoulder and leaned in close. "Listen to me, Quirino. You are my friend. We have been through a lot together. But believe me when I tell you this. You do not get to tell me about the company I keep. If I'm a bad judge of character, then I have every reason to doubt you as well. And I'd hate to do that. I treat you as my equal because I respect you. But if you start to spread rumors about Luciana, if you threaten her, if you disrespect her, or endanger her—"

"You need to back off, Daniel. This isn't your fight," Quirino interrupted.

"I am your Principe. Your future Imperatore. Any act against Luciana will be seen as an act against me."

He'd never seen Quirino so angry. It hurt Daniel to have to be harsh with him, but it was necessary. When Luciana's safety was already fragile, he could leave no room for miscommunication.

Quirino slumped against the wall, slowly sliding

down until he sat on the cold tile floor. Daniel sat against the opposite wall not long after. And so there they sat for what felt like forever, Daniel's mind swirling. He still hadn't found out what Luciana had done that was so egregious. Should he be fearful of her, too?

No, he thought. This was Luciana. She'd trusted him with her life. And when he thought about it, he would trust her with his life, too. Whatever had happened between Luciana and Esmeralda didn't matter. Even if it cost him his friendship with Quirino. Right now, he had bigger things to think about.

Like how he would convince the new Rey of Askaña not to kill Luciana. He had a few ideas, but they were all risky. The last thing he needed was for the Askanese to show up and start a war. As much as he wanted Luciana, he wanted to secure the safety of his people first.

There was also the matter of Mademoiselle Bellerose, who he hadn't seen since Luciana's arrival. She was sure to be onto him by now. He hadn't exactly been subtle with his interest in Luciana. She was likely to be offended, and if he officially called off their courtship things could get ugly. He'd have to be gentle with her. Besides, she'd really done nothing wrong, and he didn't want to hurt her feelings.

Quirino and Daniel couldn't hear anything through the heavy door and thick walls, so they continued to sit in silence until the door opened. Esmeralda and Luciana emerged from the drawing room arm in arm. They both had red and puffy eyes, like one would have after a long cry, but they seemed to have made peace with one another.

Daniel moved to stand, but when he caught sight of Luciana, he froze. She looked sad, it was true. But she also looked… healed, somehow. Like she'd been running through a dark forest and had finally seen the first hints of sunlight on the other side. She was beautiful, and he couldn't look away.

Quirino sprang to his feet and was at his cousin's side instantly. "Are you alright?" he asked.

Esmeralda nodded. "I will be."

Luciana smiled. "Well, I think Daniel and I had best be off."

"I agree," Quirino sneered. Daniel couldn't help but shoot a glare his way.

"You don't have to," Esmeralda said. "I'm sure we could arrange for you to stay for dinner."

"Are you crazy? After everything she did?" Quirino chastised her.

"She made mistakes, Quirino, but she never betrayed my trust," Esmeralda said firmly.

"And you believe her?"

"I do. If you saw what I've just seen in her, you'd believe it, too."

Quirino tried to decipher his cousin's gaze. Finally, he sighed. "Fine." Then he turned to Daniel. "I'm sorry."

Daniel smiled. Quirino was bold and liked to take swift action, but he was humble. It was one of the many reasons Daniel had chosen to be his friend. "It's alright. I'm sorry as well."

"You know," Quirino smiled a mischievous grin, "the annual military ball is in just seven days. I wasn't sure if you'd be in town for it, but if you're free you should stop by."

Daniel considered. He hadn't seen his old friends in some time.

"Where?" he asked.

"Sala de Ballo, just after sundown. Bring a date," Quirino said.

Daniel's heart swelled. This was the opportunity he'd been looking for. Even if it was attended by the rowdier gentlemen of his acquaintance, this would be the perfect way to introduce Luciana to Osmainian society. He nodded. "I'll be there."

Esmeralda asked them again to stay for dinner after that, but apparently tired, Luciana decided she'd rather head back to the palazzo. They said their goodbyes to Quirino and Esmeralda, and Luciana promised she'd visit again soon.

Then they were back in the carriage. They talked and laughed most of the way, but in the quiet moments when they both fell into silence, Daniel became acutely aware of Luciana. She smelled fresh, like a clear spring day, and the setting sun cast golden shadows on her face. She sparkled like a fine jewel.

Except she wasn't just a diamond. She was infinitely more valuable than that.

18

Day 72 of Summer

Luciana felt like a fool. And she was, for more reasons than one. Besides everything with Esmeralda, she'd made a terrible decision when she'd decided to become Reina rather than go back to Osmain with Daniel.

While she supposed the past was easy to look back on with scorn, she couldn't help but feel a pang in her chest when she saw Daniel. If she'd married him when he'd asked, would things have been different? Would she have been happy? Would things have changed enough in Askaña to keep Camila safe?

Daniel had been the greatest thing to come her way and she knew it. She also knew she'd ruined her opportunity.

Nevertheless, when Luciana saw Daniel at breakfast the next morning, he had an infectious smile on his face. Luciana couldn't help but grin herself as she sat in the chair next to him. This was Luciana's first official meal in Osmain. She'd been so out of sorts after arriving that she'd missed two meals in a row, and they'd missed dinner again last night due to their trip to Capitano Quirino's estate.

Something had changed since her visit with Esmeralda. Now it all somehow felt right. The palazzo. Daniel. It wasn't home, but it was lovely. And she knew that if she let herself, she could learn to love living in Osmain. She didn't want to let her kingdom or her people go, but Esmeralda was right. Luciana needed to move on before her duty destroyed her.

"Good morning," Luciana said as she scooted her heavy wooden chair closer to the table.

"Are you ready for another day of adventure?" Daniel asked.

"That depends," Luciana laughed. "What do you have planned?"

"Well, at first I thought I'd simply show you around the palazzo like I'd planned for yesterday," Daniel explained.

"But?"

"Yes, well, I thought you might like to see the beach."

Luciana couldn't help it. She smiled. He wasn't

telling her the real reason for getting her out of the palazzo, but she knew. She'd never seen anything but high walls. There was a whole realm outside of the Askanese castillo, and she was just now getting to explore it. She wanted to savor every moment she had in Osmain with Daniel.

Luciana's heart sank a bit as she thought about the fact that this living situation was temporary, and she wouldn't be able to stay too much longer. She had to leave to preserve his kingdom. Daniel had been much kinder than he needed to be given the circumstances. But Luciana couldn't help it. Her heart fluttered at the thought of his gesture.

"Is that alright?" Daniel asked. "You haven't said anything."

Luciana nodded. "That sounds wonderful, thank you."

"Excellent! We'll head out after breakfast then."

At that moment, the heavy wooden doors to the dining hall opened with a loud groan. They creaked as they opened, pushed by a servant on each side. Luciana looked up, and in the doorway stood Imperatore Antonio.

His towering frame and wide build had made him eye-catching in Askaña, but here in Osmain he was absolutely intimidating. Still, Osmain showed no signs of treating their citizens poorly. He might be authoritative, but from what Luciana had seen, she would have been willing to wager that he was a kind and just Imperatore.

Antonio walked to the table with a swagger that most men wouldn't be able to pull off. In fact, Luciana didn't think his own son could walk into a room with that much confidence. Daniel rarely mentioned his mother, but Luciana suspected he'd inherited his humble demeanor from her. It certainly couldn't be from Antonio.

As the Imperatore approached his seat at the head of the table, a servant ran ahead to pull his chair out for him. He sat with a flourish. Not a second later, another servant was placing a plate full of fresh food in front of him. Then, Antonio lifted his eyes to see Luciana sitting next to Daniel.

He scowled, and Luciana's blood ran cold.

He must not want her there. She'd almost forgotten about the arranged marriage. Somehow her true feelings for Daniel had overridden the memory of the political stunt Antonio and Nicolas had tried to pull. She could certainly understand how calling off the wedding might have been upsetting, and she didn't blame him for wanting her out of the palazzo. Luckily for him, she planned on being out of their hair in a few weeks at most. She would have to find a remote village to live in that no one would suspect and lie low for a while.

After several seconds of Antonio glaring at Luciana and Luciana trying her best not to do anything to upset him further, Antonio picked up his fork and violently stabbed a piece of sausage. The sound of metal on metal as his fork hit the plate grated on her, and Luciana tried not to wince. Instead, she looked at Daniel for support. He noticed her look and nodded reassuringly. Underneath the table, Daniel grabbed Luciana's hand, sending sparks up from where they touched and shivers down her spine. His hands were warm but not sweaty, firm but not calloused. Luciana gave his hand a squeeze back.

Suddenly, Antonio didn't feel like the biggest threat in the room. Could it be that Daniel had feelings for her after all? Luciana forced her pulse to settle. If her heart beat any faster, she was sure she'd explode. She needed to be reasonable, especially given recent circumstances. Even if he did return her feelings, how could they possibly be together now? It was silly for her to dream. What could she expect? That he'd give up the crown and run away with her to a farm in the Osmainian countryside, hiding from the new Askanese regime forever? That was unfair for her to even ask. So, Luciana sat there, the cold from her heart fighting the warmth of his hand.

After a silence that was much too long, Daniel said, "Father, you've met Luciana?"

Antonio simply grunted in affirmation. Daniel

looked at Luciana apologetically and shrugged. Luciana glanced at their plates, now empty. Would they be allowed to leave before the Imperatore finished eating? She glanced at Daniel and nodded toward the empty plates. His eyes widened with understanding, and he pushed his chair back and stood.

"Good talk, Father," Daniel said, "but Reina Luciana and I have much to do today."

Antonio stared directly at Luciana and an uncomfortable fear snaked around her body. Antonio didn't want her in his palazzo. That much was obvious. But there was something about that stare—he almost looked like he was judging her. Then he said to Daniel in Osmainian, "She is no Reina."

Luciana's face turned red, and without realizing it, she was on her feet as well. She could almost hear the faint sound of dishes clanging, but her mind was fuzzy. She was not a Reina. Her family was dead. Camila was dead. Her home was gone. Luciana's breathing came faster with each beat of her heart, and before she lost control of herself entirely, she hissed back in Osmainian, "Maybe not but at least my worth was earned. I didn't have my title handed to me on someone's death certificate."

Antonio dropped his fork, making another loud clanging noise, but Luciana couldn't hear it. Her mind, still churning with memories of her family and guilt about everything that happened, wouldn't let her rest.

"I want her out of my palazzo, Daniel," Antonio ordered, turning again to Luciana. "You don't belong in Osmain."

"Father!" Daniel exclaimed.

He wrapped his arms around Luciana, but she brushed him off. She fled from the room and didn't stop until she reached a place that she assumed to be a drawing room, where she collapsed in a heap. It didn't take long before she heard Daniel's familiar footsteps behind her. He knelt down beside her, out of breath.

"Luciana! Are you okay?"

She nodded.

"Look, I'm sorry about my father. He can be stressful to talk to sometimes," Daniel continued, taking her hand. Luciana considered pulling away, but while she was still recovering from her altercation with the Imperatore, she found she didn't have the strength. It was nice to have him there, keeping her steady.

"No. I'm sorry," Luciana said. "I didn't mean what I said."

"I know you didn't," Daniel replied gently.

"Do you think he will make me leave the palazzo?" Luciana asked. She needed more time before she left. She was still recovering from the shock of the past several days, and she hadn't made any kind of arrangements to care for herself yet. If she was forced to leave now, she would have to take shelter with Esmeralda and Quirino, which would be enjoyable to be sure, but she didn't want to draw extended amounts of attention to Quirino's estate since Esmeralda was also a fugitive. By herself she wasn't likely to be tracked down, but together they could be just as toxic for Osmain as if Luciana stayed at the palazzo. She would probably be able to only stay at Quirino's until the end of the summer.

"No," Daniel said. "He won't do that. I'll see to it myself." When Luciana didn't respond, Daniel squeezed her hand and said calmly, "I promise. You're going to be just fine."

Luciana nodded and took a deep breath. She didn't want to think about the Imperatore anymore. "Are we still going to the beach?"

Daniel smiled. "I'll go pack a bag for us. Wait right here. I'll be right back." He kissed Luciana's knuckles dramatically before he left, leaving her world spinning. Then he was gone.

Luciana sat in silence, waiting for Daniel to return. She tried to banish thoughts of her family from her mind, but it proved difficult. So, she stood and paced. After a few minutes that too grew boring, so she started to gently hum a waltz as she twirled around the room. She missed music. Perhaps Daniel had some instruments in the palazzo that she could play. She hoped he had a piano.

Luciana was so caught up in her own mind that she danced right into a stranger who had entered the room.

"Oh! I apologize," Luciana said, looking at her company. She seemed to be unhurt, maybe just a bit startled. She was tall, with skin as white as the snow that fell in Askaña's brutal winters, and hair the color of the sun's rays. Luciana recognized her as the woman who had been out riding with Daniel when she and Alora had first arrived at the palazzo.

"I don't believe we've been formally introduced. I am Luciana," she said, extending a hand to the stranger.

The woman shook Luciana's hand and replied, "I'm Mademoiselle Sibella Bellerose, soon to be Sibella DiAngelo."

Luciana's heart dropped, and suddenly everything became heavy. Daniel didn't have any siblings, and this woman was much too young for Antonio. "DiAngelo?" Luciana asked apprehensively.

"Yes! I'm going to be marrying the Principe soon. Can you believe it?" Sibella smiled angelically. Sibella was truly beautiful. Of course, Daniel would pick someone like her.

"No," Luciana said, suddenly feeling sick. "I can't." She sank down into a chair.

"Are you alright, Luciana?" Sibella asked. She almost

sounded knowing, like she knew this news would tear Luciana apart.

As if this morning couldn't get any worse. Lucina's hands started to tremble, and she quickly took control of her breathing to keep herself in check. How could Daniel not mention this? Had she truly meant so little to him that he'd gotten engaged right after coming back to Osmain? Or, even worse, had this woman been his lover waiting back home for him the whole time?

Luciana couldn't form words. She just sat there as Sibella continued. "You're the old Reina of Askaña, yes? This must all be very hard for you."

Of course, Sibella knew everything she'd been through. Word spread fast in any palazzo. Luciana could only imagine how fast gossip must spread to the woman engaged to the Principe.

"Weren't you engaged to the Principe once?" Sibella continued. Luciana nodded weakly.

Sibella paused, then sat down in a chair across from Luciana. She grabbed one of Luciana's hands and patted it in what was clearly an attempt at being reassuring. "Luciana, it's clear you still love him."

Luciana couldn't bring herself to say anything. What could she say? *Yes, Sibella, I'm in love with your fiancé. Could you kindly break off the engagement?* Besides, was she even in love with Daniel? While they had been engaged, probably not. But now—the thought of Sibella becoming Daniel's wife, of him declaring his love for her, of them raising children together—it was too much to bear.

Luciana knew in that moment, beyond a shadow a doubt, that she wished for those things with Daniel. She wanted him to be the first person she saw in the morning and the last at night. She wanted to spend her days going on adventures with him and her nights in his arms. But it wasn't meant to be. And she hated herself for it. If only she'd been less fixated on ruling Askaña, she could have had it all.

Sibella sighed. "It will be okay. It's probably for the best anyway."

"What do you mean?" Luciana asked, her voice trembling slightly.

"Do you want me to be honest with you?" Sibella asked. Luciana almost answered the rhetorical question, but she didn't think it would matter. "You are dangerous, Luciana. Every day that you're here in this palazzo is a day that the Askanese regime grows stronger. Before you know it, word will spread to the rebels that you're here. They will start a war, and they will destroy Osmain. They will kill innocent people, and they might even hurt the Principe—all to get to you. Make no mistake, they won't rest until you are dead. If you stay here any longer you will be the ruin of Osmain."

Sibella looked into Luciana's eyes with a steely

severity that left Luciana with nothing to say. Sibella's eyes were a brilliant blue, just like hers, although that seemed like the only thing the women had in common. That and an engagement to Daniel. Sibella had likely only sought Luciana out to ensure she wouldn't be a threat to her upcoming marriage.

Either way, she was right. Luciana was dangerous. As much as it pained her, she would have to leave the palazzo behind. She would have to leave that night, when Daniel was asleep, so that there wouldn't be a big scene around her departure. And, after all, she still had plans for the day.

"Sibella, may I ask a favor of you?" Luciana asked with all the grace she could muster.

"Of course, love," Sibella replied.

"Could you deliver a message to my former lady-in-waiting?"

"Of course, anything." Sibella smiled.

"Her name is Alora. Tell her she's welcome to stay in the palazzo as long as she likes, but I will be moving to Condesa Esmeralda's first thing in the morning. She will know what that means," Luciana explained.

"I'll do that immediately," Sibella said, standing.

"Thank you," said Luciana. She gave Sibella the warmest smile she could fake before the beautiful girl glided out of the drawing room. Sibella really was lovely. She and Daniel would be a magnificent couple, and Sibella would make a fine Imperatrice. But Luciana kept wishing she could have that future for herself.

~

DANIEL ENTERED the drawing room to see Luciana sitting on a different chair from where he'd left her and looking even worse for wear than she had before. She must have been grieving for her family. Curse Antonio for bringing it up.

"Are you ready to go?" he asked cautiously.

Luciana stood very suddenly, almost robotically. "Yes," she said quickly.

Daniel laughed to hide his discomfort at her strange behavior. "Okay then." He held out his arm to her and Luciana took it very lightly, almost as if she was afraid to touch him. What had come over her?

She walked in silence all the way to the stables, where Daniel had arranged for horses for them to ride to the beach. He didn't say anything, letting her set the tone for their outing, until he pointed to a majestic brown horse. "I asked for your horse to be saddled, if you'd prefer a familiar mount."

Luciana smiled as she greeted her horse and settled herself in the saddle. Daniel did the same with his horse. It seemed like a lifetime had passed since the two of them had gone riding in Askaña. Daniel wished he could rewind time and go back to that day. She had been unkind back then, but he would take that any day over the grief and constant threat of war that loomed over them now.

Once they were both mounted and ready, they left the comfort of the palazzo and headed into the capital city of Marea. Daniel knew these streets well, and he led her toward the ocean. "Follow me," Daniel said. "We're going to go to my favorite spot. It's never crowded."

He trotted ahead, and they followed the canals until they reached the open ocean. Luciana was still quiet as they made their way down the sandy beach toward the inlet that Daniel usually frequented. It was a bit farther away from the main path, and only those with horses could easily access it, which meant that almost no one was on this beach at any given time.

Daniel hoped to use the isolation to his advantage. He'd done enough sitting around. Over the past few days, he'd done nothing in his alone time but make plans to work things out with Luciana. His journal contained pages upon pages of scribbles. He'd tried to map out ways of winning her over, of persuading the Askanese to leave her alone, of letting Mademoiselle Bellerose down easily. But every time he came up with an idea, he found himself doubting himself or thinking of all of the ways it could go wrong.

Today he wouldn't try and plan anything. He would

just do what felt right, and with any luck, he'd be on his way to accomplishing at least one of the things he needed to do. Luciana's sour mood wasn't helping, however. He'd almost rescheduled the beach visit after things went wrong at breakfast, but he didn't want to make her feel worse. He'd have to make do with what he had.

When they finally reached the inlet, Daniel hopped off of his horse and tied it to a small tree. He held out a hand for Luciana and helped her off of her horse as well. "Here we are," he said brightly. "This is my favorite spot." He turned and pointed out across the horizon. "Look at that view. Endless ocean. And once the sun starts to set, it will set right there, across the water."

Luciana looked around. "Esmeralda's stories were right. Osmain's beaches truly are the most beautiful in the realm."

Daniel couldn't help beaming with pride. He'd known, of course, that no sight could compare to that of an Osmainian shoreline. Still, it meant more coming from Luciana. Daniel looked out at the waves again. The crystal-clear water lazily lapped up on the white sandy shores. It was paradise.

Then he looked at Luciana. The ocean breeze blew her halo of dark hair in a million different directions. She smiled at him, the warm sunlight giving her skin a warm glow. She looked like she belonged here. Daniel hoped more than anything else that she'd realize that and decide to stay.

"Come on, let's see if the water is warm," Daniel said, once again holding out his arm for her. Instead of taking it, Luciana smiled again and then ran full speed ahead toward the ocean. Daniel laughed as he tried to catch up with her.

"Wait!" he called, nearly stumbling over the small dunes of fine sand as he ran after Luciana. When he finally caught up to her at the water's edge, they were both out of breath and laughing. Daniel beamed at the sight of Luciana back to her usual self. The beach tended to have that effect on Daniel, too. There was something about the salty air that made him feel like everything would be okay.

Luciana dipped her feet into the sea. "The water is warm," she said.

"I was hoping it would be. The summer weather sometimes brings us warmer water."

"It's perfect," she said. He caught her eye for a brief moment and his heart fluttered. But just as quickly as she found his gaze, she turned away from it again.

"You know," Daniel said, "it is stiflingly hot out here today. I'm certain if we don't get in this water, you'll sweat through your gown."

Luciana rolled her eyes and replied, "I can't very well hop in wearing this though, can I?" She gestured at her gown, made of fine silks that would certainly be ruined by the salt ocean.

"Good thing I think of everything," Daniel said. "I brought bathing clothes for you."

"Where am I supposed to change, though? I can't do it here."

Daniel considered for a moment. He hadn't thought this through, had he? He sighed. "I'm sorry. I should have asked you to change before we left the palazzo."

"And have me parade around Marea wearing nothing but bathing clothes?" Luciana laughed.

"When you put it that way, it does sound ridiculous, doesn't it?" Daniel joined in, laughing at his own stupidity, but they both soon fell back into silence as they considered how to solve their predicament.

Luciana bit her lip nervously, and Daniel found his mind wandering away from the issue at hand and to her perfect lips. How he wished he could kiss those lips. He tried to snap himself out of his daze, but before he could even ask what her plan was, Luciana loosened the ties on her gown and pulled it straight over her head. She dropped it in the sand, leaving her in just her undergarments. Daniel couldn't breathe. How had he been so lucky to see Luciana standing before him, looking scandalous and tempting in nothing but a chemise and stays?

Luciana gestured to her stays, which were tied tightly behind her. "Do you mind?"

Daniel's voice cracked as he responded, "Ah, uh, yes. I mean, no." Heat rose in his cheeks as he gently tugged on the bow to release Luciana from her bindings. As he dropped her stays, all she had left on was a thin white chemise. Daniel tried not to stare, but he couldn't help it. He'd never seen her exposed like this before, and he wanted to touch her, to explore every inch of her body with his hands, his lips, his tongue. Instead, he stood there, unable to do anything but gaze upon Luciana in wonder.

"Your turn." Luciana grinned, turning back to him and crossing her arms over her chest.

Daniel shook his head as if the movement would wake him up from the best dream of his life. Of course, it wasn't a dream, so Daniel gingerly lifted off his shirt and vest and left them on the ground next to Luciana's dress, leaving him in just his breeches. Once they were both stripped down, they waded into the water.

"This might be the craziest thing I've ever done," Daniel laughed.

Luciana shrugged. "Not the craziest thing I've ever done, but definitely up there." She dove underneath the waves and came back up, hair slicked back. "Thank you for bringing me here today," she said wistfully. "I'll always think of you with fondness."

"What?" Daniel asked. They'd just arrived, and she was already thanking him like it was a goodbye. But this was Luciana, and she probably had a twelve-step plan in her head of how she would become the most respected undercover instrument maker in all of Osmain or something equally as ridiculous. So, when Luciana didn't respond, diving back under the waves, he didn't pay it any mind.

Daniel dove in after her. She was a strong swimmer, a natural, and she kept pace with him. When they stopped to catch their breath, Daniel wiped his soaking wet hair from his face and asked, "How did you learn to swim so well? I thought you never left the castillo."

Luciana shrugged. "There was a creek along my riding trail. I used to hop in during the summer months. You know when it wasn't frozen solid. Camila and I used to skate on it in the winter." Then she grew quiet. Daniel didn't need to ask her what was wrong. He could tell by the way she shrank into herself that she was envisioning her sister's death again.

Daniel quickly swam to her side and wrapped her in his arms. She didn't fight him or embrace him. She simply relaxed as he held her. Her breathing was normal, her pulse regular, and she seemed alright for now, just a bit shaken. Her body was warm where she pressed against him, and when Daniel pulled away he noticed how her wet chemise stuck to her body, outlining the curves of her breasts and hips. He stepped back to look at her and felt a wave of desire come over him.

He needed to kiss her. Luciana met his eyes, and Daniel couldn't think of anything else. He didn't care that they were in the ocean. He didn't care about his father, or Mademoiselle Bellerose, or anything else but Luciana. Daniel moved closer to kiss her, but before he could make it clear that he wanted to kiss her, she swam away into the deeper water.

Damn. Now he'd have to swim around after her while he was hard as a rock. Now distracted, he found he couldn't quite keep up with Luciana. She was unbelievably fast in the water—or maybe Daniel was just slow. Either way, Daniel gave up trying to chase after her and simply waded in the direction that she had swum.

Luciana got so far away that Daniel wondered if he should try to catch up just in case something went wrong, but then he spotted her coming back towards him. When she returned, she had a huge smile on her face. He gave her a moment to catch her breath before asking why.

"I found something," she said.

Daniel didn't say anything, just raised his eyebrows.

"Have you ever seen the cave up there?"

He'd visited this beach hundreds of times growing up, but he'd never seen a cave. He'd seen small rocky inlets that were even more secluded than the beach itself. The water there flowed gently through flower-covered trees, and he'd spent many childhood after-noons swimming to the inlets to play. In fact, he'd thought about showing them to Luciana, but then he'd changed his mind. Those were special places, and he'd take her there if he was ever able to win her over properly.

He shook his head.

"I think I found one," Luciana said. She nodded in the direction she'd come from as if to say, *Follow me.* Then she was gone, tearing off to where she'd seen the cave. Daniel swam after her, as fast as he could manage. She took him down the shoreline, deeper into the water. Daniel's limbs burned from swimming so quickly, but right as he was about to suggest they turn back, Luciana slowed to a stop.

"It's right down there," she said, pointing down. There was a sizable rock sticking out of the water. Big enough that there could be an air pocket underneath it.

Daniel, growing more exhausted by the minute, grabbed Luciana's hand. "Show me the way."

Luciana nodded and together they sank under the waves. Daniel had never been good at keeping his eyes open underwater. He'd been teased mercilessly for it when he was younger. Living in Osmain, the kingdom of the sea, it was almost expected that everyone could swim with their eyes open, but he'd never been able to do it. The salt stung his eyes and generally, he'd found it wasn't worth it. So, he didn't see when he'd dipped under the lip of the rock into the small cave hidden below.

He came up gasping for air, as did Luciana, and they looked around their hiding place. It was dark and cold, with the only light coming from a small hole in the rock. Daniel grabbed onto a ledge. He felt his way around the slick stone and then pulled himself up to sit. There wasn't much room to spare, especially once Luciana joined him.

"Well, here we are," said Luciana.

"I can't believe I never found this place before!" Daniel marveled.

"To be fair, I am unusually good at finding secret places," Luciana said. Daniel smiled, remembering the passageways in Askaña. If there was a hidden chamber in the palazzo, she'd certainly find it soon enough.

"You do have an unusual knack for it," Daniel laughed. Then he added more seriously, "For someone who likes to do everything by the book, you do have a morbid sense of curiosity."

Luciana pursed her lips.

"What is it?" Daniel asked.

She took a deep breath. "I wouldn't exactly say I live by the book."

"Well, you have your exceptions," Daniel said. "You stripped to your undergarments just to go swimming."

"No, I mean, I've done some questionable things," Luciana clarified.

"Again, I think today qualifies."

"You know what I mean," Luciana said, suddenly serious.

"I do," Daniel said, thinking of how she'd managed to become Reina.

"I just can't shake the feeling that I made a horrible mistake," Luciana confessed.

Daniel paused. What could her mistake have been? She gave Nicolas the humbling he deserved. She'd cleared the air with Esmeralda, so whatever had happened there was in the past. And her family being killed had nothing to do with her choices. In fact, whatever she'd done to Esmeralda to drive her out of Askaña had almost certainly saved her life.

"What do you mean?" Daniel asked.

Luciana's brows furrowed in concentration, but an explanation never came. Instead, she hung her head low and mumbled, "Nothing. Don't worry about it."

"Luciana," Daniel said, taking her hand, "you can tell me anything. You know that, right?"

Luciana gave him a smile that Daniel was sure was insincere and nodded. "I know."

Something was off again. Whatever burst of happiness had come over her when they'd arrived at the beach was long gone, and she was back to acting strangely. As if she was trying to distance herself from him, build a wall around herself. He was losing her, and he knew it. He had to do something. It was now or never.

"I will always be here for you, if you let me," Daniel said. Luciana shook her head slowly, almost as if in disbelief. Slowly, Daniel cupped her face in his hand and moved closer to her on the rock. She didn't fight him, drawing in a breath instead, as though in anticipation. Her body was warm as Daniel pulled her close. He was aware of his heart beating out of control.

Daniel's lips finally reached Luciana's and he brushed them gently. It wasn't a large movement, but it was enough to send Daniel's soul spiraling. Her lips were just as soft as he'd imagined them. It took all of Daniel's will power to kiss her slowly. He wanted her more than anything and she was right here, beneath his fingertips. Just for this brief moment, she was his.

He kissed her again, a bit more firmly this time, and she returned the gesture, pulling him closer until their bodies pressed together. Daniel's nerves fluttered away, leaving room for nothing but desire. She tasted like the salt of the water, and he couldn't help but run his hands over her curves. The wet chemise stuck to her, and he used it to explore every bit of her.

He ran his hands up her thigh, past her hips and

waist until he finally reached her breasts. She let out a small gasp as he ran his fingertips over the sensitive skin of her nipple. This only made him want her more. It was probably a good thing that this cave was as small as it was or he'd be tempted to take her here and now.

Instead, he kissed her even harder, with an intensity that he could only have dreamed of. And Luciana kissed him back just as fiercely. When she pulled away, out of breath, Daniel moved his lips down her neck. Her head tilted back as he trailed down her throat, and she let out a small moan of pleasure as his tongue teased her.

"Daniel," Luciana said, panting. "We can't…"

"What?" Daniel stopped for just a moment, and it was enough to jerk Luciana out of her daze. As he traced a finger up her cheek, she turned away.

"No!" she exclaimed, starting to scramble.

"What is it?" Daniel asked. "What's wrong?"

"We shouldn't be doing this." Luciana wouldn't look at him.

"What do you mean?" Daniel asked, reaching out to her. But it was no use. As much as he wanted her to, she wasn't going to suddenly return to his arms. "Whatever is going on, we can work this out together. Talk to me about whatever you're feeling, and we'll figure it out. Please," Daniel begged.

"How do you not see it?" Luciana said tearfully. "You honestly think we can be together?"

Daniel had no words. He suddenly felt like he might be sick.

"I don't belong here," Luciana continued.

Daniel shook his head. "That's not true. You've only been here a few days. You couldn't possibly—"

"I can't have you, Daniel!" Luciana cried out.

He wished he could find better words—something to say that could convince her that she did belong with him. That if they stuck together, he would do everything to protect her. Instead, he waited for words that never came.

"I should go," Luciana said, still looking away. The light was dim, but he could still see that her cheeks were red. Whatever was going on in her brain, she was embarrassed. Before Daniel could stop her, she threw herself off the ledge and back into the water below.

"Don't try to follow me," Luciana commanded.

"Where are you going?" Daniel asked, panic rising within him. He reached out and grabbed her arm. This wasn't right. This wasn't how this was supposed to go. And here he was, literally holding on to his last hope.

Luciana shook her head sadly. "Let go of me, Daniel." Then she jerked her arm away with such sudden force that Daniel couldn't stop her, and within seconds she'd disappeared back under the rock.

Heart racing, still reeling from their moment of intimacy, Daniel didn't have time to figure out what had just happened. But he forced himself to dive into the water after Luciana. Having not seen the way into the cave, Daniel braced himself, then opened his eyes. The pain was intense, and he couldn't see all that clearly anyway, only the outline of the rock and the light showing him the way out. By the time his head broke above the waves, Daniel was coughing and sputtering. He held onto the rock for support while he desperately tried to wipe the salty water from his eyes.

When he could finally see again, Luciana was hundreds of feet in front of him. He kicked off of the rock to give himself a boost of speed, but his limbs became more and more like lead the more he swam. Luciana reached the shore long before he did, and as a last-ditch effort he called out to her. But she either didn't hear or didn't care to turn around, running back to where they had left their clothes.

Daniel finally reached land right as Luciana finished dressing, and she ran off toward where the horses were tethered. Daniel didn't stop to gather his boots and shirt. Instead, he went as fast as his legs would carry him to where Luciana was mounting her horse. His feet slid in the sand, slowing him down, and as Luciana galloped away, Daniel's hope slipped away, too.

There was no way he could catch up to her now. Somehow he knew she wasn't going back to the palazzo. It was over. Daniel sank to his knees, his heart in agony.

His body was weak from the swim, his mind fuzzy. It took him several minutes to gather the strength to stand once again.

For the second time, Luciana had made her choice. And it had torn Daniel apart.

19

Day 78 of Summer

*A*s Daniel predicted, Luciana hadn't been at the palazzo upon his return. Alora had also packed up and gone, and apparently none of the servants knew where they'd run off to. He had a hunch that they'd gone to Quirino's, and he would have followed her there if it hadn't been for his father.

As soon as he'd stepped back on the palazzo grounds, he'd been whisked into the throne room to face him. And Antonio was angry.

"Where did you go?" he bellowed.

"The beach. I told you as much," Daniel growled.

"Son, please, I am only trying to keep you safe. With that girl around it's a terrible idea for you to leave the palazzo. Anyone could come after you," said Antonio.

"'That girl'—her name is Luciana, by the way—was chased off. I don't know exactly what prompted it, but I have a feeling it had something to do with your insult this morning," Daniel said, his voice almost cracking from the raw emotion that had come with Luciana's departure.

"Or perhaps the girl is not blind as you are to the reality of the situation. She is dangerous," said Antonio.

Daniel bit his tongue. He wanted to lash out. He wanted to scream like a toddler throwing a tantrum. He knew that would be ridiculous, but truly, this wasn't fair. He'd found the woman he wanted to marry, yet here he was, still forced to pretend like that girl was Mademoiselle Bellerose.

Perhaps that was just the way of things. After all, Antonio had loved Daniel's mother and that hadn't stopped her from dying. Luciana and Esmeralda loved Camila and she was taken from them. Love—of any kind, it seemed—was meant to be lost. He had just so happened to lose his before it had truly begun.

"I believe that she is taking refuge with Capitano Quirino and his cousin," Daniel explained. "I'm not giving up on her, Father. I'm going to find her."

"No," Antonio stood, towering over Daniel. "You will not. She is the Capitano's problem now. Not yours. Our kingdom is much safer with her there."

Daniel crossed his arms over his chest and stood as

tall as he could. "You can't stop me. I am old enough to make my own decisions."

"You are not just my son, Daniel," Antonio growled. "You are a subject of Osmain."

"I am the Principe!"

"That's right. You are key to Osmain's survival. And as such, I forbid you from leaving the palazzo grounds."

Daniel scoffed. "You cannot—"

"I can and I will," Antonio said. "As of this moment you are to remain under the constant surveillance of the royal guard."

Daniel saw red, scowling at Antonio. "I'm afraid that won't be possible," Daniel spat. "I've already told Capitano Quirino I'd attend a ball in just a few days."

"Very well. You may attend. But Mademoiselle Bellerose will be accompanying you. And you will introduce her to society as your fiancée," Antonio said, sinking back down onto his throne.

Daniel weighed his options. On one hand, this did complicate things. If he were to officially engage himself to Mademoiselle Bellerose, it would make things much harder to break off. On the other hand, if Quirino knew where Luciana was—

"Deal," Daniel said.

"I knew you'd see reason," said Antonio. "We may not see eye to eye all of the time, son, but I do want what's best for you. And I want what's best for Osmain. I can see that the girl means a lot to you. I'm not sure what happened in Askaña that kept things from working the way you wanted, but I'm truly sorry."

He seemed almost sincere. Perhaps some part of Antonio—a small, hidden part that wasn't Imperatore—wanted to be a better father. Maybe that part of him also wished things could be different.

THE GONDOLIER who would be taking them along the canals entered the palazzo. "Good evening, Your Highnesses," he said, bowing. "Are you ready to go?"

Daniel nodded. "Ready when you are."

Daniel held out his arm and Mademoiselle Bellerose took it. Her hands, while gloved, were still cold. He wasn't sure how she'd managed that with the summer heat, but by the time they reached the gondola that would take them to the ball, Daniel felt like his arm was going to freeze off.

Mademoiselle Bellerose carefully stepped inside the small boat and took a seat, and Daniel was glad when she finally let go of him. He then climbed inside after her, purposefully choosing the seat across from her rather than beside. With a small whistle, the gondolier pushed away from the palazzo dock and into the canal.

The ball was being held at the Sala de Ballo, which

was one of the few party venues not at a personal estate. Usually reserved for gatherings of the upper crust, tonight it would be taken over by servicemen from all stations. Daniel almost smiled at the thought. It would be excellent to see his friends again after so long. They were a boisterous crowd and knew how to have a good time. He just hoped Mademoiselle Bellerose wouldn't kill the mood any more than she already had. Just having her there with him was like having an anchor strapped to his leg. She was lovely, to be sure, and she seemed perfectly likable but her presence was stifling. A constant reminder that if his plan failed he would be married to a woman he didn't love.

Daniel watched his kingdom float past along the water. The sun was just setting, making the golden touches adorning some of the nicer buildings shine even brighter. A few of his subjects standing on the cobblestone streets next to the canals recognized Daniel, and they waved as he floated by.

Daniel smiled, proud that his people knew him and liked him. He'd made quite a reputation for himself while enlisted in the military. Despite being kept from combat, he had been known to speak to everyone, getting their thoughts and ideas on what could make Osmain better. Word had spread quickly that he was doing the best he could for his subjects.

He glanced quickly at Mademoiselle Bellerose.

Maybe his father was right. Luciana certainly wasn't the best Imperatrice for his people.

Mademoiselle Bellerose caught his eye before he could look away. "Osmain truly is beautiful," she said. "I look forward to getting to know it."

Daniel just smiled and nodded in response.

After a moment of silence, Mademoiselle Bellerose sighed. "I'm sorry."

Daniel looked at her, eyebrows raised. "What for?"

"Well, it's just... you and the Reina Luciana seemed to have a special bond. I can sense you're apprehensive about me and our marriage, and I can't help but feel like she's the reason."

So, she wasn't dumb. This didn't surprise Daniel. He'd always sensed she might be hiding a lot about herself. Still, he didn't reply. He had nothing to say to her that wouldn't be incriminating.

"I will do my best for you," Mademoiselle Bellerose continued, "but for us to be happy, we are going to have to work together. I don't expect you to love me, now or ever. But we are going to be partners."

Daniel avoided looking at her. "I just need time, that's all."

Mademoiselle Bellerose pursed her lips, then said, "I thought you might say that."

"Really?" Daniel mumbled before he could think to stop himself.

"Really. You have this look in your eye. Like you have a plan—or like you're trying to win a game of chess. And if I'm a pawn, that's fine. It's not like I've never played that role before. But if Luciana is the queen on your board, then I think you should reconsider."

Daniel almost rolled his eyes. "She's dangerous, right? She could destroy the kingdom?"

"That's not what I was going to say," Mademoiselle Bellerose replied defensively.

"What is it then?" Daniel asked.

Mademoiselle Bellerose paused, choosing her words carefully. "The Reina lost everything overnight. Her home, her family, her crown. It hasn't been very long since her life was changed forever. She hasn't even found her footing yet, and here you are, trying to tie her down. Maybe that's what she wants. But it very well might not be, and she might not be able to tell.

"Have you ever considered that she might need to figure out who she is before she commits to becoming Imperatrice of a kingdom she hardly knows? For her sake, she needs time to grieve and to learn about herself before anything happens."

Mademoiselle Bellerose's words stung. Daniel tried to argue, "But by the time she does, you and I will—"

"Already be married. Yes. But if you truly love her, if you truly want her to be happy, it's what has to be done."

Daniel had nothing to say. Everyone around him was

telling him to give up on Luciana. Antonio said that she was dangerous. Mademoiselle Bellerose argued she needed time to heal. And even Luciana seemed to object.

Daniel thought about the events at the beach. Some kind of switch had seemed to flip inside Luciana. One minute she had been kissing him fiercely, the next she was running away. Perhaps Mademoiselle Bellerose was right. Maybe Luciana had too much going on to think about him.

"I'll keep that in mind," Daniel said. He didn't want to give Mademoiselle Bellerose the satisfaction of being right. But he'd made up his mind. Once he got to the ball, he wasn't going to seek out Quirino. He wouldn't spend his evening looking for Luciana. She obviously didn't want to be found, and as much as he longed for her, he would respect her decision.

Mademoiselle Bellerose was quiet for the rest of the boat ride, clearly letting Daniel think about what she'd said. Luckily, it didn't take them too long to reach the dock at Sala de Ballo. They each thanked the gondolier as they stepped ashore, Mademoiselle Bellerose's chilly hand sneaked back around his arm, and they were off.

The building was a grand one, with large stone archways leading the way to the ballroom. Guests filed inside, some obviously higher-ranking than others. The newer recruits wore suits that didn't quite fit right or dresses that were from several years ago. Meanwhile, the higher-ranking officers dressed more sharply. The main door was marked overhead by a golden seashell, and as Daniel and Mademoiselle Bellerose entered the ballroom, he noticed how lively the group was. It was the scene he'd hoped to see. He glanced at Mademoiselle Bellerose to see her eyes wide and her mouth slightly ajar, surprised by the boisterous nature of the crowd.

Daniel couldn't help it. He laughed. Tonight, it didn't matter what his father or Mademoiselle Bellerose thought. He was going to enjoy himself.

The band played an upbeat tune, and as Daniel led Mademoiselle Bellerose down the stairs to the dance floor, he looked across the dancing crowd. Some were clearly trained dancers with perfect form, and some were clunky and unnatural. But there was not a single face without a smile. One couple in the middle of the floor caught his eye. They danced in a perfect rhythm, both clearly naturals. He was drawn to them, almost as by a magnetic force. Mademoiselle Bellerose clung to his arm as he wove his way through the crowd.

Daniel was right up on them before he realized who was dancing. It was Quirino. *How ironic*, Daniel thought. The one person he'd decided he wouldn't specifically seek out was the one he had immediately found. But then, as Quirino spun his partner around on the floor, Daniel's heart stopped.

How had he not noticed before? She was the only one in the room wearing Askanese red.

Her eyes met his in the crowd and Daniel stopped cold, shock keeping his eyes trained on the scene before him.

Quirino was dancing with Luciana.

Day 78 of Summer

*A*fter running from the beach, Luciana had fled to Quirino's estate. She rode through the streets of Osmain with reckless abandon, flying past buildings and people as she left the city. She knew Daniel would likely find her at Quirino's estate, but at least this would buy her some time to make a plan.

As she galloped the cobblestone paths turned to dirt roads, and Luciana's confidence waned. She didn't really know where she was going. She'd been too distracted talking to Daniel when they'd gone to visit Esmeralda to notice where they'd turned, and she hoped she didn't get lost. As she entered the countryside and left the canals behind, everything around her looked the same. The roads were covered with the same dust no matter where she went, the foliage the exact same types of trees. She slowed down, taking time to inspect her surroundings before she made her choices at the forks in the road.

Nothing at all distinguished any of the paths as the one that would lead to Quirino and Esmeralda. As minutes turned into hours, Luciana began to realize that she was truly lost. She couldn't turn back to the palazzo even if she wanted to.

Her stomach began to rumble, as she hadn't eaten anything since breakfast, which felt like an eternity ago. She hadn't even passed a cottage or store to ask for directions. Confused and exhausted, she decided she would try to find the city again. Maybe someone there would be willing to help her with directions.

She picked a road that looked like one she'd been on before and followed it. What felt like forever later, she spotted something on the horizon. It was so far away that at first she thought it might be an inn, but as she got closer to it, it became clearer.

Luciana squinted. The sun was beginning to dip below the horizon, making it much more difficult to see in the fading light. Luciana picked up her speed. She hoped it wasn't something dangerous, like a caravan of highway thieves. Or worse yet, someone out to turn her in to the Askanese rebels.

She sighed in relief when she saw what it was. The ornate details on the carriage, the well-dressed footman… this was a royal carriage. It couldn't be danger-ous! But then she thought about it. This was most likely Daniel, coming to try and convince her to come back to the palazzo. The carriage and those inside might not be life-threatening to her, but they were no less dangerous.

So, she galloped off of the road and hid behind a tree. She didn't doubt that someone could find her if they were looking, but it would give her an opportunity to let them pass. Maybe she could even follow them to Quirino's.

But she had no such luck.

As the carriage approached her hiding spot, it ground to a halt. Luciana sucked in a breath, prepared for a barrage of yelling from Daniel. Instead, she heard a small voice say, "Luciana?"

Luciana recognized the voice immediately, and she relaxed. She rounded the tree to see Alora standing in front of her. In all the chaos, she'd forgotten that she'd asked Alora to meet her at Esmeralda's when she left.

"Alora!" Luciana exclaimed, heart practically bursting at the sight of a familiar face.

"What are you doing out here?" Alora asked as Luciana dismounted her horse. The footman quickly led Luciana's horse to the back of the carriage, hitching it up and preparing to continue the journey.

Luciana shrugged as if nothing was wrong. "I'm on my way to Capitano Quirino's estate."

Alora's face scrunched up in disgust. "You look terrible."

Luciana didn't even want to know what she looked like. She'd tried not to think about it, as she'd been so focused on getting away that she hadn't had time to consider how embarrassed she should probably be when others saw her. All she could do was laugh. "I suppose I probably do."

Alora squinted and came closer, inspecting Luciana's gown. "Is that sand? And is that a tear here? What happened?"

"It doesn't matter," Luciana said, too sheepish to admit what had occurred at the beach.

"Come, get in the carriage. I don't particularly want to travel in the darkness, and we're running out of sunlight," Alora said, guiding Luciana into the carriage.

"Alora," Luciana said.

"Yes?"

"Thank you. For everything."

Alora smiled and took Luciana's hands. "Of course. I could never abandon you. You're my friend."

Luciana was so grateful for Alora. She'd been a loyal companion. She didn't ask awkward questions, and she always made sure Luciana was alright. Someday Luciana would have to pay her back for her kindness.

The rest of the ride was shorter than Luciana had expected. Surprisingly, she'd gotten herself fairly close to where she was supposed to be. When they pulled up to the gate of Quirino's estate, a servant opened the door for them. Upon seeing Luciana's unkempt appearance and Alora, currently dressed well enough to be mistaken for nobility, the servant's eyes widened.

"Good evening," Luciana said as diplomatically as she could muster.

"May I help you two?" the servant asked.

"Yes," Luciana replied. "We are here to see Capitano Quirino and his cousin, Condesa Esmeralda."

The servant arched an eyebrow and looked at them disapprovingly. "May I ask who you are?"

Alora and Luciana exchanged a look. "I am a close friend of Esmeralda's," Luciana explained. "We knew each other through Princesa Camila of Askaña. This is my friend." Luciana decided not to reveal that she was the former Reina, just in case someone in the household was tempted to turn her in.

The servant huffed. "I will fetch my master."

"Thank you," said Luciana.

A moment later, Esmeralda was running to the door, followed by Quirino. "My goodness!" Esmeralda said. "You look like you got caught in a sandstorm!"

Quirino looked Luciana up and down, then glanced at Alora. "Let me guess. You need a place to stay."

"Would that be alright?" Luciana asked.

"Of course!" Esmeralda said. "I couldn't turn you

away looking like this. I'll have a servant draw a bath immediately."

Esmeralda then turned her attention to Alora and said, "Luciana, who is your friend?"

"This is Alora, my maid and my friend," Luciana said, glancing at Alora, who bashfully smiled at Esmeralda.

"Welcome, Alora," Esmeralda said warmly.

And so, Luciana began her stay with Quirino. Esmeralda, who had never been practical, had packed her entire wardrobe on leaving Askaña, and she had no problem letting Luciana and Alora wear her hundreds of different gowns. It was like a breath of fresh air to be back in traditional Askanese gowns, although Luciana did miss the added comfort of the Osmainian style.

The days blurred together, and Luciana found herself missing Daniel more and more. She craved him. The more she'd had of him, the worse it was to leave him behind. If the time they'd spent apart after their engagement ended had been torturous, this was a new level of misery she hadn't expected. It seemed like every time she laid down to go to sleep, there he was in her mind. Some dreams simply had her relive the events of the beach, reminding her of how beautiful it had been before she'd left. In some nightmares he turned her away, saying that she was dangerous and that he was already in love with Sibella.

But in others, she dreamed what it would have been

like if she'd stayed with Daniel in that cave. If things had been less complicated. They usually began with him kissing her and escalated from there. In her fantasies, he touched her and teased her and left her hot with desire. Those were the worst dreams of all because they felt so real and reminded her of what she could have had. She always woke up in a cold sweat, her heart pounding. And as the false sensation of him began to fade away, Luciana found herself wishing she could stay asleep forever, inside of those dreams. It was easier than waking up to the crushing disappointments of reality.

Luciana suspected that Esmeralda and Quirino knew, or at least had an idea, about what had happened with Daniel. Thankfully, Quirino didn't seem to mind having Luciana as a house guest. When Luciana had thanked him for taking them in, he'd simply shrugged it off, saying, "I'm already harboring one Askanese fugitive and I've made no secret about it. What are two more?"

Still, Luciana didn't risk leaving the estate or revealing her whereabouts. She spent her days gardening and trying to learn how to sew. Luciana had always been absolutely terrible with a needle and thread, and by the end of the week she probably had rawer, needle-poked skin on her fingers than she had healthy.

It didn't matter, though. She was safe, and she had excellent company. Thankfully, no one asked her any questions that she couldn't answer. Quirino let her be, and Daniel wasn't spoken about. That was, until the night of the ball.

Luciana sat with Esmeralda as she got ready for the event. She wore a dazzling gown which sparkled as she moved, and fine jewelry to match. Alora had requested that she be the one to get her ready, and Esmeralda had obliged. So, the three of them sat together as Alora braided Esmeralda's hair in a complicated style.

"It looks like a mess," Esmeralda noted, watching in the mirror with a scowl.

"Give her time to finish," Luciana said, laughing. But Esmeralda was right. Clips held her loose braids in place, and they flew in a hundred different directions as Alora worked swiftly.

"It won't be too much longer," Alora promised. "Your hair has a nice texture for braiding."

Esmeralda blushed at the compliment. "Thank you, Alora!"

"I'm sure you'll be the belle of the ball," Luciana added.

Esmeralda beamed at the praise. "Thank you." She paused, and then added, "Aren't you a bit sad that you can't attend? I just assumed you'd go with… you know."

This was the first time anyone had mentioned Daniel since they had arrived at the estate, and Luciana was both surprised and anxious to answer. Just the thought of Daniel made her heart beat faster.

"I… well…" Luciana floundered, unable to make words. It was easy for her to over-analyze every second of her last interaction with Daniel. Remembering the warmth of his hand as it had traced up her body still sent shivers down her spine. She just couldn't find the words to articulate it. Luciana found herself staring at the ground, hoping they would leave it be. Unfortunately, this only made it worse.

"Oh, Luciana! I'm sorry, I didn't realize this ball meant so much to you. Are you alright?" Esmeralda asked. Alora dropped the braid she had been working on as Esmeralda moved to sit next to Luciana. She couldn't bear to admit that she wasn't fine, so she did nothing at all.

"This isn't about the ball, is it?" Alora guessed. This time, Luciana did shake her head in agreement.

"Do you want to talk about it?" Esmeralda asked, gently taking Luciana's hands.

"There is nothing to talk about," Luciana insisted. And she supposed that was true. The only thing that happened between them were a few accidental kisses. She sighed. Those kisses had been something. She'd never had time to kiss anyone before Daniel, but she was quite certain that it had been unusually good, as kisses went.

"You're lying," Alora stated plainly, squinting and crossing her arms.

Esmeralda looked at her, eyebrows raised in surprise. "How do you know?"

"Look at her. Nothing behind those eyes. Luciana always has some kind of plan, some kind of checklist. But today? Look at her! Empty. And she's been like this since she got here," Alora noted. Esmeralda shrugged, impressed.

Alora turned her attention to Luciana. "I don't know what happened between you and the Principe, but I know you. And until you fix whatever is broken, you're going to obsess over it."

Esmeralda nodded. "Luciana, we've both known you for a long while. You know you can talk to us about anything."

Luciana tried to smile, to reassure them that she would be fine. That she just needed time. But even as her lips curved upward, she knew it wasn't believable.

Esmeralda gasped loudly. "How did I not think of this before! I forgot he was all over you during your visit here." She clapped her hands excitedly and let out a little squeal, bouncing in her seat as she continued. "Let me guess! Let me guess! He's had feelings for you for a long time. Probably since before the engagement got called off. But you either didn't realize it or didn't care. You had better things to do, like becoming Reina or keeping your sister's girlfriend a secret—"

"Girlfriend?" Alora asked, eyes wide in surprise.

Luciana and Alora both stared Esmeralda down. Alora looked confused. Her head tilted to the side as if she was starting to put pieces of the puzzle together. Luciana crossed her arms defensively, one hand on her corset in case she needed to pull out the letter again to prove her innocence. Alora had packed a bag for Luciana before she left the palazzo, and thankfully, the letter from Nicolas's daughter was there, tucked safely away in Luciana's coin purse. Alora probably hadn't even known it was there, but once again Luciana was grateful to have such a competent maid.

Esmeralda's eyes got wide. "Forget I said anything." This did not ease the tension. But she kept talking. "Anyway, your all-important sense of duty kicks in and you just *have* to reject him. Now you're here in Osmain and you've realized you've made a huge mistake. Anyone with eyes could see that he's handsome, he's strong, he's in line for a throne—"

"Esmeralda!" Alora said, nudging Esmeralda to snap her out of her trance. Esmeralda looked at Alora. Luciana wasn't sure if she'd imagined it, but she thought she saw a faint blush on Esmeralda's cheeks.

"Anyway," Esmeralda finished, "now he doesn't want you back, and you're crushed."

Luciana winced a little. It wasn't exactly what happened, but she was pretty close. Esmeralda did always have an excellent sense for these things.

"Is that true, Luciana?" Alora asked, leaning forward in interest.

"The truth looks a bit different than that," Luciana insisted.

Esmeralda laughed and leaned back in her chair. "But I'm close enough, right?"

"Almost." Luciana shrugged.

"Almost is pretty good." Alora smiled.

"Luciana, when have you ever given up anything you wanted?" Esmeralda asked, raising an eyebrow.

"Well, never," Luciana admitted.

"Then don't start now. I can help you if you'd like. We'll have to invite him here. Does he know where you are? Well, that doesn't matter. Maybe we will go to him?"

"Esmeralda," Luciana said, putting a hand on the Condesa's arm to slow down her chatter. Knowing Esmeralda, she would actually arrange for a meeting with Daniel, which was the last thing either of them needed right now.

"What is it?" Esmeralda asked.

"None of this is his fault. He made his intentions clear multiple times. I was the one who turned him down," Luciana explained.

"Why?" Alora asked.

"Don't you have hair to be braiding?" Luciana countered, trying to steer the conversation away from the shambles of her love life.

Alora shrugged. "We have time. This is more important."

Esmeralda put a hand over her chest, aghast for a moment at the suggestion that something could be more important than her hair. But there was one thing Esmeralda liked more than being the prettiest in the room, and that was gossip. So, Luciana wasn't exactly surprised when Esmeralda nodded her agreement.

"Fine," Luciana sighed. "The first time I turned him down it was so I could become Reina. That was a big mistake. As it turns out, that would have been my golden opportunity." Luciana found herself trailing off into silence. She wished more than anything that she could go back to the beginning of the summer. That she would have accepted his proposal when she'd had the chance. Maybe she could have even hidden Camila and her mother away from the oncoming rebellion.

Luciana must have been quiet for too long because Esmeralda finally prompted her, "So you said no. Then you ended up coming to Osmain anyway."

"Right."

"And he still wanted to marry you?"

Luciana nodded.

"And you said no this time because...?" Esmeralda, obviously invested now, had begun to raise her voice with each prompt.

"Because I missed my chance. There are a million reasons," Luciana said, feeling the start of tears in her throat. She forced herself to swallow them. She would not shed any more tears over Daniel. She needed to move on. "For one, I'm not royalty anymore."

Alora let out a small *pfffft*. "You think he cares about that?" She gestured to the dress she wore, far too expensive for a lady's maid. "He gave me this. Treated me like I was an honored guest. Besides, have you seen this kingdom? They treat even their peasants with respect. I'm certain that your status wouldn't matter to him."

That was probably true, but it had been the weakest of her arguments. So, she gave another. "And... he is engaged to someone else."

This seemed to shock them, and it took a minute before either of them could say anything. It was Esmeralda who spoke up this time. "Who is she?"

"Her name is Sibella. She introduced herself as Mademoiselle Bellerose. She looked Esmarish."

Esmeralda shook her head. "That's strange. I've never heard of her."

"Neither have I," Luciana admitted, "but I've never been particularly close to the Esmarish court. Nicolas kept in touch with a few select noblemen over there, but I always had a feeling he was trying to keep his distance. Roi Marius never seemed to like him." A shiver went down her spine at the memory of seeing the Duc des

Étoiles at her engagement ball. How his cold stare had sent chills through Luciana's body despite the warmth of the ballroom on that summer night.

It was odd that Esmeralda hadn't heard of Sibella. While she hadn't traveled anywhere besides Osmain and Askaña, Esmeralda prided herself on knowing everything about everyone who mattered.

"Does he love her?" she asked.

Luciana thought about Sibella, about her angelic looks and captivating smile. How could Daniel not love her? Then again, he'd never mentioned her to Luciana and he had been more than willing to continue kissing her in the cave. Was it possible that Daniel didn't love Sibella? Finally, she said, "I'm not sure. She was the one to tell me about their engagement."

Esmeralda nodded. "This does complicate things. But I don't think that's a deal breaker. I think you should tell him how you feel before he actually announces the thing to the public and it's too late. It's possible that this is another arranged match like yours was supposed to be."

"It wouldn't matter," Luciana said, shaking her head.

"Why not?"

"Because I'm dangerous. My mere presence in Osmain could start a war with Askaña. Imperatore Antonio knows this. He wants me gone before more innocent people die. Maybe even Daniel."

This was the biggest bomb of all, inspiring even more silence.

Alora slowly moved over to Esmeralda and resumed the hair braiding at a snail's pace. "That's hard to refute," she said in a small voice.

"You really think the Askanese would risk war over you?" Esmeralda asked.

"To ensure there's no rightful heir to challenge them? Absolutely," Luciana replied.

"But they don't have many resources. I'm sure there's a lot of turmoil over there right now."

Thinking of the steely look in the new Rey's eyes struck Luciana with a wave of terror, and her palms begin to sweat. "Believe me, Esmeralda, these people are evil. Just ask Alora. She saw them, too."

Alora shook her head. "Keep me out of this."

"See? She's afraid of them even now," Luciana reasoned.

Esmeralda was floundering. "They're certainly bad people but—"

"They murdered Camila!" Luciana exclaimed. Even as she said it the words tasted vile on her lips, and she found herself beginning to deflate into her chair. Esmeralda's eyes welled with tears, and she looked a bit green in the face.

"Don't you think I know that?" Esmeralda ground out, her voice shaky. "I don't know who these people are, but they took everything. From both of us. We might be too outmatched to get our home back, but you're going to let them control your future with Daniel?"

Sticking it to the rebellion was tempting, but there was no way she could actually pull that off without more people getting hurt. "I don't think I have much of a choice," Luciana said, head in her hands. She'd fought so hard this summer to become Reina, to survive the rebellion, to make amends with Esmeralda. After everything she'd endured, she was tired. She knew that there was no sense in fighting the new Rey.

She heard sniffling coming from Esmeralda. "If you want to give up, be my guest," she said. "But if they want to, they're going to find you either way. You might as well have the protection of the Principe when they get here."

Luciana shook her head. "How could I put him in danger like that?"

"Do you really think these people would have the resources to harm the heir of another throne?" Esmeralda grabbed Luciana's hands firmly and pulled her up, so they saw eye to eye. "Osmain has allies. Believe me when I say that Osmain is better at foreign policy than Askaña ever was. Better trade agreements, more treaties, more influence in the realm. Harming the Principe or anyone in his close circle would mean war. Not just between Osmain and Askaña—it would be the entire realm versus these snakes. They would lose and badly. You think they'd throw away their newfound power that easily?"

Luciana found her heart beating fast under Esmeralda's intense gaze. She looked crazed, and if Luciana didn't know any better, she'd be afraid of her. Instead, she found herself only mildly intimidated, which was about right. Despite the wild look in her eyes, Luciana couldn't help but listen to Esmeralda's anger. Was this true? Had Sibella exaggerated the danger to Osmain? But then why would Antonio dislike her?

Esmeralda relaxed a little but said, "If the attack on the castillo was as well-executed as it seemed, then these people aren't stupid. But all the planning in the world can't go up against four armies."

Luciana shook her head in disbelief. "I was trying to protect him," she uttered.

"And that's very noble. But I think you should at least talk to him first."

Luciana jumped out of her chair. She couldn't help the need to pace. Daniel had known that her presence in Osmain wasn't presenting any danger to anyone. He hadn't shown any indication that he was concerned about it. Then again, he also hadn't shown any indication of being betrothed to Sibella, yet here they were.

Could there have been some kind of misunderstanding? Daniel had clearly wanted to talk through their issues at the beach, and instead of doing the mature thing—the Reina-like thing—and have that conversation, she'd run away. Just like she had when he asked her to marry him. Just like she had when she'd abandoned her country and crown to the rebellion.

Luciana stopped in her tracks. "I've made a horrible mistake. Again."

Esmeralda and Alora didn't say anything, but the smug looks in their eyes silently agreed.

"He's yet to announce his engagement, which means he will probably do it tonight at the ball," Luciana continued. "I have to attend."

Alora looked at Esmeralda, raising an eyebrow. In a silent response, Esmeralda shrugged. It was like they were having a conversation that no one else could understand. Alora then plucked a single clip out of Esmeralda's hair, and all of the locks that had yet to be styled tumbled down in waves. "It's your lucky day," Esmeralda said. "My hair's been ruined! I could never be ready in time! It looks like Quirino will have to find someone else to be his escort."

Luciana's brow furrowed. Was Esmeralda saying what she thought she was saying? "But—"

Esmeralda stood with a flourish and led Luciana to the vanity stool. "You're going to the ball tonight."

LUCIANA WAS glad that not very many of the ball's attendees were of noble birth. It made it less obvious that she was incredibly rusty on her Osmainian dances. Quirino led her around the dance floor, and as the moves came back to her, she smiled. She couldn't fully relax, still anxiously looking around for Daniel, but she was as close to content as she could get as she stepped in time to the music.

As Quirino twirled her, Luciana finally caught sight of Daniel. His jaw dropped, lips forming a shocked O as they made eye contact. But just as quickly as he saw her, he grabbed his escort—Sibella, of course—and began to lead her in a dance.

Luciana turned to face Quirino. "Did you see him?" she asked.

"I must have missed him," Quirino replied.

"He ran off," Luciana explained.

"I'm sure he brought the mysterious Mademoiselle Bellerose with him, did he not? He couldn't very well leave her behind," Quirino said, trying his best to sound sympathetic. But something about the way Daniel had broken their eye contact had been wrong. Almost like he didn't want to dance with her. He must have been angry with her for the way she'd left him at the beach. Pain and embarrassment stabbed through Luciana's chest.

She would have to clear the air as soon as she finished her dance.

Luciana tried to return to the dance she was currently having. Quirino wasn't nearly as elegant a partner as Daniel or Wes had been. His movements were stiffer than fluid but he didn't step on her toes, and while clearly untrained, he was still a natural. Luciana didn't mind though, as she wasn't dancing her best either.

At least he was kind enough to make Luciana not care about any of his technical flaws. He'd agreed to take Luciana to the ball without question, when Luciana entered the drawing room ready to go, accepting the change with only a nod of consent from Esmeralda. Still, Luciana had told him everything on their way into the city. For one, he'd deserved to know after being so accommodating. And two, she trusted him now. He could be a solid backup.

As the dance drew to a close, Luciana said, "I'm going to find him."

Quirino smiled and said softly, "Want me to come with you?"

Luciana shook her head. "No," she replied. "I think I ought to try alone first."

Quirino nodded in understanding. "Go get him."

"Thank you," said Luciana. Then she began her search.

It was harder to spot him in the crowded ballroom than she would have expected. Then again, finding someone who didn't want to be found wasn't usually easy to begin with. And as she wandered through the maze of people, she began to think that he truly was avoiding her. Luciana thought back to the first few days that Daniel had been at the castillo and how she'd ignored him. He must have felt so alone, being in a new place without a friendly face to welcome him. Luciana wished she would have been kinder to him in the beginning.

"Excuse me. Pardon me," Luciana repeated over and over again as she pushed her way through the masses of partygoers. They must have invited all of the military tonight, for a ballroom so large to be so packed.

A sweaty soldier brushed up against her, and Luciana tried to flinch away, only to back into a lady who shouted, "Watch where you're going!"

"Sorry," Luciana mumbled as she continued to fight across the crowded ballroom. Some couples danced so close to one another that she thought one of them would surely twirl straight into her. The dance floor hadn't seemed so densely packed when she'd been with Quirino. Maybe she should turn back and find him. Then he could help her find Daniel.

But as she looked around frantically, she couldn't see Quirino anywhere. There was no sign of Daniel, no sign of Sibella, and no sign of Quirino. Suddenly everything was tight around her, like the crowd was going to suffocate her. Luciana was bumped and pushed and prodded from all sides as she stood still. Luciana was struck with a stabbing fear as she remembered the last party she'd been to. Was this what Camila had seen as the rebels broke down the doors and shattered the windows? Endless people?

There was blood on the floor. Blood on the walls. Even some that had landed on the crystal of the chandeliers, dripping down on the nobles as they cowered in fear below.

She started slowly, putting one foot in front of the other. She didn't bother to apologize or be polite as she forced her way through the pulsing crowd. She was sure she was getting nasty glares, but she couldn't see anyone. Just her own two feet.

She fought back screams as Camila was kicked to the ground. Her eyes widened as she saw the sword coming for her, but it was too late.

She moved faster, even actively shoving some people out of the way. She heard obscenities from those she left behind, but she didn't care.

Footsteps coming after her. She fought for breath but couldn't let her panting be heard. Her heart was beating too loudly. She had to move quietly. She had to move swiftly.

She broke free of the crowd and bolted to the doors. The night was warm, and the remnants of the humid afternoon air stuck her hair to her cheeks. But that wasn't enough, and she ran until she couldn't hear the music of the ballroom anymore.

She stopped to catch her breath as her panic faded. She found herself staring straight ahead at the calm waters of the canal as her heart slowed to its normal pace. She sighed, then looked around. There was a bench just a few paces away, so she took a seat.

The ball had been a disaster. How could she possibly find Daniel if the crowds in the ballroom reminded her of Askaña? She shivered at the memories that had resurfaced. She'd managed to suppress a lot more than she'd thought. Despite the unpleasant heat, Luciana found herself shivering. She looked around. She could see the docks, where gondolas were still arriving carrying passengers who would no doubt pack into that ballroom. There was no way she could go back inside now.

Sighing, she looked up at the stars. They were beautiful, shining true in the night. That was one thing that hadn't changed in her move to Osmain. They were still in their same positions, twinkling down at her as a constant reminder that she wasn't entirely lost.

"Which one is your favorite?" a voice asked behind her.

Luciana jumped in surprise, turning quickly to see Sibella, half hidden by shadow. Daniel didn't seem to be with her.

"Sibella!" Luciana said. "You gave me quite the scare."

Sibella giggled, a sound almost like tinkling bells. Even her laugh was beautiful. "I'm sorry about that," she said gently.

Luciana glanced back up at the stars, analyzing the constellations. "Soleil," she said.

"I'm sorry?" Sibella asked.

"My favorite constellation? You asked?"

Sibella shook her head. "Oh, yes. The soleil. That's a solid choice. Probably my favorite as well."

"You know a lot about stars, don't you? Being from Esmar and all?" Luciana asked.

"Of course," Sibella said, beaming. "Astronomy was my best subject in school."

Luciana didn't know how to respond to that, so she simply looked at Sibella, hoping she would say something else. When she didn't, Luciana changed the subject. "Why are you out here?"

"Just getting some fresh air." Sibella shrugged. She'd seemed just fine in the ballroom a little while ago, but Luciana decided not to question it. She glanced around again. Still no sign of Daniel.

"Where is Daniel?" Luciana asked.

"Back inside," Sibella replied curtly.

"He didn't accompany you. That's unlike him," Luciana replied. It was true—Daniel would never have sent her outside alone. Something else must be in play for Sibella to be outside by herself. Sibella's face grew red, and she straightened with indignation. Luciana's mistake dawned on her almost immediately. Sibella had taken her comment as an insult, when Luciana had just wanted to figure out why Daniel was avoiding her. But Sibella's demeanor changed dramatically. The poor girl must have felt so slighted.

Luciana could imagine how it must feel to be Sibella. In fact, she'd almost been in her position. Shipped off to a country she didn't know, marrying into a position with many responsibilities. And in this case, Sibella had the added stress of knowing that her fiancé was interested in someone else.

"Yes, well," Sibella said stiffly, "he is the Principe. He is expected to mingle with his subjects."

"Is he—" Luciana almost asked if he was avoiding her, but she bit her tongue. "Is he doing alright?"

"He's perfectly fine, thank you very much," Sibella snapped. Then she slyly added, "Why do you ask?"

"He hasn't greeted me yet is all," Luciana said as casually as she could muster.

"Well, he does have everyone else here to catch up with," Sibella said, waving her off. Luciana supposed that could be true, but something in his gaze had been wrong.

Luciana shook her head. "No, I believe he's angry with me."

"I'm sure you're just imagining it," Sibella said flatly, unconcerned.

"Then bring him out here to see me," Luciana said, slowly standing to face Sibella. Despite Sibella's small heels, Luciana stood a solid inch higher than the other girl.

"I'm not going to do that. You're being ridiculous," Sibella scoffed. Luciana grabbed Sibella's arm firmly, and her nails digging into the other woman's flesh.

"What is going on?" Luciana hissed.

"Maybe he's just seen reason," Sibella said.

"What's that supposed to mean?" Luciana asked, loosening her grip.

"He can't be seen with you." Sibella shrugged. "For one, you're dangerous to Osmain—"

"I am most certainly not—"

"And he is engaged to me! We will be announcing our engagement at the end of the ball tonight. How do you think it would look if he spent the entire ball with someone else?"

Luciana's hands curled into fists at her side. She blurted out, "It wouldn't look any stranger than abandoning you halfway through the event. Some engagement. You aren't even spending time with each other!"

"You would do well to remember your place," Sibella hissed. "I will be your Imperatrice one day, a position of power. You, on the other hand, have no authority. Not here. Not anywhere."

"Do I look like I care?" Luciana said, laughing. "You think I want another crown? The first one cost me everything. Daniel is the only thing I have left worth fighting for!"

Luciana took a shaky breath and bit back tears as Sibella condescendingly put her hand on Luciana's shoulder. "Then maybe it's for the best to let him go. You don't need another crown, and that's all he would bring you."

Luciana shook with anger. There were too many thoughts swirling around in her head to put any into words. How dare Sibella tell her what was best? How dare she think of Daniel as nothing but a crown, when he was so much more? He was caring, kind, loyal, and brave. He was a better person than either Luciana or Sibella.

Besides that, Sibella was a mystery. No one seemed to know who she was. The only person who might know would be Imperatore Antonio, but Luciana wouldn't have the opportunity to ask him. Even Quirino and Esmeralda had never heard of her. Yet here she was, in line to rule beside Daniel one day.

Luciana glared at Sibella and growled, "Who the hell are you?"

"Excuse me?"

"You heard what I said," Luciana said, pushing her shoulders back and lifting her chin in the most regal way she could. "Answer me."

Sibella just rolled her eyes. "You really want me to answer a rhetorical question?"

"It wasn't rhetorical." Luciana smiled coolly. "Now tell me. Who are you?"

"This is ridiculous. You know who I am," Sibella said, crossing her arms. But her voice wavered. It was slight, but Luciana knew she'd struck a chord.

"Who is your family?" Luciana prodded. "Are you even nobility? Or just a fortune chaser?"

"Of course, I'm nobility!" Sibella narrowed her eyes. "I am the daughter of the Duc and Duchesse de Étoiles. A perfectly acceptable match for a Principe. And now I believe we're done here." Sibella turned on her heel before Luciana had a chance to say anything else. She floated back towards the ballroom, any traces of anger gone.

Luciana once again got butterflies in her stomach. There was something happening beneath the surface, Luciana could feel it. She had met the Duc des Étoiles. He'd been at the ball meant to announce her engagement to Daniel. And in all the years she'd known him, she'd never once heard mention of a daughter.

Luciana found herself moving inside. She stayed at the edge of the ballroom, away from the crowd, until she caught sight of Quirino. He was standing near the refreshment table with a group of men who must have been his friends. Luciana slowly edged her way over. When she reached him, she tapped on his shoulder.

As soon as he caught sight of her, he excused himself from the group and they pulled away to the side of the room.

"How did it go?" he asked excitedly. Noticing her pale face, he added, "You don't look well."

"Something is wrong. Daniel is avoiding me. I need you to keep an eye out for him," Luciana explained.

"Of course," Quirino nodded.

"Thank you," Luciana said. "And I do need one more favor."

"Oh, no," Quirino laughed. "What is it?"

"It's nothing big, not on your part anyway. I don't think Sibella is who she says she is. Has anyone here served in Esmar for any length of time? Or maybe grew up there and would know the Duc des Étoiles?"

"Hmmm," Quirino mused as he surveyed the room. "That one over there did, I think. I've never served with him so I couldn't be sure, but I believe he was posted at the embassy." Quirino pointed to the center of the room where Luciana saw a soldier, low-ranking by the look of his uniform. He swayed alone to the music, and the sight of it was so pitiful that Luciana's heart sank.

"Do you know his name?" Luciana asked.

"I'm terrible with names. I just know the face."

"That's okay. Thank you, anyway," Luciana said, and she pushed her way through the crowd once more, fighting down the rising panic she'd felt before. By the time she reached the man, she was keeping tabs on her breathing. In and out, slowly. She couldn't let herself get overwhelmed.

Luciana tapped the soldier on the shoulder. "Hello," she said. "Would you like to dance?"

The soldier's face lit up and he nodded excitedly, extending a hand to Luciana. She took it with a smile, and he led her through the dance with pride.

"So, you're a soldier?" Luciana asked as if it wasn't obvious from the uniform.

"Yes," he said proudly. "I've been serving for two years now!"

"Congratulations," Luciana said.

"Thank you! It's been a great experience so far and—oh, no. I'm so rude. I haven't even introduced myself! My name is Sergente Riccardo Agosti," he said.

"Nice to meet you, Sergente Agosti," Luciana replied.

"And you are?" He prompted.

Riccardo twirled Luciana. She was grateful for the extra second to think as she bit her lip, considering how to respond. She couldn't very well tell a stranger her true identity.

"Capitano Quirino tells me you served in Esmar," Luciana said, changing the subject entirely.

"Capitano Quirino? He knows of me?" Riccardo said excitedly.

"He does. You know, I'm a bit of an expert on Esmar myself," Luciana said, hoping she was convincing enough.

"Really?" Riccardo asked, eyebrows raised in interest.

"I spent many summers there as a child," Luciana lied.

"Interesting," Riccardo mused, taking note of her red gown. "You don't strike me as Esmarish."

Luciana's Esmarish was rusty, and she hoped Riccardo wasn't fluent as she said, "Looks can be deceiving."

"Bilingual," Riccardo said, impressed.

Oh, if only he knew.

"Did you work closely with the nobility there? Perhaps you and I have mutual friends," Luciana continued, dropping the Esmarish in favor of Osmainian.

"I've met my fair share of their upper crust. Who do you know?" Riccardo asked.

"Have you met the Duc des Étoiles?" Luciana asked, hoping against all odds that he knew the man.

"I've run into him a few times," Riccardo responded. "What's the relation?"

"Family friend," Luciana said. Which was technically

true. Uncle Nicolas had been very good friends with the man.

"Just between us," Riccardo said, "he's always given me the creeps."

Luciana shrugged. "I think that's a fairly common assessment."

"I wouldn't want to be too close to a man that powerful," Riccardo said.

Luciana hoped she was being subtle enough as she said, "I completely agree. Imagine being his child. I never met them but the pressure they must feel—"

"I've seen them," said Riccardo. "Nice looking boys. Worthy heirs."

"Did he ever have any daughters?" Luciana asked.

Riccardo just laughed. "The Duc? Oh, no. He couldn't even keep a wife."

Luciana's eyes grew wide in surprise. "That's awful! What happened to her?"

"She disappeared one day. Just up and left them and hasn't been seen since. I thought you knew him," Riccardo said, eyeing Luciana suspiciously.

"I didn't hear about that, no. When did that happen?"

"Almost ten years now," said Riccardo.

"I would have been a bit too young to hear about that, then," Luciana said. "So, never even an illegitimate daughter?" Riccardo adjusted his stance to be a bit farther away. She'd pried too much. "Forget I asked.

That's very personal information," Luciana said, trying to salvage the conversation.

"I know he remarried a few years ago to some peasant woman. He never had more children though." Luciana's heart was beating faster with every fact. So, Sibella had lied again! She wasn't the daughter of the Duc and Duchesse—she couldn't be!

Out of the corner of her eye, she spotted them. Daniel was standing next to Sibella at the top of the stairs, overlooking the ballroom. He looked almost solemn, a stark contrast to Sibella's sparkling smile. This must be it. The big announcement. Luciana stopped abruptly, throwing off Riccardo.

"I'm so sorry," she said. "I have to go. Thank you for the dance!" She ran toward the stairs as quickly as she could, not looking back. She didn't think she could bear to see the look of shocked disappointment on Riccardo's face at her departure.

Luciana pushed and shoved her way through the crowd, stepping on toes as she went. She most likely only had until the end of the song to reach them. Finally, she reached the staircase and ran up it, skirts bustling behind her as she flew.

She reached the top of the stairs panting and out of breath, but Daniel and Sibella were already gone. They'd left their perch above the crowd. Luciana scanned the ballroom but didn't see them anywhere. Turning, she looked out at the walkway to the canals. There they were, arm in arm, leaving the ball.

Without thinking, Luciana ran full speed after them. She didn't have time to consider logistics. Hopefully Quirino wouldn't worry too much when she disappeared.

As Luciana's legs carried her to the dock, she knew that this was it. Her last chance.

21

Day 78 of Summer

*D*aniel had known she was coming. From the moment he saw her in the crowd, he knew she would do something to ruin the engagement announcement. Whether out of spite or regret he wasn't sure, but when he'd looked at Mademoiselle Bellerose to ask if they could announce their engagement another night, she seemed to already know what he was thinking.

Before he could make a sound, she sighed in frustration, then said, "You're going to put it off, aren't you?"

What was he supposed to say to that? So, he just nodded.

"Are you doing it to protect me or her?" Mademoiselle Bellerose asked with a steely gaze he'd not seen from her before.

"I'm doing it to protect myself," Daniel said. He hadn't been thinking about Mademoiselle Bellerose at all. In this case, he didn't think he could bear to see Luciana's face as he declared his love for someone else. Would she be happy for him or would she be as devastated as he was? Neither idea sounded particularly appealing. Of course, his father wouldn't be happy with the change of plans, but what could he do?

"Let's just go," Daniel said, offering Mademoiselle Bellerose his arm.

"But—" she protested.

"Not tonight," Daniel said firmly.

Without another word, Daniel led her from the ballroom and toward the dock where their gondolier was waiting for them. He was napping and awoke with a start as Daniel cleared his throat.

"Your Highness, I'm sorry, it's just—" he stammered.

"We've decided to leave early," Daniel said. "That is not your fault."

The gondolier nodded and quickly readied the boat for departure. Mademoiselle Bellerose and Daniel stepped aboard carefully, and the gondolier untied the last rope holding the boat to shore. Daniel looked back at the ballroom one last time. Instead of a calm lawn behind him, he saw someone running toward the dock.

He had a feeling. Who else could it be? And as the gondolier pushed off from the dock and the figure drew closer, he knew his gut had been right. Luciana was running to him, her long curls flowing behind her in the wind, skirt flaring behind her as she held the hem up to run.

Daniel was captivated. He tried to look away, but he couldn't. He'd only seen her running with such determination one other time—when she'd run away from him at the beach.

"Wait!" Luciana cried, reaching out to Daniel.

"Don't wait for her," Mademoiselle Bellerose commanded the gondolier. The gondolier, unwilling to refute orders, kept moving. Daniel didn't know whether to stay or go. She'd hurt him on more than one occasion, but when it came down to it, he didn't care. He wanted to hear what she had to say at the very least.

"Stop the boat!" Daniel ordered, but it was too late. Luciana reached the edge of the dock as they began their cruise down the canal. Daniel's heart sank. Mademoiselle Bellerose let out a small snort of triumph.

Daniel had to tear his eyes away from Luciana. He couldn't stand to look at her as he floated away.

But he didn't have to.

The gondola rocked violently, almost taking on water. The gondolier yelled angrily, holding on to the side to keep from falling into the canal. Daniel and

Mademoiselle Bellerose yelped in surprise, then Daniel looked up. Luciana stood in the middle of the gondola. She'd clearly jumped a few feet off the dock into the moving gondola, and she looked just as shocked as the rest of them that she'd made the landing.

"What are you doing?" Mademoiselle Bellerose shrieked.

"I need to speak to Daniel," Luciana said.

"You can't be here! Gondolier, turn this boat around! I want her off now!" Mademoiselle Bellerose whined.

"No," Daniel said, finally finding his voice. "Keep moving."

The gondolier glared at Luciana once more but said nothing. He just kept rowing along.

"What is going on?" Daniel asked.

"Sibella isn't who she says she is!" Luciana said, pointing accusingly at Mademoiselle Bellerose. Despite this clear indication, it took Daniel a second to remember that Mademoiselle Bellerose did, in fact, have a first name.

"I told you who I am," Mademoiselle Bellerose—Sibella—sneered indignantly.

"The daughter of the Duc and Duchesse de Étoiles, is that right?" Luciana clarified.

"Yes," Sibella confirmed.

"I've known the Duc for years. He's never mentioned

a daughter. And I spoke to a well-connected Osmainian family, they'd never heard of you either," Luciana challenged.

Sibella huffed and crossed her arms. "This is Osmain. How could you expect people here to know everybody at the Esmarish court?"

"Oh, please. Esmeralda knows nobility in every corner of the realm," said Luciana.

Sibella looked at Daniel, confused. "Who is Esmeralda?"

Daniel, who had been listening intently, finally said, "She's right. Esmeralda likes to talk."

Scowling, Sibella said, "Again, who is Esmeralda?" But rather than filling her in, Luciana kept talking.

Luciana said, "But then I spoke to Riccardo, a soldier who was stationed in Esmar for a while. He had met the Duc and his sons—"

"Yes, yes, Leo and Simon. My brothers. What's your point?" Sibella interrupted.

"He never met any daughter. He'd never even heard of a daughter," Luciana continued.

Daniel looked at Sibella, raising his eyebrows. He'd never much thought about her official social ranking. He'd just trusted his father had done his research when he'd invited Sibella to the palazzo. Now he was curious as to her true identity.

She scoffed. "That's typical. They've always been his pride and joy. Why would he mention me?" There was a sad look in Sibella's eyes that struck pity in Daniel. Suddenly, Sibella's lack of attachment to the people of Esmar made sense. She'd been outcast by her own family.

"Well, you're not a failure," Luciana reasoned. "So, either you're lying or—" Luciana cut herself short, a hand flying to her mouth, eyes wide. Daniel looked at Sibella, who had the appearance of a cornered animal.

"I feel like I'm missing something here," Daniel said. The stare off between Luciana and Sibella was so tense it sent shivers down his spine.

Luciana brought a trembling hand to her back. Loosening her top slightly, she pulled a slip of paper from inside. It was crumpled and worn, but Daniel knew what it was. The letter from Nicolas's daughter.

Daniel looked at Sibella. No. She couldn't be. Although she did have the same uncommonly blue eyes as Luciana... and Nicolas's strong cheekbones.

"I believe this is yours," Luciana said, holding the letter out to Sibella.

"I don't know what you're talking about," Sibella said. Still, she took the letter. As she read each line, she gripped the paper tighter, shaking with rage. Sibella shook her head. Then she tore the letter in half, tossing the parts into the canal.

"Sibella, no!" Luciana screamed.

"Oops," Sibella said smugly.

"Is it true?" Daniel asked.

"You can't prove it," Sibella hissed.

"I have all the evidence I need. Do you want to come clean or should I tell Daniel how I figured it out?" Luciana asked.

Sibella's lips hardened as she considered her options. She looked back and forth between Daniel and Luciana, then seemed to give up with a sigh. "Nicolas met my mother on a trip to Esmar. She was a lowly seamstress at the time, but he loved her. At least that's how she tells the story. Anyway, he wouldn't marry her. Too poor, I suppose."

Daniel was surprised Luciana didn't bring up the fact that Nicolas had been an Ambassador of the Sun. That alone would have been reason to refuse a marriage. Instead, she let Sibella continue her story. "We were poor. And I was bitter. So, I decided I'd get my revenge on him for abandoning us. It worked, by the way. He managed to convince the Duc des Étoiles to marry my mother."

"The second wife," Luciana muttered.

"Wait," Daniel said. "If you had a great life in Esmar, why come here?"

Sibella was quiet.

Luciana was expressionless as she said, "You wanted

a crown, didn't you?"

Daniel shook his head. "Of course, she does. Why else would she come here to marry me? This changes nothing."

Sibella let out a shaky breath. "Thank you."

Luciana took a step closer to Sibella, looming over her menacingly. "No. It changes everything. You knew the price of a crown. You saw it tear your own family apart, how your father disowned you in his pursuit of power, yet you still wanted it. That changes everything," she spat.

Sibella stood, rising to meet Luciana's scrutinizing gaze. "You know nothing about me. You know nothing about my situation."

"I know enough," Luciana said, crossing her arms.

"Daniel, please," Sibella begged, turning to face him. "Don't break off the engagement."

Daniel shook his head. This was so much all at once. So, he just said, "We will discuss this tomorrow. I need time to think."

From there, the group fell into silence as the gondolier guided them through the familiar waterways back to the palazzo. Daniel couldn't look at either Sibella or Luciana. His stomach was churning with the implications.

Cousins. Luciana and Sibella were cousins. He certainly wouldn't have thought it, with Sibella being ghostly pale and Luciana having a warm brown complexion. But it made sense. The two girls were so alike otherwise. How had he not noticed the similarity in their builds? In their faces? Not to mention they both apparently had an attraction to power. Although it seemed like Luciana had moved past her desire for a crown. It was probably best to leave her alone then.

Like it or not, Daniel came with strings attached. Strings that Luciana probably wouldn't want.

Before he knew it, they'd docked at the palazzo. The gondolier tied off the boat, then helped the three of them ashore. Daniel slipped him a few coins from his pocket. While he didn't say anything, the message was clear. *Not a word of this to anyone.*

Sibella cleared her throat to get Daniel's attention. "I think I'd better retire for the night."

Daniel nodded. "I think that would be best."

Sibella left, her head hung low.

And then it was just Daniel and Luciana. He shook his head. What was he going to do with her? It was much too late to send her back to Quirino's. She'd have to stay at the palazzo. With him.

"I'll have Gabriella prepare a room for you," Daniel said dismissively.

"Wait!" Luciana called after him. "I need to speak with you!"

"Can't it wait?" Daniel asked, fully intending to put her off. As much as he'd love to spend more time with Luciana, it would hurt too much knowing he could never have her.

"No, Daniel. It's important. And it needs to be now." Luciana looked around. They were in a corridor that carried an echo. Any conversation held there would certainly attract the attention of half the staff. "Although I'd hoped to do it somewhere more private."

Daniel shook his head. He knew her well enough to know she wasn't going to give up. "Fine," he said. "Follow me."

DANIEL'S ROOM wasn't at all like Luciana expected. Back in Askaña, her bedroom had been on one of the highest floors. Their philosophy was the higher-ranking you were, the closer you should be to the sun. But Daniel's room was on the very first floor. Water level. Where the servants should have been. When he'd opened the door, Luciana had been expecting a study. But instead, there was a bed and a wardrobe, and a million books. Luciana was impressed.

"You like to read?" Luciana asked, running her fingertips along the clothbound volumes.

"Books just serve as inspiration for my own writings," Daniel said, blushing slightly.

Luciana turned her attention to the rest of the room, the floor-to-ceiling windows giving her an impressive view of the canals and the city in the distance.

Daniel cleared his throat from behind her and Luciana turned back to face him.

"What are you here to discuss?" Daniel asked.

And there it was. In the heat of everything, she hadn't prepared a speech. How was she supposed to start this? She took a deep breath.

"Daniel, I... I'm sorry. For everything," Luciana said. "I should never have run away from you at the beach. Up until tonight you've been good to me. Much better than I deserve. So, thank you."

If she could have slapped her past self, she would have. She'd behaved like a child, putting her selfish wants above him. And she was done with that. That would be a good place to start.

Daniel crossed his arms and leaned against the wall. "That's not why you needed to talk to me," he mused. "But thank you for the apology."

"It's difficult to just tell you this," Luciana admitted. If she was honest, she had no idea how to convince him not to marry Sibella. Daniel made a strange face. Almost as if he knew what she was going to say and couldn't decide if he wanted to hear it or not.

"I know you think I'm dangerous. I know you think I could destroy Osmain. And I think those fears are well-founded but—"

"You're not dangerous. I don't think so, at least," Daniel said.

"But your father—"

"Do I look like my father?" Daniel asked. He was suddenly very tense, his hands curling into fists at his sides. Then he just snapped, deflating. "He is a good man, but we don't see eye to eye on everything."

"So, you're just mad at me, then?" Luciana blurted before she could help it. "I left you at the beach, so you decided not to talk to me anymore?"

Daniel took a step closer. "No! I mean, yes, I was hurt. But that's not why I was staying away."

Luciana couldn't look at him. She averted her gaze, hoping Daniel couldn't see the pink heat rising in her cheeks. It was embarrassing to think that maybe he was in love with his fiancée after all. "Do you love Sibella?" she asked, the words stinging as she said them aloud.

Daniel laughed. "What? No! I thought our little boat ride made that clear."

"Then why?" Luciana asked softly.

Daniel gently took Luciana's hand. His touch was warm, and she couldn't help it—she looked up at him.

His eyes were like pools of warm honey, and she could get lost in them forever. She was suddenly aware of just how badly she wanted him to kiss her. No. She wanted much more than that. Her heart beat fast, even at such a small touch. She wanted all of him.

But instead of taking her in his arms and sweeping her off to the bed, he just shook his head. Luciana tried not to be disappointed. What could she have expected?

"Luciana, I don't blame you for anything you've done. You are more courageous than anyone gives you credit for," Daniel said. "But you've been through hell this summer."

Luciana pursed her lips. What was he implying there? What he said was an understatement. She'd lost everything. Well, almost everything. And she'd had more worries than she could count. Every night, if she managed to sleep, she had nightmares. If she wasn't dreaming about Daniel—which was its own breed of torture—she had to witness Camila's death over and over again.

Daniel was right. She had been through hell and now words escaped her. When Luciana didn't respond, Daniel continued. "The last thing you need right now is more responsibility. Another crown, another country to learn. Not to mention, you need time to make sure your decisions aren't based on grief."

Luciana yanked her hand out of Daniel's grasp. The

air was suddenly suffocatingly heavy, like everything was happening in slow motion. Her cheeks grew red-hot. "And who are you to tell me what I need?"

"I don't want you to resent me. I want you to be happy in who you are before you commit to anything. Your world was rocked, Luciana," Daniel said, reaching back out to her. But it was too late. Luciana was angry now.

"When have I not known who I am?" Luciana asked, raising her voice. "I might not always know what I want, but I know who I am. That hasn't changed a bit." She stood tall, facing him. She did know who she was, and she was proud of herself. She was someone who made mistakes, sure. But she was also someone who owned up to them.

She smiled at that thought. Because her worth didn't come from any of the things she'd always imagined it did.

Luciana straightened her back and squared her shoulders. She took a deep breath and said, "I am not eager to become royalty again. That much is true. But I am sure of two things, as I have been since long before my home was destroyed. I know myself... and I know you."

She continued. "I have always put reason before anything else, and reason pushed me away from you. But you're all I have left, Daniel. And if you think I'm going to let some perfect, pretty girl take you away from me, then you don't know me at all."

Daniel looked shocked but he was smiling from ear to ear. And that infuriated her. Here she was, being completely honest, telling him the deepest desires of her heart, and all he could do was grin like an idiot. She stomped up to Daniel, getting into his face. She was so close to him that the heat from his body went down to her bones. "And another thing—"

He cut her off with a kiss.

Gone was his slow melt into her. This time he dove straight in, kissing her with an intensity that left Luciana breathless. As her initial shock wore off, she kissed him back with the same fire. She ran a hand through his thick curls, pulling him closer.

This was what she had come here for, and it was better than she could have imagined. This was the feeling of victory Luciana had pictured when she'd dreamt about him. As Daniel held her in his arms, everything seemed to fade away. None of the problems that had plagued them seemed to matter when she was at his side.

Daniel grabbed her ass to pull her right up against him, and even through the layers of her gown she could feel the hardness of his manhood. This made Luciana pause in surprise, but it quickly gave way to arousal as Daniel traced his lips down her neck, kissing along her collarbone. He left trails of fire everywhere he touched, and Luciana found her breathing getting faster. As he teased her and touched her, Luciana became aware of the growing heat between her legs. She knew that feeling. Desire. She'd felt it every time she'd imagined being alone with Daniel.

When Luciana didn't think she could contain herself anymore, Daniel broke off their kiss. He brought his hand to her back where her bodice was tied, but he didn't pull the string just yet. Lingering close to her lips, he muttered, "Is this too far?"

Breathless, Luciana shook her head. "Not even close."

"How far do you want to go then?"

"As far as you'll take me."

Daniel grinned devilishly and kissed her again. Then, with expert fingers, he unlaced her corset. He pulled off petticoats, skirts, and shoes, kissing her each time he removed an article of clothing. Each time she lost something, she smiled more and more with excitement.

Before she knew it, it was just her, standing before Daniel. He kissed her softly then took her hand, leading her to the bed where she laid down.

"Your turn," Luciana teased, gesturing to his clothes, which were still very much on his body. Daniel wasted no time fixing that. As his torso came into view, Luciana was once again reminded of just how muscular he was.

He even had the faint outline of muscles along his stom-ach. The army had done him good.

Daniel followed Luciana to the bed, positioning himself above her. He leaned down to kiss her once more. It was a deep kiss, and when he broke it, he said softly against her lips, "I love you, Luciana. I always have and I always will."

Luciana's heart soared. "I love you, too," she said, taking his face in her hand and pulling him closer. He was somehow even more intense in his kiss, pressing his tongue into her mouth. His hand ran up her body, then he cupped her breast. Luciana gasped at the sensation, and he gently brought his mouth to her nipple, kissing and licking it gently. Luciana let out a small moan of pleasure.

His hand traced down the length of her core again, making her shiver. She instinctively opened her legs as he touched her carefully, as if she were a delicate flower blooming before him. His caresses sent a different kind of feeling rippling through her body. No one had ever touched her there before. It was a strange sensation, yet she wanted more.

"Do you like this?" Daniel whispered in her ear.

Luciana nodded, then gasped as he touched her more fervently.

"Do you want more?" Daniel asked. Breathless, Luciana could barely form words. She nodded again.

"Tell me what you want," Daniel said, moving down to kiss the place he'd just been touching. Luciana moaned again as Daniel indulged her.

"I..." Luciana tried to say between breaths. "I want you."

Daniel lowered himself to her body, their skin pressing together, and she fought the urge to gasp at the sensation of the tip of his cock against her opening.

"Are you ready?" he asked.

Luciana nodded vigorously. Her nerves twinged with anticipation as Luciana waited for him to push into her. The butterflies in her stomach were flying out of control.

Daniel entered slowly, but Luciana still gasped. It was slightly painful, but Daniel was gentle. He rocked back and forth, pressing a little further each time until he was fully inside. Then he moved slowly, gently pulling in and out. Luciana tried to keep her breathing steady.

"Are you okay?" he asked. Luciana nodded. He continued, "It won't hurt much longer, I promise."

Daniel continued to touch her and tease her as she became accustomed to having him inside of her. Luciana couldn't tell the exact moment that it happened, but as he moved, pleasure spread to every inch of her body. As the warm feeling grew inside her, she softly cried out his name. He moved with a passion that

Luciana had never expected from him, and they fell into a rhythm, their two bodies perfectly in sync.

She didn't know how long they did this. Time seemed to disappear as they moved. Luciana touched him and kissed along his collar bone, smiling every time he sighed in enjoyment. They were the only two people in the world, and Luciana had never been more at home.

Daniel kissed her everywhere until it seemed like the world might explode. He tickled the side of her neck with his tongue, ran his hands through her hair, and he kissed her breasts. All the while, Luciana grew closer and closer to what she knew must be the release.

Finally, the pressure inside of her built up to be too much, and with one last cry she threw her head back in ecstasy. It was almost like she had left her body, overcome by wave upon wave of breathtaking, wordless bliss.

It only took Daniel a few minutes to follow, pulling himself out of her just in time as he finished. Daniel collapsed on the bed beside her, content. They both caught their breath, coming down to earth together, then fell into a comfortable silence.

Luciana had never experienced anything like that before. She had known generally what went on between a man and a woman, but she hadn't expected it to be as incredible as it was. She looked at Daniel and saw that the heat of their passion had left him coated in a light sheen of sweat. In the candlelight, it was handsome, accentuating his muscles. She reached out and took his hand, feeling a surge of pride that it was hers to take.

He squeezed her hand, and that broke the spell of silence. "Come closer," he said, pulling her toward him. He held her, the now familiar sensation of his skin against hers spreading across her body. They fit together like pieces of a puzzle, and Luciana relaxed in his embrace. He kissed her forehead lightly and pulled his comforter over both of them.

"Luciana," Daniel said.

"Yeah?" she replied.

"I think we should... I mean..." Daniel took a deep breath. "I know it's not very conventional, but nothing about us has been so far."

Luciana smiled, hoping he was going where she thought he was with this. "Yes?"

"I don't have a ring. I know they're a tradition in Askaña. I could get you one if you'd like. I would ask you somewhere more romantic, but I've never been surer of anything or anyone, and I know that I am meant to be with you."

Luciana smiled. "Are you asking for my hand?"

Daniel nodded. He was right. None of this was conventional. But Luciana wouldn't have had it any other way.

She answered him by kissing him deeply. Luciana

could feel Daniel's smile against her lips as he held her tight.

"There will be things to work out. I'll talk to Sibella tomorrow, let her down easy. Well, as easily as I can with her. And of course, my father…" Daniel said.

"Let's worry about that tomorrow," Luciana said. "Tonight, I just want you."

22

Day 79 of Summer

*T*he morning sun reflected on the water outside of Daniel's window, illuminating the room in golden waves that ebbed and flowed with the canal. As he slowly opened his eyes, an overwhelming sense of calm washed over him. He could barely believe that the night before had happened. It almost seemed too good to be true.

Everything was so perfect, so serene, that he lay in silence for a few minutes wishing he could pause the moment. But he had a whole lifetime of mornings like this to look forward to.

As he finally yawned and turned his head, he smiled to see Luciana was still next to him in bed. She rested her head on her hand, lying on her side in a pose that could only be described as sensual. Like Daniel, the only thing covering Luciana was a blanket. He smiled at the proof that somehow he wasn't just dreaming this.

"Good morning," Luciana said, stretching out. As she yawned, her breasts peeked out from under the blanket and Daniel was overcome with the urge to kiss her. So he did.

"I could get used to this," Daniel said, grinning. "When we're married, I'll never get out of bed."

Luciana laughed. "That sounds awfully lazy."

"Oh, don't worry," Daniel said, running his hand up Luciana's bare side. "We'll get plenty of exercise."

Luciana had a gleam in her eye as she said, "Show me."

And he did.

She was glorious. Just as hungry for him as she'd been the night before, but now she knew what to do. She touched him more, and every time her fingertips trailed along his bare skin he thought he might explode.

When they'd finished, Luciana curled up in his arms and he held her. He didn't think he could ever go back to waking up without Luciana next to him ever again. He knew he had things to do, but he didn't care. As long as Luciana was there in his arms he knew he couldn't leave.

"What are we going to do?" Luciana asked, breaking their perfect silence.

"What do you mean?"

"I mean, this isn't going to be easy, is it? Convincing everyone to agree with this."

Daniel sighed. He couldn't lie to her. "No, it won't be. But don't worry about it. I'll take care of everything."

"So, I should just keep your bed warm while you work things out?" Luciana said.

"If you can think of a way to help, I'm open to ideas. I just don't want you getting into hot water." Daniel hugged her tight. "Trust me on this one."

He kissed her on the neck, and she sighed contentedly. "Fine," she conceded. "But promise you'll come to me if you need help."

"I promise."

A little while later, Luciana finally forced him out of bed, saying she needed to find Gabriella to send word of her whereabouts to Quirino's estate. Daniel whined, but eventually he got dressed and went to find Sibella. He'd decided to speak to her first. If Antonio still saw Sibella as an option for Daniel it would be much harder to convince him to be understanding of Daniel's decision. Also, Daniel didn't want Sibella to hear that their engagement was over from anyone but himself. He wanted to be as kind as he could about breaking off their arrangement.

He started his search at her bedroom but had no luck. Then he walked the grounds, thinking maybe she had gone for a stroll near the canals. He even checked common areas like the dining hall and drawing room, but she seemed to have disappeared into thin air.

Finally, Daniel decided to check the last place he hadn't searched—the south tower. It was the tallest tower in the palazzo, and it took Daniel several agonizing minutes of climbing stairs to reach the top. By the time he got there, he was huffing and puffing from the effort.

There was only one room at the very top of the tower. It was usually used for servants' quarters, but Daniel had converted it long ago into an office of sorts. It was the only room in the palazzo with a view of the ocean in the distance instead of the canals that surrounded the city. When he reached a particularly difficult spot in his writing, he'd come to the office for inspiration. He didn't know what he would do with the room now that Luciana was here. If he needed inspiration he wouldn't have to look out a window. Now he could just look at the woman he loved.

As he opened the door, he saw her. Sibella was looking out that same window, gazing at the water in the distance. She turned with a start as the old hinges creaked, and she gasped when she saw him. "Oh, no. I'm so sorry. I could tell this was a private space, I shouldn't have come in here—"

"It's quite alright," Daniel said. "I came to talk to you, and this is as good of a place as any."

"Are you sure?" Sibella asked. Daniel nodded. He didn't mind that she'd found this little nook of the palazzo. Someone might as well use it if he wasn't.

Daniel cleared his throat. "Sibella. I... uh... well. There's really no easy way to say this."

"You're breaking off the engagement," Sibella guessed.

Daniel let out a breath. "I'm sorry."

Sibella shrugged. "I figured as much. Honestly, I'm surprised it took you this long to sleep with her."

Daniel's eyes widened and he rushed forward. "What? How did you—"

"Look at you," Sibella laughed. "I've never seen your lips so pink. And what is that at the base of your neck?" Daniel instinctively touched the spot Sibella pointed to. When his hand came back, there was a faint smudge of lipstick on his fingertips.

"Oh, no need to be embarrassed," Sibella said. "I've seen worse."

Daniel cocked his head to the side and chuckled. "Sibella, what have you been up to?"

"Not me, you nitwit! My brothers," she clarified.

"The Duc's sons?" Daniel asked, and Sibella nodded. Then she sighed. "I don't know how I'm going to break the news to them. To any of them." She flopped down in the desk chair and put her head in her hands. She looked more tired than anything, but something was wrong in her tone.

"Sibella, what is going on in Esmar? Is everything alright?" he asked, sitting on the floor next to her.

"It's nothing," she said, but Daniel didn't believe that for a second.

"You can tell me. I don't want to send you back anywhere unsafe."

She shook her head. "I'll be fine."

It was obvious she didn't want to return home, but Daniel wasn't going to force her to explain why. Instead, he took a different approach. "Maybe that'll be for the best," he said. "I'm sure there will be plenty of respectable men vying for your hand. You never know, you might find one who you can love."

He'd meant it to be hopeful, but Sibella laughed his suggestion off. "I wish. But the kind of love that you've found? It doesn't come to girls like me. I'd be lucky to marry a merchant, much less a man of noble birth."

"Why not?" Daniel asked. "Esmar has social seasons, right? Everyone turned you down?"

Sibella said nothing and just looked at him with a grim expression. The truth dawned on Daniel. "You were never given a season, were you?"

Sibella shook her head.

Daniel sighed, then shrugged. "Then I'll sponsor one for you."

Sibella cocked her head to the side. "You? Sponsor me?"

"Certainly! I'll send you money for dresses, carriages, anything you need."

"But—"

"Why shouldn't I?"

"Well because… because you don't have to," Sibella said. "Besides, he'd never let me go."

"The Duc?" Daniel asked.

Sibella looked at him, pursing her lips in a manner very similar to her cousin. Finally, she exhaled sharply and sunk back in her chair. "He knows. About my parentage. And he holds it against me. I've never once been introduced anywhere as his child. I may claim support from those in high places, but for all intents and purposes I'm no better off than a peasant."

"So, you don't want my help?" Daniel asked, confused.

"No," Sibella said. "I accept your offer of sponsorship. Thank you. It will just be hard for me. You know? To find someone to marry while avoiding the Duc."

Daniel laughed. "You of all people can do it, I'm certain."

"Thank you," Sibella said, showing a slight hint of a

smile. "I'll be leaving for Esmar later today. The sooner I can get home, the better."

"Are you sure?"

"I need to get back to my mother. But please do invite me back for your wedding," Sibella said.

"Really?"

"I wish you the best, truly," she replied softly. Daniel had no doubt that she would find a husband who would adore her in Esmar.

"I do need to tell you something important, though, and it's about Luciana," Sibella said.

"What? What is it?" Daniel asked, springing to his feet.

"I've made a horrible mistake. I'm so sorry. You've been so kind to me, and I've blown it."

"What is it, Sibella?" Daniel shouted, heart racing. What had she done?

She looked him directly in the eye. In a voice that was bone-chillingly cold she said, "They're coming."

Daniel's heart stopped. He didn't need her to tell him who "they" were. He already knew. The Askanese.

"You tipped them off?" he yelled.

"I'm sorry!" Sibella cried. "I shouldn't have! I sent a letter the day she arrived. By the time I had second thoughts, it was much too late."

Daniel didn't say anything. He just shook with rage. It took only about seven days to travel between Askaña's

Castillo and the Osmainian Palazzo. They would be here any day now, no doubt searching for Luciana. Reports from the border would likely be arriving soon, warning of their oncoming threat. He'd known this confrontation would happen eventually. It was just coming a lot sooner than he'd expected. He only hoped no one would be hurt by the Askanese.

"I thought you should know, I don't blame you if you don't want to sponsor me anymore. Heaven knows I don't deserve it," Sibella continued.

Daniel held out a hand to silence her. "No," he said, as calmly as he could muster. "I'm a man of my word. I will sponsor you. But only for one season. After that, you're on your own."

Sibella exhaled sharply, clearly relieved that he wasn't going to immediately have her drawn and quartered for what she'd done. In all honesty, Daniel didn't even know how he managed it. If he thought Antonio had been hard on him before, he could only imagine how it would be when he found out the Askanese were on their way.

And what would he tell Luciana? She wasn't stupid. She knew the rebels would come just as well as he did. The Askanese weren't likely coming to wage a war, but they would no doubt want her head on a platter. Would Daniel have to send her away? Perhaps with Sibella, to Esmar. Except that he didn't want her to leave Osmain.

Some primitive part of him needed to protect her, and as much as he trusted Roi Marius of Esmar, he didn't want Luciana out of his sight.

No, she would have to remain at the palazzo. And he'd have to somehow keep the new Rey of Askaña from murdering her.

DANIEL DIDN'T BOTHER KNOCKING as he burst into the throne room. A craftsman kneeled before the throne, pleading his case for something or other, and Antonio stopped listening to glare at Daniel as he entered. The craftsman didn't seem to notice and kept talking. Daniel shrugged and hugged the wall, waiting for the man's appointment to end. He spoke for what seemed like forever, and Daniel unconsciously began tapping his foot impatiently. Still, he stayed silent until Antonio thanked the man and sent him on his way.

The craftsman bowed in passing as he spotted Daniel. As soon as the man was gone, Antonio sighed. "What do you want, son?"

"Your help," Daniel said flatly.

"What have you done this time?" Antonio asked, crossing his arms in irritation.

"Well, it's hardly a matter of what I've done and more

what Mademoiselle Bellerose has done," Daniel said flippantly.

"Have you chased her away, too?" Antonio said, sounding disappointed but not exactly surprised.

"Kind of?"

"Daniel," Antonio said sternly, "you must get her back. How many times do we need to have this conversation?"

"But that's only part of what I'm here to discuss," Daniel interrupted. "She and I came to a mutual agreement to break off the engagement. So, you see, you can't blame me this time. Besides, she's already left. I saw her to her carriage."

"What did you do to suddenly turn her off of marrying you?" Antonio pressed.

"We'll get to that but first—"

"It's the Askanese girl, isn't it?" Antonio interrupted.

"Yes, but also—"

"Daniel, I thought we were clear. She is to stay away from the palazzo. She is dangerous and, quite frankly, the last thing you need right now. You need to be focused on finding a wife."

Daniel laughed. "Well, funny you should mention that. Funny on multiple levels actually—"

"Spit it out, son!" Antonio shouted.

"I've been trying!" Daniel yelled back. "Days ago, Mademoiselle Bellerose tipped off the Askanese rebels that Reina Luciana is in Osmain. I'd expect a report from the border any time now that they've entered our kingdom. But Luciana isn't going to be leaving Osmain or even the palazzo. Because I love her and I'd rather be killed along with her than live without her." Daniel sucked in air, realizing that he'd said all of that without pausing for even a moment.

"You *what?*" Antonio seethed. Then he considered and said, "That stupid girl, bringing death to our doorstep like this."

"It wasn't her," Daniel said firmly. He tried to keep a cool demeanor as he defended Luciana, knowing he'd need to keep his wits if he was going to go toe to toe with his father. He continued, "She tried staying away from me. Tried protecting me. I'm the reason she's back here now."

"Not Luciana," Antonio said. "Mademoiselle Bellerose. How could she expose Osmain to danger like this after our generosity?" Daniel didn't have a good answer, and he certainly didn't want his father to know that he pitied the girl and her desperation. So, he just shrugged.

"I expected you to be a bit more concerned, Daniel," said Antonio. "After all, this is your heart and your kingdom at stake."

"I know," Daniel said grimly. "But this was inevitable. If they didn't find her now, they would likely have figured out her whereabouts after Askaña's political landscape settled down. Then it would be harder to negotiate a peace treaty."

"That's true," Antonio mused, twirling a long strand of his beard between his fingers.

"I think we can settle this peacefully," Daniel said.

"And if you can't?"

"Then you'll be right. I'll be a fool, and Osmain will be ruined."

Antonio sighed. "There is no going back for you, is there?"

Daniel shook his head. He'd made his choice. Antonio stood and descended from this throne to stand with Daniel. He held out a hand to his son, and Daniel took it tentatively.

"Then it looks like the three of us have preparations to attend to," Antonio said, nodding solemnly to his son.

Day 85 of Summer

The rebels arrived at first light, just like Antonio had predicted. Every day since Sibella had left, Antonio, Daniel, and Luciana had woken up before the sun and sat in the drawing room, awaiting a visitor who could be arriving at any time.

Luciana was still surprised by Antonio's change of heart. Whatever argument Daniel had used to plead for them had worked. Perhaps Antonio just wanted peace between Askaña and Osmain. Or as Luciana was convinced of more and more each day, he knew what it was like to be in love.

Luciana and Daniel spent their days planning what to do when the Askanese arrived and preparing for the worst. Daniel reached out to his comrades in the military, making sure the palazzo would be well-defended when the Askanese arrived. Luciana reached out to Quirino's household, instructing Esmeralda and Alora to lie low until they heard word from the palazzo.

Luciana hadn't been sure at first if Alora should stay with Quirino or if it would be safe for her to return to the palazzo, but the more she thought about it, the more certain she was that Alora should stay with Esmeralda. Luciana had seen the glances between them. She'd never seen Alora act the way she did when she was with Esmeralda—shy at first but then warm and comfortable, even flirty. Maybe it was too soon since Camila's death, but Luciana held out hope that Esmeralda and Alora might fall in love one day.

Daniel had also made arrangements for Quirino's family to escape to Esmar if the Askanese came after them. He'd written to his ally, Roi Marius, informing him of the situation with Askaña and requesting that he keep Esmeralda and Alora concealed should the need arise. He'd yet to receive a response, but the two were on good enough terms that Daniel had assured Luciana they could rely on him.

Despite their preparations, when Gabriella knocked on the door, fear in her eyes, Luciana's heart stopped. It was time.

Antonio stood abruptly and looked at his son.

"Stay here until you're summoned to the throne room," he said. "Remember the plan."

Daniel nodded grimly. Antonio followed Gabriella into the hallway, and the door clicked shut behind him. The air suddenly felt very thin in her lungs as her nerves began to get the best of her. Would their plan even work? These people had killed her mother, her uncle, her sister. Stole her crown. Who knew what else they were capable of?

As her thoughts swirled around in her head, she found herself staring straight ahead, eyes wide, unable to concentrate on anything. She was faintly aware of Daniel's calming touch on her hand, but even that wasn't enough to snap her out of her trance.

Finally, Daniel said, "Luciana?"

"Sorry," she said, blinking and shaking her head to bring herself back to reality. She was suddenly aware of the sweatiness of her palm, and she wiped it on her dress before taking Daniel's hand.

"It's going to be okay," Daniel said gently, tracing circles on her hand.

"It's just... who knows what these people will do?" Luciana said. "They obviously have no qualms murdering royalty."

"If they know what's good for them, they'll go along with our plan. But I'll fight by your side even if they don't see reason. We've thought this through. Trust me. Trust my father," Daniel said.

Luciana forced a smile. Daniel was right. Their plan was solid. She tried to tell herself that she would be okay, but it was difficult to believe it when murderers were in her midst.

Daniel pushed himself out of his chair and held out a hand to Luciana.

"It can't be time to go yet," she said.

"No," he said.

Luciana took his hand, and he pulled her to her feet. "What is it then?" Luciana asked nervously.

He gave her a goofy smile, then pulled her close, placing one hand on the small of her back, and the other holding her hand. Daniel leaned in close to her and whispered. "You need a distraction, and I need a dance."

Luciana let out the only words she could think to say. "A dance?"

"You think I haven't noticed you dancing before?" he asked.

"Well, I just never really thought about it," Luciana admitted.

"You owe me a dance," Daniel said.

"We've danced together already," Luciana laughed.

"Yes, but back then you weren't mine. Now that you are, well… I think we need to have our first dance again."

Without giving her a chance to say another word, he swept her into a dance. There was no music. No melody to sway to, no beat to keep their feet moving. But in her soul Luciana could feel the sweeping song that should have been playing. Daniel kept up with her, and together they floated around the room in perfect harmony.

Their eyes met and he smiled as he twirled her, and Luciana's heart fluttered. She wondered how long it would take for her to get used to that. It had been six days since he asked her to marry him, and it was still surreal to wake up next to him each morning, to feel his sturdy arms around her as she fell asleep. As they gradually slowed down, Daniel leaned in and lightly brushed Luciana's lips with his.

"No matter what happens today," he said, looking her in the eye, "I will always love you."

That was one part of this she knew she'd never get used to. She only hoped that he knew how much she loved him, too. She closed the distance between them once more, and at that moment there was another soft rapping on the door. Any ease that Luciana had felt a moment ago froze as reality set back in. It was time.

"Let's go," Daniel said. He took her hand and together they walked to the throne room. When they finally arrived, Daniel gave her hand one last squeeze then let go as the doors opened and their names were announced.

Antonio sat high on his throne, and before him stood several officials, all wearing the black wardrobe of the rebellion. The man that Luciana recognized as the new Rey stood at the front and glared at her as she walked by. Luciana fought to keep her panic in check as fear spread through every inch of her body. This was the man who had killed her family in cold blood.

The only thing that kept her calm was the presence of the Osmainian royal guard. Several heavily armed men were stationed all around the room, ready to intervene at a moment's notice. And if they had done their jobs correctly, they would have made the rebels surrender any weapons before entering the palazzo. Luciana figured that conversation wouldn't have gone well, but the fact that the Askanese were in the throne room without a trail of blood behind them meant they'd ultimately agreed to the terms.

Daniel led her to the dais, where Antonio had arranged for Daniel and Luciana to have thrones of their own next to his. Luciana took a deep breath, then sat on the ornate golden throne that had been set up for her. Luciana tried to harden her face as much as possible as she gazed at the small crowd before her.

If everything had gone according to plan, Antonio would have made sure that the introductions went smoothly. He would accept any offerings they brought, then when they tried to bring up negotiations, Daniel and Luciana could join him. Which meant that this was when things would get serious.

"State your business," Antonio said firmly.

"You have something I want," the new Rey said in the same deep growling voice that she remembered from the night of the massacre. His eyes found Luciana, and a shiver crept down her spine under his penetrating gaze.

"You are a new monarch, yes? I'd be happy to renew our former trade agreements, if that's what you'd prefer," Antonio said, playing dumb.

"No," the Rey said, looking directly at Luciana. "We want her."

Luciana fought to keep herself from panicking, but despite her best efforts, all of her limbs had turned to lead.

"Ah, yes. Well." Antonio shrugged. "I'm afraid I'm not looking to barter for her."

"That would be a very foolish choice to make," the Rey said.

"Threatening me already?" Antonio said. "I was hoping you'd be more civilized than that."

"I will not rest until that girl is dead. Refuse me now and my armies will attack Osmain. We will not only kill her, but everyone you hold dear. One girl cannot be worth all that," the Rey said.

"Go ahead," Antonio said. "Kill me, kill my son, kill my guards. Your new government is in no position to fight my army, which will descend upon you should you make a single move against me. Not to mention our allies in Esmar and Tatria, who would surely join the fight against you as well. You—and all of Askaña—will fall."

The Rey scowled. "I am not leaving without that girl."

"You mean my wife?" Daniel interjected, and both Luciana and Antonio turned their heads sharply to look at him. His wife?

"That's right," Antonio said, improvising. "You haven't heard?"

"The Principessa and I haven't even had time to enjoy a honeymoon, and here you are trying to steal her away," Daniel continued, clicking his tongue as if in disappointment.

"I don't see a ring," one of the Askanese men huffed under his breath.

"How dare you!" Daniel said sternly. "Rings are not traditionally used in Osmainian marriages. What a culturally insensitive thing to say."

Luciana was almost moved to laughter at the sheepish look on the man's face. Even the Rey seemed to be stumped.

Antonio said, "As our Principessa and future Imperatrice, she is under the full protection of Osmain."

"Is this some kind of trick?" the Rey asked. "It hasn't even been a whole season!"

Daniel shrugged and looked at Luciana, his gaze calming her nerves as he said, "When something feels as right as this, it seems silly to wait."

The Rey stammered. "But the throne of Askaña—"

Finding a strength, she didn't know she possessed, Luciana stood from her throne, glowering down at the men below. "The throne is yours, you foul creature!"

This earned her angry looks from both the Rey and Antonio, but she didn't care. "You murdered my people and stole my crown before I even had a chance to rule. I could have made Askaña a better place to live, but you'll never know that because you chased me away."

Luciana's confidence made her feel ten feet taller as she descended the stairs and stood face to face with the Rey. "Listen to me when I say this. I don't want the throne of Askaña. You need not worry about me returning to stake my claim. Take care of the people and you will never hear from me again.

"I've found a home here in Osmain. A home that I don't intend on leaving. And there will be no war between Askaña and Osmain. I don't want to hear that a single drop of blood has been spilled, Osmainian or Askanese, or I will personally make sure your goods are tariffed beyond belief. You and your country will crumble should you attempt to undermine the authority of myself, the Principe, or Imperatore Antonio. Now get out of my home and never return. Are we clear?"

The Rey looked down at her with cold eyes, but Luciana didn't feel the chill she thought she would. The moment lasted longer than she'd expected, and Luciana began to worry that the man would pull out a hidden sword and slice into her right then and there.

Instead, he said, "Come on, men. You heard the Principessa. Let's go."

"Not so fast," Antonio said, stopping the men in their tracks. "I would like to get this agreement in writing."

"Why?" the Rey asked. "Don't trust my word?"

"I'd rather think you'd like to have an official document proving that Reina Luciana has abdicated the throne and formally renounced her claim," Antonio said. "Am I wrong?"

"Very well," the Rey growled.

What followed next was a lengthy process. A scribe drafted up a contract, and when each term was clearly outlined and agreed upon, the Rey, Antonio, Daniel, and Luciana all scribbled their names at the bottom.

"Thank you for your visit, gentlemen," Antonio said after the new treaty had been signed. "You will be escorted back to the border by members of the Osmainian military. I do hope you enjoyed your stay."

As the group left, the Rey turned back one last time

and said to Antonio, "Just don't come to me for help when she destroys your country."

The door slammed shut behind him, and with that, the Askanese were gone. Luciana was happy that Antonio hadn't offered them a room in the palazzo. She let out a breath, relieved, and stumbled backwards right into Daniel's arms. He'd ran down the stairs and caught her just in time, holding her tight to his chest.

"It's alright," Daniel said. "You did it."

"The negotiation wasn't as finessed as I'd planned, but well done, Luciana," said Antonio. "You are sure to make Osmain proud."

Luciana beamed. "Thank you."

"I'm truly sorry," Antonio continued, joining them on the floor. For once, he looked like a regular man instead of the high and mighty Imperatore. "I'm sorry to both of you. I've been harder on you than I should have." He clapped Daniel on the shoulder. "I'm proud of you, son."

Daniel smiled. "Thank you, Father."

"I suppose you two have a wedding to plan, now that Askaña believes Luciana to be our Principessa," Antonio said, heading toward the door. "I'll leave you to it."

When they were finally alone, Luciana didn't hesitate. She kissed Daniel right there in the throne room. He pulled her close, leaving Luciana hot with desire once more. She breathed in his scent. He smelled like ocean air and summertime. Carefree and safe. Luciana smiled as they broke apart.

"What is it?" Daniel asked.

Luciana held him close and said, "All this time, I've known I was born to rule. And it turns out, I was always meant to rule by your side."

Year 767

Day 55 of Spring

The day had arrived. Daniel, older now, stood in front of the mirror, making sure he looked ready to face his people. The long purple cape flowing out behind him was ridiculous, but it was what had to be done. It was tradition when a new Imperatore was crowned.

He'd been more than ready for his wedding to Luciana. When their first son had been born three years later, he'd been nervous but prepared. But despite holding the title of Principe for fifty-five years, he still didn't feel quite ready to step up to Imperatore. He'd known it was coming. His father's health had been declining for years. But that didn't make this moment any easier now.

He heard a soft knock at the door, and Luciana entered. The years had been kind to her. She had a few streaks of silver in her hair and laugh lines around her eyes but given the stress she'd endured in her youth and the challenge of raising three children, she was still incredibly beautiful.

"There you are," she said. "Everyone is waiting for you downstairs."

When Daniel didn't answer, Luciana shut the door. She took his hands and sat him down. "Nervous?" she asked.

"I just don't want to fail them," Daniel admitted.

"Believe me, I know the feeling," Luciana said, tucking a stray lock of hair behind his ear.

Daniel couldn't help but smile. She knew him better than anyone else. "I suppose this is the part where you're going to tell me that we can face anything if we do it together?" he joked.

Luciana rolled her eyes. "I was not!" Then in the silence, she mumbled, "Fine, that's exactly what I was going to say. I mean, it's worked every time before. How could it fail now?"

She was right, of course.

"You aren't nervous?" Daniel asked. "After last time?"

Luciana's face grew grim, just like it always did when

she reflected on the deaths of Camila and her mother. "This feels different," she said. "Better. I know I should be scared. But I'm not."

Daniel looked at his wife. He was still deeply in love, even after all the time that had passed, and he was still in awe of her strength. Luciana had been hurt by power before, yet here she was, willing to become Imperatrice of Osmain for him. He'd seen her struggling in the early days of their marriage to feel like she belonged, to assimilate to a new culture and leave Askaña behind.

If she could look at her past and still decide to move forward, Daniel could surely do the same. After all, he had all the tools he needed to succeed as Imperatore. He knew he could go to any ruler in the realm for help and they would gladly give him counsel. His children would always humble him and challenge him to make the world a better place for them. And he had Luciana. With her by his side, he could not fail.

Daniel took a deep breath and smiled. Luciana stood and held out her hand to Daniel. "I'm going to your coronation. Care to join me?"

Daniel stood and nodded, taking her hand, and feeling her warmth and reassurance. Together they walked into the future.

ACKNOWLEDGMENTS

Thank you to everyone who supported me during my writing and publishing process, but especially to the following:

Mom, Dad, and Tim. I couldn't have done this without your advice and support.

My fabulous editors, Hannah and Hilary. Thank you for polishing this book to perfection!

My amazing coworkers who have kept me accountable for my writing goals, supported my work, and stayed invested in the world I've created.

ABOUT THE AUTHOR

A lover of storytelling, Madison has been writing since she was in middle school. When she's not typing away at her computer, she can be found sewing fantasy gowns or visiting the Orlando theme parks.

You can find her online at
www.madisonhortonauthor.com